Memoirs of a Reluctant Archaeologist

an Elise Marquette adventure

Yvonne Kjorlien

ISBN CreateSpace: 9781542915700

ISBN print: 9781738644223

ISBN electronic: 9781738644230

This book is a fictionalized work using true events as inspiration. The characters are productions of the author's imagination and used fictitiously.

Cover photo by Tim Foster on Unsplash

Contents

To Dad, the wisest man in my world.

"This is bullshit."

~ E. Marquette

Chapter One

Finger in a Haystack

Picture this: It is 10:04 am, a May Tuesday morning, and it's rained the night before. Two people dressed in bright blue fire-retardant Nomex with reflective strips on their arms, legs and other relevant places of importance, white hard hats on their heads, and shovels in hand, are attempting to walk across a cultivated field that spreads across the rolling prairie for as far as the eye can see. One person is wearing a large red surveying vest. Mud cakes their steel-toed boots.

"I don't know which I hate more, the hard hat or the Nomex," I muttered again.

"Just focus on each step, Elise," Cam said. I glanced at him and thought that maybe, for him, being covered head to toe, in fire-retardant safety gear was a good thing. Poor kid was one of those freckle-faced, carrot tops that would roast in the heat. At least I didn't have the freckles. What the hell were we doing in archaeology?

"This is a big load of crap," I continued to mutter. It really wasn't the sort of impression I should have been giving my new assistant. At this point, I was far too crabby to care. I hated working for Mountain Oil and their stupid safety standards.

Cam halted. "How much further have we got?"

I thrust my shovel into the cultivated mud, grumbled as it toppled over (but Cam's hand shot out to catch it), tucked an escaped lock of my moppish red hair behind my ear, then unzipped my back vest pocket to pull out the survey plans. I turned the plans right side up then scanned the horizons again. "We've got.....um," there wasn't a fenceline in sight, only a landform vaguely resembling a ridge up ahead, to the north. But it wasn't the sort of landform a surveyor would find important enough to put onto the pipeline plans. "Looks like about another 400 metres and then the pipeline branches north-east and southeast."

Cam stood beside me and took in the plans. He ran a gloved finger along a line to the east of our position. "Is this a road?"

I nodded. "There's a residence in the next section and this is their land. I'm guessing that's their road."

"But we've got landowner permission, right?"

Again, I nodded, trying to keep my precariously perched hard hat upon my head. "We wouldn't be out here if we didn't."

Cam took a breath, hesitated, then said, "This is just a suggestion," another hesitation, "but why don't we split up. I can finish this bit and you can drive around and do the branches. We can meet at the truck for lunch."

I nearly smiled. I'd been working with Cam for nearly three days now and, granted, it was because I wanted to make sure that he was seeing things through my eyes before I cut him loose, but he was impressing me. Not too many assistants did that. Maybe it was because he had a brain. "Okay," I said. "But if you find anything, a rock, a piece of wood, a piece of plastic, ANYTHING, collect it and get a UTM coordinate point. I want to see everything. Got it?"

"I thought you didn't like GPS and all that technology," Cam grinned.

Yeah, it was a good thing he was on the tiny bit of good side I had left. "Just make sure you got more than 10 metre accuracy on that stupid piece of technology."

"Got it," Cam nodded and his hard hat tipped over his eyes. I gave him one last suspicious glance before I turned, ripped off my hard hat, and headed back to our white half-ton in the distance.

The truck was in sight again as I was finishing up the northeast branch. My legs were aching from hauling around an extra twenty pounds of mud on my boots. I had given up taking pictures as the north landscape looked the same as the south, east and west landscape. There was a little, collapsing shack in the distance to the east from the 'Y' in the branch, but it was too far off the pipeline right-of-way to be impacted by the development.

I veered off a little. A bail of hay sat in the middle of the sea of mud and beckoned my muddy boots. If I could just scrape a bit of the mud off for a few blissful moments of freedom, I'd be happy. I didn't care that in just a matter of steps it would all be back with a vengeance. I propped my trusty shovel against the bail and started to wipe my boots down the side, watching with satisfaction as the mud left long brown streaks on the bail. I let my boot gently fall to the ground, savouring my new freedom, when I heard it hit something. I immediately picked up my foot and looked under it. I expected yet another rock, a souvenir of glacial till in the area. Instead, what I found was white. White and muddy. I picked it up out of the mud and rubbed it on my leg, again, watching with satisfaction as the mud left a brown streak down the bright blue Nomex.

My heart skipped a beat. It was a metacarpal.

Or, a metatarsal.

Yeah, I was a little rusty. Being an Archaeological Consultant for three years since finishing an M.A. in Anthropology would probably have dulled anyone's intelligence. But seeing bone, human bone, always had that same effect. "Holy shit!"

Holding the prized bone between my muddied fingers, I began lifting my feet, looking at the accumulating mud on my boots, and scanning the ground for more bone. I suppose I must have looked comical: idiot in blue Nomex, red survey vest, long red pony-tail, and white hard hat on the prairie, half crouched, half walking backwards while try to look at the bottom of her feet.

Then a sound rang through the air. I froze in mid-crouch. My racing heart kicked up the pace. My mind groped for a rational response. It was a backfire. Or, a farmer doing something on his machinery. Yeah. That was it. Nothing to worry about. Just over-reacting as usual, Elise.

I did a scan of the horizon and saw nothing. I was beginning to relax again when another shot rang out.

I don't remember moving. I was suddenly face down in the mud, bone still clutched in my hand, and terrified. Apparently, my survival skills were still intact even if my osteological skills were lacking. And my survival skills said that was no backfire.

I glanced back and saw the bright white of my Ford half-ton gleaming in the morning sun, not 100 metres from where I lay. Of all the times I wish I wasn't wearing Nomex, this was number one. It only made it worse that on the back of my red survey vest was a big yellow 'X.' I was begging to be shot. So much for being safe.

I squirmed in the mud, attempting to get my feet back under my legs and get a hold of the cell phone in my vest. I managed to find a clean spot on the inside of my vest to wipe the keypad clean and called Cam. It rang and rang. I muttered a string of obscenities as I split my ever-shortening time between scanning for Cam and looking for more bone.

A third shot rang out.

Okay. That was it. I grabbed my hard hat and sprinted back to the truck, phone still tucked to my ear and bone still clutched in my hand. As I rounded the truck, trying to find the keys while not letting go of the phone or the bone, I saw Cam high-tailing it across the field, mud flying from his boots. We piled into the truck and pealed out of there.

"Whoa, Marquette! What happened to you? Get run over by a herd of cattle?" Frank snickered, coffee in hand, and watched as I tromped across the attic to my desk, fully mud-encrusted.

I was trying really hard to keep my temper in line. The only thing helping was the bone in my pocket. "I got shot at."

Frank's eyebrows rose, "Wow. You're the first one in the office."

"I'm all a-tingle with glee. Can't you tell?" That comment was loaded enough for even Frank to notice and he finally went back to his own desk.

I rifled through the papers lining my cubicle until I found the file. I dialed, as specks of dried mud flew, and waited. "Hi, Tom. Elise Marquette here, from Human Strata Archaeology. I was just out trying to do the pre-impact assessment for that pipeline by Bassano...yeah, that one, and I got shot at." I waited as my client backpedaled and threw out apology after apology. "Yeah. I know. Look, all I want to know is that you actually contacted the landowner and got permission." As usual, the client himself hadn't. The land agent, however, had. I silently cursed again. Goddamn meddling land agents.

I got the number of the land agent and, after putting on so much sugar in my voice that I wouldn't need to sweeten my coffee for the next week, I finally got the landowner's number. I dialled it.

My desk was now a veritable mess. Dried mud was everywhere. I didn't mind being dirty. Frankly, I was dirt magnet. You could put me in a vacuum-sealed, sterile room and I'd still find a way to get dirty. But, doing a face plant in the mud because I was being shot at was in the realm of 'how to piss off Marquette.' I'd have to add it to the growing list on the lunchroom joke board.

The phone was finally answered. "Hello?" The voice was far away, shaky, and hesitant. It was a sweet old lady. I put my temper on the back burner.

"Hi. My name is Elise Marquette. Is this Harriet Lamnell?"

"Yes."

"Hi Harriet. I'm an archaeologist with Human Strata in Calgary. I was hired by Mountain Oil to do an archaeological assessment for a pipeline they plan to put through some of your land. Were you contacted about this?"

"Oh, yes. I remember that. They called last week."

I didn't know whether to blow up or simmer. "Were you told that I would be walking on land and what I'd be doing?"

"No." My temper shot up, but Harriet continued, "but I said they could do whatever they needed to do."

Now I was just confused. "Well, I had a bit of a problem today. I could have sworn I heard gunfire while I was out there. Do you know of anyone shooting anything today?"

"Oh, my. No, no. My son is away in Saskatoon to visit his daughter and usually he's here to take care of the farm. There's no one else out here. I don't know who would do that."

I told Harriet that I would be out again to finish my assessment, gave her my number, and thanked her for her time. I hung up, perplexed. As more dried mud littered the carpet of my cubicle, I fished out the bone from my pocket. Without the stress of someone trying to kill me, I could now see the features of the metacarpal. I grabbed my dusty edition of 'Anatomy of the Human Skeleton' from the back of my bookshelf and managed to identify the bone as the fourth metacarpal of the left hand. But that wasn't what was nagging at me.

It looked to be in really good condition. Almost no bleaching or weathering. More out of instinct, I held it to my nose. It didn't have the musty smell of old bone. I brushed more of the dirt off it then stopped as my heart skipped a beat. There were tooth marks on the distal end.

Scavengers liked fresh bone more than old bone.

I left the Nomex at home this time. Even my survey vest with the big 'X' on the back was absent. Cam was sitting in the truck with a two-way radio. "Check in, Elise," the radio crackled.

"Yeah, yeah. I'm here," I said. It had dried up overnight. Without the mud, the Nomex and the hard hat, I was in a much better mood.

"See anything?"

I had been reluctant to tell Cam anything regarding the bone. I knew the implications of having a fresh human bone in my possession. But I also knew that once I turned it over to the cops, I'd become non-existant real fast. Call it ego, call it ambition. All I knew is that I could figure out what happened a damn sight faster than any cop. Even if it was a Mountie.

I was rusty at identification, yes, but I hadn't earned the nickname 'Bone hound' for nothing. It was like dirt; if it was here, I'd find it.

"No," I toggled the radio, "nothing yet. Let me know if you see anything."

"Can do," Cam said and I continued my sweep behind the hay bail. Now looking at the bail without my temper blinding me, I could see that an animal had been rummaging around at the base of it. Hay was spread across the ground adjacent to a small dugout area at the base. My instincts said a coyote was probably chasing a mouse. I swept a foot across the hay and heard a faint knock against my boot. I bent down and pushed back the hay. Bingo. Coyote scat. And in it, something shiny.

There's dirt and then there's scat. Thankfully, I had remembered to put a couple pairs of latex gloves in my pants pocket. I donned the gloves and pried apart the dried scat. The 'something shiny' turned out to be a ring. A wedding ring.

Things were definitely getting serious.

"Okay, Elise," I said to myself. "Think like a coyote." I scanned the distance. "Where would I get this and where would I take the rest of it?" I noticed the few trees to the south and the collapsed shack to the east. "Not much shelter out here. Well, gotta start somewhere."

I tried to follow the coyote's tracks but soon gave up as the rain had obliterated everything. I headed to the shack, "I'm heading east, Cam." I voiced into the radio. "I'm checking out an old shack."

"Roger that. Be careful."

The shack was on the edge of the cultivation as the slope deepened into a small seasonal drainage. It was the sort of structure that I would normally loathe recording as an historic structure. There was nothing distinct or of interest in structures like this, but it was out of archaeological duty that any structure older than 50 years was recorded. At times like that, I was tempted to use the Bic lighter I kept handy in my survey vest.

The door was still attached and latched. All windows were boarded up. I noted gaps in the boards of the exterior, big enough for a coyote to easily scoot through. I had a good look at the nail holding the latch of the door shut. Unfortunately, it looked the same age as everything else -- indeterminate. I hammered at the nail with the base of my radio. It finally let go and I pried the door open. That's when the smell hit me.

I paused and collected my wits.

Okay. When was the last time I saw a dead body? At the Medical Examiner's Office during my internship. Next question: Do I really want to see a dead body... correction, decomposing body, probably on the really gross and green side of things? Well, I'd never puked during my internship, hadn't even come close. It was more of a 'do I want to have nightmares for the rest of my life' question. Then I realized that if I didn't do this now, I'd never do it. And I'd regret it.

I took a deep breath, said goodbye to the blue spring sky, and ducked inside.

It was hot in the shack and it was only mid-morning. There was no body. When my eyes adjusted to the dimness, I saw the stain. There were flies all over the place. I knelt down and had a closer look. The stain was fresh. No clothing. No bone. No pupae cases. Strange.

The radio squawked and I nearly died right there, next to the body stain. "Elise? You there?"

I forced my racing heart back down my throat, "Christ, Cam, you scared the crap out of me! What?"

"I'm just checking in. Haven't heard from you in 15 minutes. Where are you?"

"I'm in the shack."

"And?"

"And there should be a dead guy in here but there isn't."

"What do you mean 'should be'?"

"There's a body stain but no bones or clothing. Oh wait," I knelt back down. It looked like a squashed maggot.

Even over the radio, I could hear the tremor in Cam's voice, "Elise, I think you should come back to the truck. I don't think we should be out here any more."

"Cam, I'm fine. Calm down. I'm going to do some more checking around and I'll be right back. Give me another 15."

"Elise, I ..."

"Cam, I want you to dig out those books that I brought. Find out when flies hatch and pupate. Can you do that?"

"Yeah. Just don't turn off your radio, okay?"

"Okay, Cam." I was tempted to turn off the radio but instead turned the volume way down. I needed my wits about me.

It was mid-May. The shack would have acted like a furnace and increased the rate of decomposition. I was pretty sure that flies hatch within a few days of laying and pupate a couple weeks after that. Conditions like this would have accelerated everything, including the attraction of scavengers. However, scavengers usually don't haul off all the bone and clothing; there was always something left behind. It was possible that the person had been naked and that there were lots of really hungry coyotes in the area, but that was on the improbable side. What was it Sherlock Holmes said? Whatever remains, however improbable, when all else is excluded, must be the answer. Or something like that. I still wanted to look around further.

I stepped back outside and suddenly the sky seemed very blue.

The drainage bottom was still muddy from the rain two days ago. Aspen and willows lined the banks as the drainage snaked through the prairie. I began wandering around, aiming generally for the drainage and its treed shelter, but wasting some time along the way.

There were an awful lot of coyote tracks in the plowed field between the shack and drainage. I tried to follow their general direction hoping they'd lead me to a den. Instead, they led to a spot with freshly turned dirt. And boot prints. The coyotes had apparently found the new resting spot of dead guy. Nothing gets past them.

I kicked at the spot the coyotes had been digging at. Green garbage bag poked through the hole. Typical criminal, I thought. Lazy and unwilling to dig a deep hole. Then I started to piece together the evidence so far and form a scenario. "Oh, that's just gross!" I couldn't imagine trying to pick up the slimy pieces of a decomposing person, bagging them and transporting them. Yuck. But I had see if what I suspected was true.

I kicked away a decent section of the dirt and, with a deep breath again, pried a hole in the plastic bag. As luck would have it, I picked the head end. Amidst the bloating, maggots, and decomposition, I saw that it was a male with short brown hair and brown eyes. He was wearing a blue checked shirt.

I stepped away from the bag and breathed in the fresh morning air. I had been prepared for a dead body, but this was different. Nobody expects to see a dead guy in a garbage bag. It was so different than the sterile atmosphere of the M.E.'s office. "Cam. Cam?" I toggled the radio but heard nothing. I was breathing hard and the radio was beginning to blur. Then I remembered I had turned down the volume. As I turned it up I heard Cam's frantic voice, "Elise? ELISE? Are you there?"

"I'm here." But not for long. Everything was so blurry. "Call the cops. I found him."

"Where are you? I can't see you."

"Down by the drainage." Then I heard Cam's voice coming from the distance. I looked up and saw him just before my knees gave way and my butt hit the dirt. Then Cam's freckled face was right there in front of me.

"Are you okay?"

I tried to push him away and stand up, "Yeah, yeah," but my legs didn't seem to work. "I told you not to leave the truck."

The freckles on Cam's face were so numerous they almost seemed comical. He reminded me of Archie and I wondered if he liked Betty more than Veronica. "You wouldn't answer your radio. I've been try-ing to call you. A truck drove by."

"A truck?" Panic rose in my chest. I fumbled in through the many pockets in my cargo pants. "Cell phone, cell phone." I finally found it. I turned it on and began dialing. Then it rang mid-dial. "Hello," I said hesitantly. Things were getting very strange around here. "This is Elise."

"Is this Ms. Marquette?"

"Yes, it is."

It was the shaky voice of the old woman. "Hello, Ms. Marquette. This is Harriet Lamnell. We spoke yesterday about a pipeline."

"Yes, I remember."

"I just got a phone call from my granddaughter in Saskatoon. My son has not arrived. I began to get very frightened especially since you say that you heard gunfire yesterday. I wanted to warn you. I don't think you should continue your work on my land until I've contacted the police."

I glanced at Cam as my stomach began to knot. "Mrs. Lamnell, we are already out on your land. May we come and see you?"

"Well, okay. You shouldn't be out there anyway. I'll put on the tea kettle."

I hung up. "What's the number for the nearest police station?"

Cam said, "It's on the safety forms in the truck. Can you walk?"

"I'll walk," then prised myself off the ground.

Cam took a moment to rise. "Hey! Guess what I found?" He held up something shiny and black. His grin was huge. "An obsidian flake!"

He was a real archaeologist, this one. The excitement on his face was palpable. "That's nice, Cam."

Great. Now I had a dead guy AND an archaeological site.

Cam phoned the Bassano RCMP as we bounced down the gravel road to have a cup of tea at Harriet Lamnell's place. I was still shaking, my palms were drenched in a cold sweat, and that knot in my stomach was growing harder by the second.

I had an uncanny feeling that when we got to Harriet's place, the pictures on her fireplace mantle would be of the guy I saw in the garbage bag.

Cam rifled through our safety forms to find the address of Harriet's place to give to the police. "They want to talk to you," he held the phone out.

"I'm driving. It's against safety protocols. Tell them I'll call them back."

Cam had known the answer but repeated it to the police. He signed off as we made our way up the driveway to a blue two-story house. It was in the Victorian style even if it wasn't that old. It had a nice veranda with bay windows and a second storey with dormers. The house sat in the middle of a yard surrounded by sheds, shacks, more outbuildings, and finally barns and stables in the outer perimeter. A nice plush spread for farmyard. The curtain in one of the bay windows drew back then fell as we pulled up.

I grabbed my business card from its place on the truck's dash and exited the truck. Cam said, "They wanted to know what we were doing out there, snooping around. They didn't seem to know anything about archaeology."

"Not surprising." I had encountered this when I was lucky enough to be invited onto searches with my supervisor in grad school. Cops knew what they knew and nothing more. It was difficult get them to understand that there was often more than one way to do something, especially if is was a better, more efficient way to do it. Like searching for human bone.

I climbed the stairs to the front door. Cam was a few steps behind, hesitantly scanning the surroundings. I knocked on the door and called out, "It's Elise Marquette, Mrs. Lamnell."

The door opened a crack and a small wrinkled face peered out. I held out my business card to her. She opened the door, took it, and said, "You are look a lot younger than you sound, Ms. Marquette."

"Thank you. This is my assistant, Cam Tucker." Much to Cam's credit, he leapt up the stairs and held out his hand to Harriet.

"Nice to meet you, Mrs. Lamnell."

And, in a heartbeat, she'd been won over. "Please, call me Harriet." There's much to be said about having a mixed-sex field team.

We'd just stepped inside the farmhouse when I heard a vehicle pull up outside. I leaned back out the front door, expecting to see an RCMP cruiser. It was a blue Ford half ton. The knot in my stomach tightened. A man was getting out. "Hey," Cam said. "That's the same truck I saw before." The man was pulling a shotgun from the front seat of the truck.

"Inside!" I shoved Cam and slammed the door shut. I threw the seldom-used deadbolt. "Close the curtains! All of them. Hurry."

Harriet, who had been on her way to the kitchen in the back of the house, turned back, "What's going on?"

"There's a man outside with a gun."

All colour drained from her face, but then her mouth screwed up tight. "Many people out here have guns, Ms. Marquette." And she strode to the door as best as her seventy-something legs could manage and unlocked the door.

I motioned Cam to the back of the house and tried some hand gestures asking him to find a gun or weapon of sorts. I scurried down the hall and hid behind the stairs. I wanted to see the interchange between Harriet and the man but stay out of sight.

"Max," I heard Harriet's voice from the veranda, "why are you carrying a gun on my land?"

Max, my mind registered the name.

"Why are you letting them build a pipeline on our land, Harriet?"

"Our land? There is no 'our land.' It's mine and you know it." I had to hand it to the woman. She was doing a good job of standing her ground. But for how long?

"My father left it to both of us. I have a say in what happens." That voice was dangerous and I was torn between staying put and trying to pull Harriet back inside. Where the hell were the goddamn police??

"Samuel said you lost it to him in a poker game, fair and square."

"I was drunk!" That's it. I started for the front door.

"It's not my fault you can't handle your liquor, Max."

"I want my land back! My father left it to me."

"No, Max." I heard the waver in her voice. "It's my land and the pipeline's going through. It's no matter to you. Go home." I crept up between the door and the window. I could see Harriet's red sweater.

Max's voice was suddenly very close. "All the profits will go the government, Harriet. They're only buying you off so they can get onto the land. Within a year, they'll pollute everything then offer to buy your house for a buck. Then you'll be living out of this new fancy truck."

New fancy truck? Oh, crap. He was talking about my rental.

"Go home and sober up, Max." Harriet took a step back and I raised a ready hand.

A crash sounded from in the kitchen as a shot rang from outside. I didn't know whether to duck or run. Instead, I grabbed Harriet's sweater and pulled for life itself. I'd overestimated her weight. She flew past me into the hallway and I threw the door shut again. When I looked back, Harriet was in a crumpled heap on the floor. Cam was standing at the end of the hallway, his face white with terror and a frying pan in his hand.

I scurried over to Harriet, "Are you okay?" She merely groaned.

"I want my land back!!" Max shouted from outside.

Where the hell were those damn police?? The thought had no more entered my head when sirens rang out. I nearly fainted with relief. From the look on Cam's face, he nearly did too.

I peeked out the window and saw the Mountie descend on Max. I also saw that the windshield of our rental truck had been the target of his last shot. So much for Human Strata's insurance.

I opened the door as a Mountie climbed the stairs to the veranda. "I'm Elise Marquette. My assistant phoned into Bassano earlier about the remains we found. I think Harriet is hurt. Can you call for an ambulance?"

He stopped and stared at me with the cold blue eyes of a cop. I stared back. Then he stepped around me to have a look at Harriet. He knelt down and asked if she was hurt. Yup. Typical cop. Didn't trust anyone. His nametag read "Sgt. Campbell." "See? She's hurt," I urged. Sergeant Campbell didn't look at me. Instead, he called into the detachment.

Sergeant Campbell questioned us while we waited for the ambulance. A couple more cruisers showed up. Every Mountie in a fifty-mile radius must have been in that yard; we were the next-best thing to a coffee shop. After Harriet was whisked to the nearest hospital, Sergeant Campbell finally asked the question I was waiting for. "Can you show us where the remains are?"

Cam and I rode in the back of Campbell's cruiser and directed him to the road, then led him on foot to the garbage bag. He stopped us before I got to the garbage bag and said they'd take it from there. "By the way," I said. "You might want this." I dug out the metacarpal and wedding ring. "There's also a body stain back in the shed indicating the original point of deposition. He wasn't there more than a couple days before the coyotes found him and was then moved. I found the metacarpal and ring at the hay bail by the road. The ring was in coyote scat."

Campbell looked at me as I handed over the bone and ring. It was the same look he'd given me at the house; listening but not buying a word of it. Fine. Whatever. One of these days they'll realize the value of multi-disciplinary investigation. Too bad he was a cop. He was kinda cute. In a cop way.

I was fuming. Cam remained silent as we walked back to the house and retrieved the truck. It was a windy ride back to Calgary.

Convincing my boss, Morris, that having the windshield shot out of the rental truck wasn't actually my fault was difficult, to say the least. It also took a lot of talking to finally get some information from the Bassano RCMP office. After swallowing my sugar and playing it straight, it turned out that Sergeant Campbell was an alright guy. I nearly jumped for joy when he told me that the dead guy was Harriet's son. Max had shot him in a drunken rage three days before we got out there. With all the activity going on due to the pipeline, Max was getting paranoid and up tight. He'd shot at me to scare me off, then moved the body. Because he was a farmer, Max had no problem handling gross, dead things.

Oh. And I found out that Harriet had tried to charge me with assault. Apparently, breaking someone's ribs while trying to save them wasn't a good thing.

Case solved. I had figured it out. But hadn't even got a 'thanks for the help.' I didn't know whether to spit at the phone or do my Stampeders-won-the-Grey-Cup dance.

I sipped my coffee and stared my notebook. Frank appeared around the corner of my cubicle. "So, Cam said you guys found an obsidian flake on that pipeline project. Are you going to excavate?"

"It wasn't found on the pipeline right-of-way, Frank."

"Did you find anything on the right-of-way?"

"It's under police investigation. I haven't been allowed back out there."

"Oh. Sucks." Frank left.

I slid the survey plans aside, uncovering my dusty edition of 'Anatomy of the Human Skeleton,' and continued to brush up on my human osteology.

Chapter Two

Post-Impact

A file folder landed on my desk beside me. "Need this to be done right away," Morris said.

"Why?" I asked as I leafed through folder full of survey plans, maps, draft budgets, and emails. "It's a post-impact assessment."

Post-impact assessments were uncommon as the archaeological site, if there was one, had already been impacted by the construction of the development. The government, and archaeological community, weren't fond of looking at already impacted sites. It's kinda like saying, "Yup, there was something here, but now there's not. Carry on." In some cases, where the development is urgent -- usually with winter coming on -- and the archaeological potential is moderate, the government will okay the process.

The whole thing never really made sense to me. But I was going to be in Grande Cache and that more than made up for the crappy project I'd been dealt.

"They said they wanted it done right away so that's all I know. Besides what else are you doing?" Morris raised his greying eyebrows to my computer screen.

I couldn't argue. Not like there was a lot of words there. I think I was typed out. It had been a long winter spent typing permit report after permit report. I'd pushed myself because I was looking forward to a well-earned vacation in February. I wanted – needed -- to get the first draft of every report from the previous summer into Morris for review before I left. It was the only way I could vacation with a clear conscience. And, frankly, if I didn't do them before I left, I wouldn't have the motivation to do them upon my return.

But that was a couple months ago. Now I was revising the same material I'd written before Christmas.

I looked at my screen, the word "Results" standing stark on the whiteness of the page, then glanced at the picture tacked to my bulletin board. It was a landscape shot I'd taken in County Meath. The greenness of Ireland never ceased to amaze me. "Any word on the insurance for the windshield on the truck?"

Morris' gaze flitted over my desk and finally came to rest on my photo of Ireland. "No. Let me know when you submit the permit application for the post-impact. Nice photo." Morris said then made his way back to his office at the front of the building.

I'd hung up that photo three months ago. Ugh. Maybe I was depressed. I pulled up the internet and searched for flights to the UK. Again.

For my vacation in February, I'd wanted to get as far away from work as possible. Since work was essentially paying for it, I figured that, with the three months of banked time I'd accumulated, I'd make this good. Santorini seemed like too many flight connections so I opted for the English countryside. Three trains and 24 hours of traveling later I was cursing the lack of insulation in English buildings and their ignorance of forced air heating. I'd arrived the day before the worst snowstorm in 20 years. I'd curled up into a ball, fully clothed under a flimsy quilt, and shivered my way through two weeks of humid hell. Santorini had looked pretty damn good then. The four days I spend in Ireland afterwards barely made the whole trip worthwhile. Not even the young and very nice lecturer I met at Trinity College could save my dismal vacation.

I did a search on the internet. Gavin Cleary was a lecturer of Roman History and Archaeology at Trinity College Dublin. He had told me he was applying to work on the Dakhleh Oasis Project in Egypt. Digging up Roman stuff in Egypt. Wow. Things just didn't get any better. Except unless things involved digging up skeletons. And working with Gavin Cleary.

His web picture didn't do him justice.

That very nice lecturer, Dr. Gavin Cleary, had offered to take me up to Connemara. Stupid me, I refused because I was due back at work. I was going to beat myself up about that for sometime. Half a year at least.

I had goofed during my undergrad. I took classes that I enjoyed without the thought of how I was going to get a job afterwards. The Department of Archaeology at the University of Calgary specialized in Plains Archaeology and Physical Anthropology. I'd managed to find and take a fieldschool in Tunisia through the History and Classics department. We'd dug in a Roman fort. Real archaeology with pottery, coins, and social stratification. It was the next best thing to digging up dead people. But I'd discovered the History and Classics department and their academic delicacies late in my program, too late to switch my major. Seven years later, I was still paying for that fieldschool. And I was now stuck looking for arrowheads and tipi rings in Alberta when all I wanted to do was fondle some bones. Hell, I'd even take some coins or pottery at this point. But there was none of that in Alberta, barely any in Canada, for that matter.

God, I hated looking for rocks.

"Come on, Elise," I muttered to myself. "Get a hold of yourself. You're dreaming. Not like you're ever going to do Archaeology outside of Alberta."

But damn, the man was beautiful. He wasn't your typical Irish-type with dark hair and blue eyes: he was blond. He was nice too. Maybe I should have taken a picture of him instead of a bunch of green hills.

He'd given me his card and I'd tried emailing him a couple of times. I got a bounce-back. It was no use. I would have to give up. It had been three months since I'd seen and talked to Dr. Gavin Cleary. Three months since I'd been in the UK, away from my job of looking for rocks and shuffling papers.

"Besides, I'm only an M.A. What would I have in common with a Ph.D.?" Now my mother's voice was popping into my head. The woman wasn't dead so I couldn't rightly concede she had supernatural abilities. Then again, she did resemble evil incarnate.

My phone rang. My hand wavered over the receiver as I considered my last blasphemous thoughts. Knowing my mother, she'd been reading my mind and was now calling me on it. I finally grabbed the nagging phone and shoved it to my ear, "Elise? Hello? Elise? Is anyone there?"

I let out my held breath, "Yes, Theo, I'm here."

"Okay, that was fucked up." I wasn't the only one in the family with trucker-mouth. I tried to blame it on the fieldwork, but the field just brought out what was already there.

"What's up, Theo?"

"I need you to stop by my office some time. When are you available?"

A chill ran up my neck. I didn't know why; Theo was my eldest brother, not my mother. "I've got some work up in Grande Cache. I'll be back in a few days."

"Okay, I'll tell Margaret you'll be dropping on Friday at ten." Margaret was my brother's assistant. Only lawyers and doctors and Hollywood actors could afford assistants, I told myself. This was why I don't have one. I just couldn't compete with my lawyer brother's paycheque. Or, his arrogance.

"Fine," I suppressed another shiver and signed off. Yes, Friday's fine, Theo. No really, I'm not busy. Friday is good.....

I took one more look at the Trinity College website. If only I could have few more miles from my family, I thought.

Then finally I gave up on Dr. Cleary, and procrastination in general. I called the Provincial government Historical Branch and talked to the regulator who looked after the Grande Cache area, Mark van Gutten.

"It's regarding this telecommunication tower. You issued a post-impact requirement. Is there something I should be aware of?" I asked.

"There were a few sites recently located in that area. This area has higher archaeological potential now. You'll see it all in the new Historical Sites Listing next month." Okay, that made sense. The Historical Branch revised the Listing every year. Archaeologists used the Listing as a tool to estimate the likelihood of finding new archaeological or historic sites in the same area and what kind of sites those might be, such as historic buildings or precontact campsites. People are so predictable in their patterns.

"What kind of sites?"

"Couple of precontact campsites. They should be included in the site form documentation you'll request from the library. If they aren't, let me know. I'll send them to you."

I thanked him, noting his support – he used to be a Consulting Archaeologist after all -- then asked, "Did you get my Arctic Power report yet?"

Mark sighed. "Yeah, I got it. Been a busy winter though. Lots to review. I'll get to it soon. I won't let it impact your permit-holding status, though. Don't worry." Frankly, I wouldn't have minded if Mark took a year to review it. I could do with some sitting around without the ability to hold permits for archaeological fieldwork.

I picked up my coffee cup and I did a detour through the lab in the lower back part of the building. Melissa, our lab madame, sat in the far back corner behind tables of washed stone tool debitage and boxes full of bagged and tagged stone tools debitage. Melissa was surrounded by rocks. Needless to say, I didn't come back here much. I waved to her frizzy blonde hair and carried on.

Cam sat hunched over a microscope surrounded by catalogue sheets and stone tool debitage. There were times I did not envy assistants, not many, but some. I nudged him and he looked up, massaging his eyes, "Are you available to go up to Grande Cache in a couple days?"

"Can't," he shook his head before regaining sight again. Cam blinked back at me, "John's booked me for the next two weeks in the Yukon."

"The Yukon. Wow. Okay, I can't compete with that."

Cam took a swig from his 7-11 Gulp-sized coffee cup. "Sorry, Elise. Hope you have a good time."

"Yeah, me too. Hey, have you processed that obsidian flake you found last week?"

Cam beamed and spun in his chair. From amongst the multitude filed across the tables, he plucked a single plastic baggie with a white index card tucked inside. The whiteness of the card made the stone artifact seem blacker. "Yup. It's obsidian all right. It's a biface reduction flake too."

"That's nice." And I left to find coffee and an assistant.

I should have stayed in the UK.

The Human Strata Archaeology Company had office space in downtown Calgary. I wasn't overly joyed about their location, what with lack of parking and all. But the building was neat, in an antiquated way that would only appeal to someone who didn't have to work there. It was a converted shoe factory built in the 1920s. The owner of HSAC, Tim Bowden, bought it for cheap during the 80s when they couldn't even give away real estate in Calgary. Since then, it'd been renovated a few times, piecemeal of course, as the company had grown. Now, Tim could have probably sold the place and retired the entire staff on the profits, but it's not like Tim would have done that. Nope.

So, in the meantime, I put up with the parking but tried to walk to work whenever I was actually in town. Usually I didn't have the energy to walk. Instead, I drove my 1992 Toyota Tercel and swore at the downtown drivers.

It was one thing to drive and park downtown in a small car, it's another in a large pickup truck. Over the course of the couple years working with HSAC, I'd driven just about every rental truck and SUV under the sun, whether that sun came up this year or last. And let me just say this, Calgary wasn't designed for pickup trucks, especially the ones they make for the oil patch guys. I mean, really, who needs to sit four feet in the air and four people across anyway?

I jumped the curb, as usual, as I swung the F250 down the alley to our backdoors. I did a 52-point turn to back into the small parking area we got as part of the building agreement. Thankfully, Tim wasn't here; I unbuckled my seatbelt and swiveled around to see that I was backing into his meager parking space.

The budget on this post-impact was for three days of field time. It was actually twenty hours of driving time to Grande Cache and back just to do four hours of fieldwork. I don't mind the driving; it was the assistant I inevitably got stuck with. What do you talk about for 20 hours? I had to hope we had compatible tastes in music.

I'd stacked my gear inside the back doors last night before leaving so I'd only have move it into the truck the next morning. At 7am on a May morning, I was already sweating and panting with exertion. If only all girls were so lucky.

After loading up a sherpa and two donkey's worth of gear, I stepped back to do a check. "Fire extinguisher, bear spray....make that two bear spray, bear bangers, rechargeable air horn...where's my pump for the air horn," I dug around in my Rubbermaid bin, "Ah, there. Okay, truck kit with tow chain, flares, emergency blanket, booster cables, first aid kit for the truck, first aid kit for me, GPS, survival kit, survey vest, rain gear, winter gear, bug spray, sun block, water bottle, hat....where's my hat? Hello, hat." I dug out my wide-brimmed, ele-phant-can-crap-it-out indestructible Tilley hat and placed it atop the gear. "Camera, baggies, Sharpies, pencils, laptop, battery for camera, batteries for GPS, charger for cell phone, cell phone, satellite phone, charger for satellite phone, manual on how to use the satellite phone, maps, safety manuals, safety forms for when all else fails......" There's always a nagging feeling at the back of my mind I've forgotten some-thing.

"Shit." I ran upstairs, my steel-toed clomps echoing through the empty building, and picked up the shovels, survey plans, permit, and my notebook. I lost count of how many times I'd written my notes on the back of the safety forms because I'd forgotten my notebook. And I also had to turn around after driving an hour and a half because I'd forgotten survey plans and permit. If that isn't an excuse for a sherpa, I don't know what is. But when I brought that up at the last safety meeting, I wasn't taken seriously. Neither was my comment about breaking my back with all the safety equipment. Things really went down hill when I suggested we should all wear bubble-wrap.

I threw the safety forms, survey plans, permit, and notebook on the dash of the truck, plugged in my cell phone to charge, plopped my water bottle into the console and checked that my wallet with my personal credit card with a $25,000 limit was still in my back pocket. I checked inside the console again. My other wallet, with my two thousand and one safety certificates, lay there bulging. One of these days, that wallet was going to burst. I was going to file an expense claim when it did.

My assistant's name was Ron and he lived in an apartment in some part of Calgary I'd never heard of. It was one of those hidden parts where people I knew did a summer fieldschool and dug up what is now the suburb where they lived. Whatever. I was angry at not having Cam at my side, at not looking for bones, and at not having a Timmy's coffee in my stomach yet. I was aware that anger was becoming a part of my daily life. It wasn't good. The picture of County Meath at my desk only fueled it.

Ron was sitting outside his apartment building when I pulled up. He was wearing jeans, a T-shirt, and a ball cap. Ron was also plugged into an iPod. Yeah, I could see where this was going already. Good thing I'd remembered to bring extra water and sunblock. I really missed Cam.

Ron flung his bag into the truck box. When he opened the truck door I said, "I don't know what kind of weather we're going to be driving through. You might want to put your bag in the cab."

Ron shrugged and climbed into his seat. Okay. I definitely could see where this was going.

I plucked the safety forms from the dash. "Before we take off, we have to have a tailgate meeting. How long have you been with HSAC?"

"Just got hired last week."

"You got all your safety training? First aid? H2S?" Ron nodded. "How about the Bear Awareness online course?" Ron nodded. I wasn't sure if he was on automatic mode. "Do you have a driver's license?" Ron shook his head.

Great. Here's to me driving the 20 hours there and back.

The definition of a permit holder according to the Alberta government was a person qualified through their education and experience to perform assessments for Historic Resources. Said persons would provide documentation and recommendations regarding the preservation of these resources. If these resources could not be preserved, said persons would provide recommendations as to the mitigation of the impact to the resources.

My definition of a permit holder was this: I had a duty to conserve the past. If that meant re-routing a pipeline to preserve a precontact campsite, or photographing the hell out of a scatter of stone tool flakes, then that was my job. I'd tried running this line about having a duty to the past to a landowner once. He didn't buy it. He thought I was working for the oil company. Sure, the oil company paid me. An Historic Resource Impact Assessment was part of the process for them to get their clearance. On the other side of things, I submit my reports to the government, but I don't answer to them either. They depend on my recommendations regarding the preservation of the resources and, pending the destruction of the resource, my documentation will likely be the only thing left of it. I was an objective, non-partisan party and my only responsibility was to the Historic Resources of the province.

Note that neither of these definitions mention anything about safety or survival whilst doing the fieldwork necessary to assess the Historic Resources. I had my own rules regarding that.

Regarding my assistants, rule number one: Elise's assistant must be able to drive. Rule number two: Elise's assistant will not drive unless told to do so and, thus, will take up the position of Navigator. The Navigator position has specific responsibilities such as catching maps and safety forms as they fly across the dash and, of course, giving driving directions. Other than these simple rules, I didn't expect much. I didn't make assistants take notes, like other people did, and I didn't ask them to keep track of their shovel tests. I was a control freak and I liked it that way.

I flipped over the tailgate form and checked off what safety training Ron had. I started running down the list of what was on the form, "This is the project number and client. This is where we're staying. This is the number of the rental company for the truck. We won't be using radios because we'll be staying together." I glanced at Ron to make sure he was paying attention. "Grande Cache is right smack in the middle of grizzly bear country. And," I put down the form to further make my point, "It's also where Fish and Wildlife ship all the delinquent bears. We will be staying together, understand?" Ron nodded. I stifled a sigh and continued. "All emergency phone numbers are also on here, including the local RCMP.

"I usually keep the safety forms in the console of the truck while we're driving and on me, in my vest, while we're in the field."

Ron nodded.

I nodded. My ass was getting sore just thinking about the drive.

We were five hours into the drive when I began to see the tree line turn from aspen to spruce. In May the aspen are just starting to bud. The landscape changed from flat and yellow in the south, to aspen trees looking like vertical match sticks in the undulating topography near Edmonton, to a dense, dark green of pine and spruce to the northwest. In the boreal forest, it's always shaded and it's always green. Kind of like the perpetual green of Ireland.

Four hours later, the sign for Grande Cache appeared. It was a tiny town of 1200 people. There was a reserve nearby; the First Nations group knew their paperwork and was organized.

I managed to make good time because I didn't stop for lunch. I also didn't stop because Ron slept the entire trip. "Are we there yet?" Ron mumbled, wiping at his eyes.

"Yup. Welcome to Grande Cache."

"God, that took forever." I bit my tongue. "I'm hungry."

I wasn't. After nine hours of sitting in a vehicle, all I wanted to do was go for a nice long walk. But I had a responsibility to my assistant: I was supposed to feed him.

"We have pizza and steak in the mall and two chinese restaurants."

"Where's the McDonald's?"

"It's called Alberta archaeology, Ron." He gawked at me. "You're lucky you have a choice."

Ron shut his mouth, then muttered, "Pizza."

We ate pizza staring out at the brown tiles of mall floor. The dollar store and the rest of the mall had closed. "I need to stop at the band office tomorrow morning to ask if there's anything of First Nations' significance where we'll be. We might get some information before we even go out there. I'll meet you in the lobby at 7am. Be ready to leave."

Ron gawked again. It was short-lived. Maybe he was starting to get used to it.

At 7:05 I was in the lobby and impatient. Ron wasn't there.

My cell phone rang. I frowned and looked at it in amazement before answering it. "Hello, Elise speaking."

There was silence on the other end.

I looked at my phone in amazement again, checking the number of service bars I had. Yup. Still had exactly a half a bar. "Hello?" I tried again. Still nothing.

I don't know why I left my phone on in Grande Cache. There was no cell reception out here. I pretty much kept it on to tell the safety coordinator that I did. I had already called into Morris from the landline to tell him we were on the road.

I disconnected, still baffled. Oh well, I thought. If they need to reach me they can call the office or email me.

It was now 7:10 and still no Ron.

I asked the front desk to call his room. It rang five times before a muffled voice answered. "You have a job to do," I said. "If you're not downstairs in 15 minutes, you're fired."

Ron was downstairs in twelve.

I got no information from the First Nation band office. They weren't too concerned about the area and no one knew of any Traditional Land Use sites in the area. Not even any trappers' cabins.

After an hour of driving and a half-hour of getting lost, we finally arrived to the development area. I pulled the truck down a gravel road, through old spruce forest, to arrive at an open rectangular area containing a brand new telecommunications tower. I was still steaming because Ron and I had just learned that Ron couldn't read a map.

I slipped down out of the truck onto the bark mulch that lay across the site. I muttered an expletive. Mulch prevented us from seeing the ground and, therefore, from seeing if there are any artifacts lying around.

I pulled out my cell phone. I knew there would be no reception. Contrary to popular Western belief, there were places in North America, even capitalist Alberta, where there was no cell phone reception. Better yet, there were places where satellite phones didn't work. Grande Cache was one of those mythical places. On both counts. I often wondered if they knew about that before deciding to put delinquent Grizzlies here.

I donned my survey vest and my Tilley hat and asked Ron to come around to my side of the truck. I gave him a run down of the equipment, where it was and how to work it all. I even showed him where the satellite phone and instruction manual were, despite their uselessness. I gave him a bear spray and clipped my own to my belt. I pumped air into my air horn and put the two parts to a bear banger in my top pocket. I turned on my GPS, double-checked that my camera, notebook and survey plans were with me. I fumbled with a plastic bag of food and slipped it into the back pocket of my vest. Rule number one of archaeology: never get separated from your lunch.

I was set to go.

Ron had disappeared around to the other side of the truck and was rooting around in his backpack. "Ready?" I urged.

"Um, yeah." After a few minutes, I closed up my side of the truck and fetched both shovels from the box of the truck.

Ron put on his reflective vest but continued to root around in the truck. I stood and waited.

"Did you forget something?"

"Um, no."

"Then, come on. We won't be far from the truck. You can come back if you've forgotten something."

At long last, Ron finally abandoned his rooting. I held out a shovel to him. With apparent reluctance, he accepted it. "Will we be digging?"

"It's called archaeology, Ron."

Ron began to walk away to my left, kicking at the mulch. "Remember," I told him, "stay within sight. Don't wander off." I was pretty sure I saw Ron nod, but I couldn't be certain.

I tucked my shovel under my arm and pulled the survey plans from my back pocket. They showed the site for the telecommunications tower, the access road we'd just driven, and a river to the south, about 100 metres away. There was a greater possibility of an archaeological site on the south side of the telecommunications lease because of that river. I tucked my survey plans away again and began to wander toward the south, kicking the mulch as I went.

Forty-five minutes, a page of notes, and twenty pictures of mulch-covered ground later, I was at the western end of the telecommunications lease. I'd kicked up the southern half of the mulch without finding any archaeological artifacts. I climbed a backdirt pile, looking intently for that special shard of rock that might be an artifact. After another fifteen minutes, I was finished with the backdirt pile. I finally looked up. I heard a sniff behind me. I turned. There was a bear not twenty feet in front of me in the bushes.

I froze.

I didn't know whether it was a grizzly or brown bear. Frankly, I didn't really care. It was a bear and too close.

I did a slow dive into panic. *Okay, Elise, just calm down. It's not running toward you, it's not charging. Just back away slowly.*

I obeyed my mind, not thinking of the air horn or the bear bangers in my vest. I inched back a few steps, I found the incline of the backdirt pile and my mind re-engaged. The noise-makers wouldn't work – the bear was too close – they'd just scare the bear toward me. *Just keep backing away.* My hand found the bear spray and fumbled it from its holster.

The bear sniffed the air in my direction and kept its eyes on me. Then, it stood up on its hind legs and I nearly shit my pants.

My feet stumbled and I broke into a sweat over my own gracelessness, but I managed to continue backing slowly away over the backdirt pile.

I'd walked backwards halfway across the lease before I couldn't decipher branch from bear. Nothing was following me.

I started to breathe again. Then it hit me: *Where's Ron?*

While I kept one eye on the location of the bear, I scanned the rest of the clearing and the surrounding forest.

Ron was nowhere in sight. I didn't know whether I was pissed or scared.

"Fuck, fuck, fuck, fuck," I said in time with my steps as I continued back across the lease.

I finally felt it was safe enough to turn around and head toward the bushes at the northern edge of the lease. Ron emerged over the top of a backdirt pile, engrossed in his own investigation of the dirt, iPod in his ears and another bear looming in the bushes behind him.

I came to a sudden halt.

"Ron," I whispered out a scream.

Ron continued to be oblivious.

"Shit." I took another look at the bear.

I loaded the bear banger and put it in my pocket. I took out my air horn and took a deep breath. Later, I thought, I will wonder how to fill out the safety paperwork for this.

While holding the air horn and shovel high above my head, I bellowed, waved my shovel, and blew the air horn. The bear stood up and looked at me. Before I lost my nerve, I dropped the air horn, fired the bear banger and headed toward the bear. It wasn't until the bear banger fired that Ron finally looked up, then collapsed into a crouch, hands over head and eyes wide. I ran over the backdirt pile past him and charged the bear.

The surprised bear turned and galloped through the bush. I was right. It was a yearling. He had yet to figure out that puny little human females with big barks can't hurt him.

With adrenaline still surging, I returned to the backdirt pile and hauled Ron up by the collar. Then I did something I've wanted to do since I met him. I yanked the earbuds from his ears. He flinched.

"We're leaving," I growled.

Ron nodded.

Chapter Three

On the Range

"So what's the deal giving me an assistant who can't drive?"

It was Friday and I was in Morris' bright office. The southern exposure was potent compared to my dark northern cubic cave. The gleaming uncluttered surfaces of his desk and matching office furniture didn't help.

"What if I had been hurt? Got bear spray in my eyes? Am I still expected to drive myself to the hospital?"

Morris looked up from his computer screen. The man was nearing fifty and seemed to think that looking over his bifocals at me made him appear distinguished. At least that's what I thought. "Michelle didn't tell me Ron didn't have a driver's license."

"Did you ask? Did she ask when she hired him?"

Morris' gaze drifted back to the computer screen. "If I had known, Elise, I would have found you someone else. You're right. It was not safe."

"Thank you!" I said to the ceiling tiles. I was victorious. I was going to have to find some way to gloat about this.

"Did you submit your paperwork to Joe?" The mouse clicked and Morris typed as he reviewed email and debriefed me. He was the only man I've ever known who could multi-task.

"Yes, Joe has all my safety paperwork in triplicate." I hadn't told him about the bears. Neither had Ron apparently. That would involve weeks of paperwork.

"Everything go well?"

"Got the job done," I responded.

"No bear spray in the eyes?"

"Nope."

"No old ladies with broken ribs?"

"Nope. Smooth as silk, Morris."

The keyboard chattered as his fingers fired off yet another email. "The day you stay out of trouble is the day I am back in the field." Morris' dissertation was on something about longhouses in Ontario. It didn't involve bones so I'd quickly forgotten.

I gulped. "Then we both want the same thing. How about the insurance on the truck?"

"They'll cover it." Morris' eyes hadn't wavered from the screen.

"Really?" I leaned on his polished desk looking for the lie in his face.

Now Morris' hazel eyes found mine. "Yes. I said they'll cover it. They'll need your police report though."

"Wahoo!" I couldn't help it. I punched the air and did my Stampeders-won-the-grey-cup dance. This definitely deserved some gloating. I bellowed into the cubiform expanse of our second floor office space, "They'll cover the windshield on the truck."

Ida's head popped up from behind a cubicle wall. "Hooray, Elise!" then disappeared again.

From behind I heard, "Are you done?"

I paused, panting, and readjusted my ponytail. "Oh, come on, Morris. This is good news. Let me savour it. Just a little."

Morris spun in his chair and reached behind to the tidy rows of files on the table. "I need you to go to Cold Lake next week, if you're up to it. You had expressed an interest in doing some work with First Nations. This project involves working with the Cold Lake First Nation."

I pulled up a chair and plunked myself down. I'd only 'expressed an interest in doing some work with First Nations' as a way out of looking for rocks. It was a diversionary tactic, I admit. "Is it arky work or consultation?" I'd only ever done consultation over the counter with the group in Grande Cache, never any on-site work.

"It's arky, but you'll be working with a Cold Lake First Nations' representative."

"Are they going to be an observer or my assistant?"

"Your assistant."

I pulled back, leery. "Do they know archaeology involves hard labour? Digging by hand, with a shovel, making holes in the ground? "

Morris looked over his bifocals at me again, "Yes. See if you can book Lorraine. She comes highly recommended. Russell's worked with her." Russell was a coworker I barely ever saw. He did a lot of oilsands work in Fort McMurray and was gone for months at a time.

"You'll be working on the air weapons range too. I suggest you talk to Russell so that you know what you're supposed to do. There are very stringent protocols that you need to follow. There is no room for error." There was a pause as Morris let this sink into my thick skull. "Russell will let you know." Morris turned back to his computer screen. "The Historic Branch said they can issue your permit Monday morning if you send in the application right away." I'd been dismissed.

I got up but paused at the door. "I gotta run out for a little bit to visit my brother."

"Which one?"

"The lawyer." Morris nodded and sniffed into his moustache. "Did you call me on Tuesday morning?"

Morris frowned but continued typing. "No. I got both your call-in and call-out messages so I had no need to talk to you. Besides, I know you have no cell phone coverage there." He also had a near photographic memory. I had to be very careful when I lied to him. "Maybe it was your mother." A hint of a smile played upon his lips as he continued to type.

"Don't even go there, Morris." I left and started my trek to Theo's downtown office.

Theo's office was the epitome of masculine design. Every time I walked into the office of Torrington Willis and Jones, I felt like my jeans and long red hair were an affront to law-abiding society. Maybe just law-creating society.

I opened the plate glass door to the dark leather and oak interior and told the receptionist I was here to see Theodore Marquette. The brunette with false eyelashes eyed me suspiciously. Not like she didn't know who I was. I blamed the jeans.

Margaret appeared from a corridor a moment later and she smiled at me. "He's on the phone but is expecting you." Margaret, a 50-something widow with a sharp mind, red smile, and a quick step lead me down the familiar hall. "Where are you back from this time, dear?"

"Grande Cache."

"Oh, my Roy used to like fishing up there. Pretty country."

"Yes, minus the bears."

"They're nasty little buggers aren't they. Roy tried to make me believe he once fought a grizzly for a trout." She smiled then as she pushed open Theo's door and glanced in.

She nodded and turned back to me. "He's just about done. Go on in and have a seat. Can I get you a coffee?"

I declined and stepped into Theo's world.

Besides being a lawyer, my eldest brother was a decent guy. On his good days. When he had them. Life as a lawyer was stressful. My bookshelves were loaded with reference material for my job – The Historical Resources Act, a few dozen books on the who's who of the tree, plants, and animals in the boreal forest world, writing style guides, government regulations, soil and surficial geology books -- but I had nothing on Theo. His office was floor-to-ceiling bookshelves. Packed. And his desk was the same – packed but messy. I guess I measured stress by how much was on a person's desk and how many bookshelves they needed. Morris' desk was pristine and he was Buddha.

Theo had his leather chair's back turned to me. His elbow rested on the arm, his hand cradling the phone to his ear. His brown curly hair was shiny with product, as usual and I could already smell it mingling with his cologne. No matter how many times Theo balked at me, threw me off-centre, and backed me into a corner, the smell of him seemed to mellow the blow. Sometimes I wondered if it was because he reminded me of dad.

Theo's voice stopped. The phone fell. The chair turned.

Theo replaced the phone and saw me standing in front of his desk. "Sorry. One of my clients was being an asshole. Did you get a coffee?"

"It's okay. I've had my daily quota already."

Theo looked at his watch. "It's only ten."

I shrugged. I didn't want to be here any longer than necessary. I'd catch Starbucks on the walk back to the office. "What's up?" I took a seat in the wingback opposite him.

Theo jerked on his tie. Today it was a burgundy and pink stripe to offset his navy suit and white shirt. Then, he leaned back in his chair. His hazel eyes never leaving mine. That's when I knew I shouldn't have agreed to a personal visit.

He pulled his chair forward, placed his interlaced fingers upon his desk and leaned toward me. "How's work, Elise?"

"Fine. How's yours?" I knew how this worked.

"Things are still busy despite the economy?"

"Fine. We've barely had a hiccup. Looks like you're doing well too. Lots of divorces?"

"You apartment is still good?"

"Yes. It's fine. How's the house?"

"And your car? You're still driving that little Toyota?"

"Yes. And how's the Beamer? Still driving like an idiot?"

Theo's head bent down then. We've been playing this game too long. I knew his diversionary tactics and he should have known better. I waited.

Theo leaned back and met my eyes again. The chill raced down my back again, but I ignored it.

A manicured hand ran down his tie and refitted it inside his suit jacket. Just because my eldest brother got my father's good looks didn't mean he was handsome. Too much maintenance.

Then Theo sighed and looked up at the ceiling. That's when I knew I was in trouble.

"Elise, I need you to pay back the money I lent you for school."

"Well, yeah....."

Theo's eyes dropped back down to mine. "All of it. Now."

Shit.

"And I have money stuffed up my ass for just such an occasion."

"Elise...."

"What the fuck, Theo?" A cold sweat was pooling down my back and into all the other places that were usually warm. "The four hundred bucks a month I give you isn't enough? Where did this come from?" Visions of pawning my second-hand TV and my prized books were flashing in front of my eyes.

"You could take out a bank loan."

"The whole idea was to avoid crippling interest. Hello. Student. Archaeologist. Remember?" I would be living on the street, every paycheque going to my unscrupulous brother just because he was having a bad day. "Is the business not going well so you're taking it out on me?"

"No, Elise...."

"I know you're a divorce lawyer, but, geez Theo, this is really low."

"Elise, will you shut up!" Theo shot to his feet. My mouth clamped shut. But the rest of me was shaking.

I owed my brother a lot of money. I hadn't been able to get a student loan because the-wisdom-of-student-loans stated that if your parents earned over a certain amount of money, you shouldn't need to borrow money from the government. My mother, however, had refused to fund my journey into self-exploration and happiness in the Department of Anthropology, and later the fieldschool in Tunisia. My three part-time jobs hadn't cut it. Sebbie had just finished school and gone through the wringer with his first wife. Theo had been my last hope.

Theo rounded his desk and leaned against it, arms crossed. "Look, I have a compromise."

I was now numb to any further suggestive shivers.

"Margaret needs some help. She is willing to train you. You work here, I pay your rent, utilities, groceries, etc. and I get to write you off. You'd be a kept-, albeit working, woman."

My life had really only just begun and now it was ending. After years in undergrad, I finally found a discipline that made me happy. After ten years in school, I'd finally finished. After a year of looking, I'd finally found a decent paying job. It wasn't Physical Anthropology, but the runner-up discipline of Archaeology. I hated the government bureaucracy but managed to cope with it. All in all, I'd finally found my own way, despite the lack of fulfillment and happiness, and now Theo wanted to rip it all out from under me.

"That's just fucked up." I finally managed.

Theo sighed and rolled his eyes back up the ceiling. Shit, again. "Okay, I'll settle with you. I need to settle my accounts so that I can make partner."

"Why don't you ask mother for the money?"

Theo raised his eyebrows. "Do you really want mom to know where you got the money for school?"

"You're such an asshole."

"I'm sorry, but that's the way of it." Theo walked back to sit at his desk. "Think about it." He straightened his tie, "I want to make partner by the end of the year." He picked up the phone and dialed.

He'd won and he knew it. Unfortunately, I knew it too. He'd been trying to make partner for over four years now. I was sick of hearing about it. I'm sure everyone was. At nearly every family function, Theo would find some way to rant about it. It was going to take $50,000 dollars to get him to shut up.

I left and dragged myself to Starbucks for what I felt would be my last fluffy coffee ever.

When I got back to the office, I sat numbly at my desk and sipped my coffee. Like a quad stuck in the muskeg, the wheels of my mind spun, flung mud, and me got nowhere. By the time I'd reached the bottom of my paper cup fifteen minutes later, I'd bounced through the internet attempting to find answers, only coming back to the Trinity College website once again. Yes. Gavin Cleary was lovely, but he wasn't going to give me $50,000. Too bad I knew nothing of Hellenistic Archae-ology; I could run away and forget about all of this. But knowing my family, Theo would probably follow me and Mother would fund his expedition.

I went in search of Russell for my Cold Lake project.

Russell vouched for the proposed assistant, Lorraine. "She's won-derful." Score one for Elise. "But protocols on the Weapons Range are intense. If you don't follow them, they can kick you off and never let you back on." Okay. I could do that. Russell gave me a handful of papers outlining what I'd need.

My client was an old favourite. I'd worked with Erinson Power quite a bit over the years and their project managers were communicative and on the ball. Nice guys, all around. When I looked at my survey plans again, I saw they had come not from a project manager, but an administrative assistant. That was strange.

There was also some ambiguity to the plans. It didn't show the proposed right-of-way, only the existing road. I needed to clarify exactly where the right-of-way was so I called the administrative assistant. She was in training. Please leave a message. So much for this being urgent.

I emailed the administrative assistant instead, asking her specific questions regarding the right-of-way limits wherein I needed to assess. While I was at it, I emailed the HSAC Cold Lake liaison and asked him to book me Lorraine for next Monday and Tuesday. I figured I could get all this figured out today, have one day off, drive up to Cold Lake on Sunday, and start work on Monday morning.

My phone rang. Instead of Erinson Power, I got, "Elise, mom's in the hospital." It was my other brother Sebastian, the engineer. My day just wasn't getting any better.

"What's it this time?"

He sighed. I could picture him running a hand through his curly chestnut hair sans all the mousse and other products Theo put in his. "Elise, don't do this."

"Do what? This is, what, the third time in the last year she's been admitted. I told you she does this for attention, but you and Theo don't seem to believe me."

"Can you just listen for once?" His voice rose. I paused. When we were kids, any word against mom got him in a tizzy. I admit I used to take advantage of that, now, as much as I wanted to, it was sometimes difficult to avoid the topic of mother. Theo was the Teflon Man and Sebastian was a Momma's boy. Not that Theo wasn't under mother's thumb too but he didn't display it the way Sebastian did.

"Fine. Talk."

He sighed again. "Mom's got pancreatic cancer."

I was stunned. Stunned because I didn't feel anything. I searched my gut, my heart – all I found was a bit of guilt over not feeling something more.

"What's the prognosis?"

"It's iffy. They can't do surgery. She's starting chemo and radiation tomorrow." I let the silence hang between us. Mostly because I had nothing to say. At least, nothing nice. "Why don't you come over for supper tonight and we'll go over and visit mom together."

"I don't want to visit mom."

"Why not?"

"For all the same old reasons."

"She might be dying, Elise."

"What? So you want me to play nice so she can think she'll get into Heaven after all? Nuh, uh."

Sebastian's voice rose again. "She wrote you into her will, Elise."

"There's more to life than money, Sebbie."

I fully expected the phone line to go dead after that. Instead, my brother decided to take the high road, "Why don't you come by the office later this week? We'll do lunch."

"I can't. I have to go into the field soon and I've got a pile of logistics to figure out before I go. Maybe when I get back, okay?" I signed off and I looked at the calendar. It would be June when I got back and field season would in full swing. Score two for Elise.

I felt bad for Sebastian. He wasn't going to have a life until mom died. Maybe I should go back to the UK, at least until all this was over.

I was just about to go get another coffee, maybe go for a walk to clear my head when my phone rang again. I was fully expecting to hear from my mother, or maybe one of my brothers' wives. I was surrounded by people who either objected to everything I did or thought they knew what was best for me. And Morris wondered why I was always in a fighting mood.

It was the administrative assistant from Erinson Power. "I need to know where exactly the right-of-way is in relation to the road. My permit from the government will only be valid within the right-of-way. Is this the new road or the old road on the plans?"

"I don't know," I was stunned. I pulled the phone away from my ear and glared at it. "I can find you someone who knows." Then there was silence. I could only assume she was hunting for someone. *Be patient, Elise. Be patient.*

Then a nice male voice came on the line, "Hi, I'm Todd, the project manager. What can I help you with?"

At last, the project manager!

He was able to answer my questions exactly as a project manager should. Todd knew his project inside and out.

One task done. Score again for Elise. Next!

The phone rang. I looked at my empty coffee cup longingly. "Elise, why aren't you coming to dinner tonight?" It was the phone call I was expecting. It had taken Trisha , Sebastian's wife, twenty minutes to pick up the phone. I know Sebastian had told her not to call. Twenty minutes must have been an eternity for her.

"I'm busy."

"We're going to go see your mom afterwards...."

"Look, Trisha. I really don't want to see my mother or come for supper. I'm really busy."

"You're too busy to see your mother?"

"Yes, and she's my mother so please stay out of it. Now, I'm sorry, but I have work to do." I was really trying to keep the edge out of my voice. I felt I was failing but this truly was none of Trisha's concern.

I hung up and lunged away from my desk before the phone could ring again.

When I returned, coffee cup now full, I turned to the list Russell had given me. I needed to lay my hands on some new 'Range approved maps.' What the hell were 'Range approved maps?'

My computer beeped. An email from the HSAC Cold Lake liaison told me Lorraine was available for work Monday and Tuesday. Score again. I was on a roll!

I called the orientation office at the Cold Lake Air Weapons Range, or CLAWR for short. Sometimes these military acronyms kill me. "I need a Range approved map," I told the woman.

"Where are you working?" the very efficient Francine asked.

I told her. "Okay, you need to call into the Bonnyville office. Tell them I told you to."

Okay.

So, I called the Bonnyville office and asked for the same thing. He asked the same thing as the very efficient Francine. "That's okay. Come by the office on your way out to the Range and we'll get you sorted out."

Score for Elise again! "Oh, and by the way, does your project have DND approval?"

Department of National Defense approval? "I guess so. The client should have taken care of all that."

"Well, can you do me a favour and check with them? I'd hate for you to get kicked off the base."

Yeah, me too.

I called DND and left a message. Ten minutes later, my phone rang. "Elise, I think you should come for supper tonight." I was being jostled back to Theo, who apparently wasn't satisfied with one victory over me today.

"What's got into everybody? Yeah, mom's in the hospital. So what? Leave me out of it." I propped the phone between my shoulder and ear as I dug into my bag.

"Look," Theo said, the edge in his voice taking a backseat. "Why don't you come for supper? The gang hasn't seen you in a while. We don't have to go visit mom afterwards if you don't want to."

I pulled the ibuprofen container out and popped a couple in my mouth followed by a swig of coffee. "I have to go into the field."

"Jesus, Elise. Isn't family more important than work?"

I nearly shot back, "Isn't my happiness more important than money?" but I just wasn't ready to step into that argument with Theo yet. I was still sore -- raw and bristling, in fact -- but I needed to do some research. I need to figure a way out of my predicament before standing up in his defense box.

"Fine," I finally caved, already feeling the pressure of being under Theo's thumb. "Dinner's at 6:30, right?"

He confirmed and signed off. At last, peace! It would be mine until 6:29 tonight.

I looked at the clock. It was 12:10 and still no word from DND. This was going to be a very long day, I could just tell. I was beginning to have doubts that I would be able to start work on Monday morning. I decided I should probably eat lunch in addition to gather more coffee.

After lunch, I stopped by Russell's office and told him about being jostled between CLAWR and DND. He frowned at me. "Sounds strange. I never got a run-around around like that. I have some old Range approved maps. They're from last fall. Take 'em but stop in at the orientation office on your first day to make sure they haven't changed." I could have kissed his scruffy face.

Next, I stopped in at Morris' office. He was on the phone, so I sipped my coffee and waited.

"What's up, kid?" He scribbled on a notepad while he hung up.

"What's the protocol for doing a project on the Range? I was just asked if my project had been approved by DND. Shouldn't Erinson Power have done all that?"

"Yup. But follow up just in case."

Despite the coffee, ibuprofen, and my lunchtime reprieve, my head was beginning to hurt. I wanted to blame Theo for starting it all.

I sat back down in my cubicle and called DND again. No answer. I left another message. I called the orientation office again and explained what was going on. "I need an answer ASAP," I told Francine. Francine and I were becoming fast friends.

"Call Kenneth. He's my supervisor. He'll know what's going on."

I was getting bruises from being handed around so much. But okay. I called Kenneth.

Kenneth was an ex-fighter pilot and ex-RCMP. And Kenneth knew what was going on. "Anything not concerning First Nations, I can process," Kenneth explained in his clear and succinct Mountie voice. "If it concerns First Nations, it has to go through DND. Sorry, I can't help you."

So I was back with the non-responsive DND.

"But," Kenneth continued. "email me all your information. Explain exactly who you are, what you want to do, and why. I'll forward it to DND. Hopefully you'll get the response you need."

I hung up and downed my coffee. I dug in my bag for some more ibuprofen. I had suggested to the HSAC social committee that we really needed a punching bag installed in the lab. They thought I was crazy. Maybe they hadn't dealt with DND.

My phone rang again. Oh god. Coffee and over-the-counter drugs just weren't cutting it. I picked up the phone. "Holy Hanna, Batman! You're in the office."

Finally someone to make me smile. "Hey, Mikey! How's the dissertation?"

A groan, loud, long, and hard, erupted at me. Mikey and I had done our undergrad together at the University of Calgary. I left to do my Master's elsewhere. He stayed and was now into the fourth year of his Ph.D. It wasn't good to do all your education at the same school. He was brilliant and could have got into any grad program in the country, fully funded. I suspected Mikey was just too lazy to move. "Llewellyn wants a chapter by the end of June. He's seriously putting a crimp in my Halo competition time." Mikey was also a video game addict.

"You had to put out sometime, Mikey. Not like they'll keep you around forever." I looked at the caller display on my phone. "You're calling from the department. What's up?"

A sigh. "Llewellyn got a call this morning from the Mounties. They need someone out on a search this weekend." Electricity shot through my body. Searching for bones. Suddenly Theo's threat didn't seem so bad.

"No one else in the department?" I asked, trembling, salivating.

"No. They're all doing studies on teeth. They wouldn't know a bone fragment if it hit 'em in the face. What the fuck, Elise?"

"Hey, you're preaching to the choir on that one." I tried to sound nonchalant despite the itch gnawing at my palms. "Two hundred and six bones in the body, why the thirty-two in the mouth? I don't know. Llewellyn still off fieldwork?"

Lance Llewellyn was a great Physical Anthropologist and a fantastic professor at the UofC. He'd spent many years doing archaeological fieldwork in foreign countries digging up cemeteries. Now hell and highwater couldn't get him back into the field. It was all due to a stint with Physicians for Human Rights after the bad stuff in Croatia. Even a Physical Anthropologist can be turned off dead people.

"Yeah. He asked me right after he demanded a chapter. Apparently I'm an all-powerful god. Can you do it?"

He'd asked it. Finally. Me. Looking for bones in Alberta. Human bones. In ten years, I'd only been asked one other time. And no one outside of academia gets asked. No one.

Then reality descended. Life. Work. Lack of life. I looked at the picture of County Meath again.

"Dude, I can't. I'm trying to organize fieldwork for next week."

"But that's next week. What about the weekend? I'll have Halo and all the fixins – chocolate, pizza, chips waiting for you when you get back in." Little did Mikey know how tempting that was to me at this very minute.

"I can't." The words lodged in my throat and made me choke. I tilted the dregs of my coffee cup into my dammed throat. "I wish I could, dude, but life sucks right now. Seriously. I just can't." I tried to shield the emotion from my voice, but more than a little got through this time.

"Geez, you alright, Ellie?" He was the only one who called me that. "Anything I can do?"

I swiped a hand across my watering eyes and righted myself. "No, no, it's alright. I'll figure it out. Like usual."

Mikey sighed. "All right. But let me know if I can help okay? You still up for a night of Halo?"

My headache was coming back. "Yeah," I managed, "maybe in December."

I walked a lap around the attic, taking stock of the other attic-rat desks. Frank hadn't cleaned up his desk and it would remain that way until he got back from the field in three weeks. Ida left about noon to go out on a survey for a week or so down south. It was the time of year when instead of saying, "See you later," we said, "See you at Christmas." We were lucky: the quick sand folks downstairs who worked up north in oilsands country never saw each other.

I refilled my mug, retraced my steps, cracked my knuckles, and hunkered down at my desk. I worded my email to Kenneth, the Mountie at Cold Lake, very clearly and included the survey plans. I then changed my accommodation and truck bookings from the Monday to Tuesday.

I phoned Lorraine, my assistant, and told her that our start was postponed until Tuesday. I arranged to meet her at the Range where we would both be included in the orientation session. That was two hours of fieldtime down the drain. I booked a radio – I would need a special radio for calling into CLAWR Range Patrol.

Meanwhile, it was 430. An email showed that Kenneth had forwarded on my message to DND and copied me. There was no response from DND. Friday business hours were over. I hoped that I could get everything straightened out on Monday. However, it wouldn't be the first time I'd have to re-book truck, hotel, assistant, and accommodation multiple times.

I left the office and picked up a bottle of wine on the way home. I had two hours of peace before my appearance at Sebastian's and I intended to make the most of it.

I threw my bag and jacket over the old school chair that stood in the hallway of my apartment and promptly tromped into the kitchen to open the wine. I'd been so intent on wine that I'd forgotten to pick up some food to complement it. Any food would have done, I sighed as I looked in my empty fridge. Supper would be slow in coming at Sebastian's place. Trisha never seemed to order in until at least an hour after everyone got there. I cracked a can of Cream of Mushroom soup, stirred it up with the last of the milk in my fridge, and popped it into the microwave. I poured myself a glass of wine then stood breathing and sipping while my soup cooked.

As I stood waiting I took stock of what I could possibly sell to fetch Theo's $50,000. My TV, sofa and kitchen table were all hand-me-downs from friends during my undergrad. Yup, that's how long I kept stuff. At least ten years. And it had all been moved six to eight times, into various apartments and storage places. The wooden chairs around the kitchen table were ones I'd picked up at garage sales over the years. I had managed to buy a new bed when I started at HSAC – it'd been a treat to myself for finally getting a job in my discipline, well, sort of. I'd proudly walked into Ikea and fitted myself up with one of the cheapest and simplest beds going. It was a double and I was very proud of that. It felt as if with a double bed I was finally growing up. It was far stretch from the futon Mikey had given me.

I had a small one-bedroom apartment. The sofa took up most of the living room. Cheap bookshelves and make-shift shelving, lined the room and were crammed with my prized possessions – books on ancient Egypt and Mayan culture. I'd started collecting them in junior high. They ranged from National Geographic coffee table books of glossy pictures to textbooks on deciphering hieroglyphics and mummies and mortuary practices. I loved every single one of them like they were my biological children. They were the reason I was fascinated with dead people and ancient cultures.

The kitchen table and chairs were shoved against the back wall and were piled with papers and books. I was still trying to publish a journal article or two from my graduate work. One of these days I'd realize that was a lost cause.

I took the two steps from the kitchen toward the bedroom. It was the same theme. My double Ikea bed took up most of the room, with a hand-me-down dresser and chair fitting in along the walls.

And that was it. That was my life in 400 square feet for $1500 a month.

The wineglass in my hand was shaking as I lifted it to take another sip.

I really had nothing.

Tears began to well in my eyes.

I had been happily living in denial when my eldest brother had to come in and crashed it all. And Mikey's fateful call this afternoon had shown me -- quite plainly -- that even the life I'd managed wasn't all that blissfully ignorant.

Fuck, my life sucked. And I hated Theo for showing me.

The microwave beeped as the tears began to roll. I gulped the rest of my wine.

Had I really chosen wrong? Should I have chosen profitability in a university degree instead happiness? Should I have done an MBA or an MD and been miserable? Should I have been married at 18 and become a baby-making slave to an oil-industry husband?

I just didn't know any more. I'd tried so hard to find something that made me happy, to do something worthwhile and fulfilling, but recent events had been telling me that all my efforts had been in vain. Why bother to try to be happy? There's no money in it and money makes the world go round. Without the money cushioning you, buffering you from the outside world, you don't have a hope at happiness.

I knew there were probably several Buddhist monks and commune-living hippies that would have disagreed with me on this point, but they didn't live in Calgary. Frankly, I wasn't too sure they lived in reality.

I poured myself another glass of wine.

I retrieved my soup and pulled myself together enough to push some food down my throat.

I glanced at my laptop. It was a used one, picked up when I realized that my old 486 wasn't going to cut it for writing a graduate thesis. It wasn't often that I wished I had internet at my apartment. I hated being connected: I hated that I needed a cell phone for my job; hated that my clients expected me to respond to emails within ten minutes of them being sent; hated that people were willingly giving up their souls for technological toys and the sake of "convenience." Does everyone really need to be glued to a cell phone 24/7? Are there that many life-threatening bombs in the world? No. If we could survive 10,000 years without cell phones and the internet, we could do an hour commute without needing to phone our friends and clients.

That being said, however, this was one of those times I wished I had internet at home. I wanted to check into bank loans. Maybe even check into working for an escort service, who knows?

I was now convinced that a bank loan was my only hope. Getting a second job was out of the question. My schedule barely allowed for me to pay my rent on time. But I knew enough about banks to know that I wasn't a sure thing. I didn't own my home, didn't own anything except my old clunky car. And I had nothing saved. The only thing I had going for me was a credit card that was maxed because of the cycle of work expenses. When I'd started at HSAC, my card had a $5000 limit; four years of fieldwork forced it up to $25,000.

That escort service idea was beginning to look better all the time. I could work a couple, three jobs in the one week a month I was home and get, what, a couple thousand dollars. Sure. By the end of the year, Theo would have his $50,000. And I would have syphilis. And no self-respect.

I finished my soup and refilled my wineglass.

So, the escort service is out. I can't live without self-respect. And even though syphilis looked really cool in skeletal remains, it wasn't so cool when you're living and that's if I didn't contract HIV and die first. What about drugs? I could sell drugs. I didn't do drugs, never have. Me doing drugs was right up there with me getting along with technology. But I could sell 'em. Yeah. It's not my fault others caved in and were intent on ruining their lives. But it was illegal. Mmmm, it was bad enough that I was stressed out about being on call 24/7 eight months of every year for my current job, what would I turn into with the paranoia of being caught and thrown in prison?

Okay. Drugs were out. Not that I'd know where to start on that venture.

I sighed. It was 6:20. I put my bowl in the sink, setting it to soak, then downed the rest of my wine. I wasn't even getting a buzz. Bummer.

Maybe I should go work on the oilrigs in Fort Mac. Just when I thought my life couldn't be any shittier.

I picked up my jacket from where I'd thrown it and gathered my car keys. My life wasn't getting any better any time soon, but at least I was in a ripe mood to greet my brothers.

Sebastian and Trisha lived in Mount Royal, one of the poshest and most expensive places in Calgary. It was also on the banks of the Elbow River. I refused to live on the floodplain. If the Elbow River and the Bow River had a floodplain, that meant they'd flooded before and probably would again. But, then again, if you're rich enough to live by the river, you're probably rich enough to rebuild after a flood. I lived in an apartment building on the ridge overlooking downtown; out of the smog and the floodzone.

Maybe I could ask Sebbie for the money….no, he'd just tell mom. Shit. I needed to do some research on bank loans.

I'd managed to finish the bottle of White Zinfandel I'd picked up after work. It wasn't having any effect. I was disappointed and, by the time I'd rung the doorbell on Sebastian's place, I was sincerely hoping Ashley, Theo's wife, would have brought something other than a double-malt scotch.

When she opened the door, Ashley was, in fact, holding a bottle of Chardonnay. "I love you," I blurted, surprised that I almost slurred.

She smirked, hand on her hip, "I figured you might need something, but it sounds like you already started." As she took my bag, she leaned close and added, "I need to catch up."

I leaned back. I could smell Ashley's Chanel No 5 and how it mixed with the products that made her dark hair look perfect. "Have they started yet?"

"You've been the topic of conversation since Theo and I got here at quarter to six." Ashley twisted her arm through mine and led me down the hall to the kitchen. The cedar lined walls and tiled foyer had ceased to amaze me long ago. The kitchen, however, always made me wish I could cook. Stainless steel. Marble. It was macho Italy with more than a touch of Chris & Steve.

I could hear my brothers in the living room just beyond the counter. "I'll crack the bottle and put another in the fridge." Ashley left me in a rustle of black silk. Sometimes I wished I could wear silk – I'd just end up wrecking it, though, or getting it dirty.

I was left to face the family, to walk onto the firing range alone. Some things never change.

Voices died down when I stepped into the living room. "Hey," I began.

"Hey," Theo offered. Sebastian was quiet. Trisha leapt up and hugged me, "Hey, Sweetie." These had been my family dynamics for three years; Theo sitting on the bridge with Sebastian and Trisha on either side. It would have been nice to have someone on my side of the bridge for once, if only she wasn't always trying to get me to cross it.

"So, how's work?" Trisha broke the silence. "Where are you off to next?"

"Cold Lake."

"Where's that?" Trisha gazed at me with her green contacts and lined eyes. How could anyone so pretty be so...so blissfully ignorant?

"Um, north-east of Edmonton," I bumbled as Ashley appeared and put a glass in my hand. "Drink," she whispered.

"I saw my hairstylist today and he thinks you have the coolest job," said Trisha, merging into her 'holding court' routine – bangles banging and hair flipping --- "He's got you pictured as an Indiana Jane, with a whip and everything."

I wished I had a whip right then.

"Trisha," Theo warned, "leave Elise alone. You know she doesn't like talking about her job."

"Yeah, she only does it to piss off mom." These were the first words Sebastian had said to me since the phone call.

Unfortunately, instead of having just enough wine to not care, I'd had just enough to loosen my inhibitions. "Yes, Sebbie. Unlike mom, my life revolves around pissing other people off."

"Mom only ever wanted the best for you." And we were off. Sebastian's face was red and blotchy; he must have started on the wine early too.

I felt wine slosh onto my wrist, "My 'best' is my happiness. If she cared, she'd let me do as I wanted."

"Since when are you happy? You haven't been happy since you started archaeology."

"And since when are you an expert in happiness? Not like you're happy in engineering."

"At least I'm making money."

"Yes, Sebastian; I'm poor, you're rich. Life suddenly makes sense." I felt my back burning as Theo looked on. I wanted him to say something, anything, because I wanted to start into him too. The itch to tell him to shove his offer was burning a hole in my tongue.

Instead, I gulped my wine. Ashley returned with appetizers to feed the silence.

Finally, Theo made his move. "Can we just sit and have a nice family dinner? Can we talk about something other than our jobs and mom?"

"Is that possible?" Ashely's mumble was more than a little audible.

The wine was taking effect. I snorted and burst into a laugh. "She's right," I finally managed. "I don't know what else we could talk about."

Trisha stood up again to hold her court, "Oh, I know. This is like a game. We can play 'what we have in common'."

Ashley rolled her eyes. "I've got a better idea." She strode to the sideboard and pulled out a bottle of double-malt scotch. "Who's up for a game of poker?"

Did I mention that I loved Ashley?

We ate, we drank, we played poker, and thanks to some ingenious prompting from Ashley, we talked. I think it was the first time since I was five that I'd ever spoken to both my brothers without any of us trying to get a rise out of the other.

No one visited mom that night.

On Monday, I arrived at work to an emailed response from DND: "As the road you intend to assess has been in existence for 12 years, an archaeological assessment does not need to be done. Access denied."

"FUCK!" I slammed down my Starbucks latte on my desk. My five-dollar coffee sloshed dangerously against the lid.

I immediately looked up Todd's number at Erinson Power. "Todd, this is Elise at HSAC. I was told to follow up with DND to make sure this project has access. I was just denied. I think you need to do some checking."

I sat and waited. Or, as my friend Kara says, I simmered in a soup of my own aggression. I barely tasted my coffee as I waited for a response from Todd.

It took a half hour. Todd called. "It was a bit of a mix up. It's alright. DND will be contacting you."

Five minutes later, an email from DND appeared. "There was a misunderstanding. Access is granted."

I think the score was tied between me and DND.

By the time I'd completed all my safety forms it was 3pm. My rental truck arrived and I had to put in another two hours of checks and sorting and gathering of equipment. Every permit holder needed a stellar assistant like Cam. But I didn't even have a Ron. Without an HSAC archaeology assistant on this project, I was on my own. My mind and my mind alone needed to remember everything I needed. Consequently, I kept waking up that night remembering things I'd forgotten. I had to return to the office with a revised list of equipment to pack. I didn't leave for Cold Lake until nearly 10am.

Eight hours later, I was put into a smoking room in a hotel inundated with fisherman for the annual Cold Lake Fish-Off. Switching rooms didn't solve my problem; it only substituted it for another. The couple next door had loud sex until after midnight. I'd forgotten my earplugs.

5:30 am came way too early.

I met Lorraine at the Range orientation office. Lorraine endured a re-training while I watched the orientation video in awe. I knew this was a national air weapons range, but it hadn't really sunk in. The orientation straightened me out. There were zones where the fighter planes practiced their bombing and, um, lasering. Calling in on the radio ensured that you aren't in those zones, which can sometimes change weekly, if not daily, and to ensure that you won't get blown up or blinded by the lasers.

The orientation informed you of many things: if you see a bomb, don't touch the bomb, back away from the bomb, but first take lots of photos to show your friends and security. Then there was the radio: call in when you are about to leave high-grade gravel road. Next, call in when you've left high-grade gravel road (two feet later) and tell them where you're going. Then, call in when you get there (10 minutes later). Reverse and repeat all day. Good thing I'd brought ibuprofen.

I understood now. This was working on the Range. The good thing was I had fantastic cell phone reception here. At least I could call Morris to tell him I'd been blinded by lasers.

I got to meet the amazingly efficient Francine. She was an older lady, with maroon hair and long red fingernails and she chewed gum like a cow chews its cud. She was everything I knew she would be – fantastic.

I introduced myself and she practically threw herself over the desk at me. "Hello, Elise. I gather you got everything sorted out?"

I nodded. "I just need to know how to call into security on the radio. I'm going to be traveling down the length of the road. If I'm supposed to call in every time we leave the road, I'll be calling every few minutes."

She chewed and considered. "Call security on your cell phone and ask them what they want to do. I suspect that since you're only going to be within the treeline beside the road, they will only want you to call in once in the morning and call in once at night."

Out in the parking lot, Lorraine in the seat beside me, I called security. "How far from the road will you be?" the officer asked. "Within 50 metres."

"Don't worry about it then." I blinked and cleaned out my ears.

"Sorry, I need to clarify. Are you saying you don't need me to call in at all?"

"Yes, that's correct. If you're that close to the road, I'll just notify Range Patrol and everything will be fine."

Okay! I dumped the fully charged and ready-to-go radio in the back seat and forgot about it.

After two days, Lorraine proved herself worthy. She was a good assistant; she kept up, dug 40 centimetre by 40 centimetre by 40 centimetre holes without complaint, and she knew her way around the area. She was everything an assistant should be.

On Monday, I faxed in Lorraine's timesheet to Erinson Power. Twenty minutes, I got a phone call from the administrative assistant. "How come Lorraine drove to the Range?"

I frowned at the phone, "She wanted to."

"If Lorraine drives, she gets to submit for use of her vehicle. You should have picked her up."

"Nobody told me this."

The woman snickered into the phone, "Yeah, she's not going to tell you because she makes money off of her vehicle this way."

"You should have specified anything like this in the project description. As it was, I had to go through three people to get the survey plans sorted out and five people to tell me I did, in fact, have DND clearance. You should take a lesson from the folks in the pipeline section; they know what they're doing."

The phone went dead. Maybe Erinson Power wasn't such a loyal and beloved client after all.

Chapter Four

Wisest Man in the World

A sliver of dim light leaked into my bedroom as the door opened. "Elise, are you awake?"

My father needn't have asked.

I threw the blankets off and, already dressed, grabbed my Barbie backpack from under my bed. I'd chosen the hideously pink pack over my beloved Star Wars pack because I knew what Dad and I would be doing today.

My dad was grinning. I could see in him the itch that had already begun to play in my stomach.

In unison, we crept down the hall, gently put on our shoes, and picked up the cooler Dad had already packed.

We loaded ourselves and the cooler into the old Landrover Dad kept parked in the yard out back. I pulled on my lap seatbelt. As Dad started the Landrover, I prayed that Mother didn't wake and demand a halt to our activities. She hadn't found out yet. Or, if she had, nothing had been mentioned to me, at least. A moment after the Landrover's engine turned over, a curtain in a second-story window was pulled back. My breath caught before I realized who was awake.

As the Landrover back out of the yard, I watched as Sebastian's eyes grew sadder the further we retreated.

The next spring, Dad had a surprise. He'd bought a cabin near a pond off the end of that muddy road. "What do you think?"

It was a cabin of vertical logs, angled roof with a large deck jutting out over the bank descending toward a pond. There was an outhouse a hundred yards or so into the bushes behind. Firewood was stacked along the cabin by the front door. I could hear the wind and the birds in the trees. It was perfect.

I didn't think my dad could smile any bigger than when I'd lit a fire in the stove by myself that summer. We made smores, snuggled in our sleeping bags, with the moon peaking through the patio doors. "What do you want to be when you grow up, Elise?"

"I want to be me." My Dad laughed, his head tilting back and his laugh bouncing off the bare ceiling of the cabin.

"I think that's very wise. But what are you going to do to make money so that you can live?"

I remembered thinking very hard at this question. I hadn't actually pondered the whole concept of jobs and making money before. I hadn't needed to. "What can I do?"

When you're young, everyone believes their parents are gods. At that moment, my Dad was the wisest person in the entire world. To this day, I still think he is. "You can do what ever you want to just as long as you do your best, you're happy, and you're not hurting anyone."

By the end of that summer, two quads had appeared by the side of the cabin. I spent the fall helping my dad build a shed to shelter the quads from the winter. "The thought of these will get us through the winter, Elise." And they did. There were times that winter when I'd look at my father in his office at home or even at the dining table. He would have a dreamy, far away look, a small smile daring to chase across his face. His reverie would break and, in seeing me looking at him, he'd wink and smile.

If my mother ever suspected what my father and I were doing on those weekends, she never let on. When Dad and I left on Saturday mornings, I would often see Sebastian at his window. In the beginning, I felt guilty for leaving him there. Then, when Dad and I started leaving Friday after I was done school, I forgot about Sebastian in his window.

The summer I turned ten, I learned how to ride a quad. I had a small 75 that fit me just right. Dad had a winch on his and it only took one outing before I found out why. My little quad could run right over the muskeg and mud; his sunk in and there was nothing I could do but watch as my dad winched himself out.

We took it slow after that. The wilderness versus the quads became an experiment. We got maps from the forestry office and Dad made friends when he began to ask questions. My father, the wise man he was, knew enough to know that he didn't know. He asked questions and talked to people; in this, he was in his element. And in this, I wished I was more like him. In the span of a couple of summers, he'd acquired an encyclopedic knowledge of our small spot of forest. We traced our path from the cabin, where the muskeg was, and where the nice lunching spots were. We watched how the country changed with the weather, with the changing season, and how our catalogue of experiences grew over the summer. It was September before we put the quads away. "It's just about hunting season, Elise," my father said our last day out. The forest was turning into a picture; gold, orange, red and green spread out across the valley below us as we sat and had lunch on a hillside. "I don't want you to get hurt."

"But I'm not a deer, Daddy."

"Sometimes the hunters don't look at what they're shooting and they just shoot."

"Then how do they know if they're shooting what they have a license for?" The forestry guys had been talking with the fish and wildlife guys. We'd had a few visitors at the cabin over the past summer. Apparently, a father and his ten-year old daughter were quite the talk of the countryside; we had to be seen to be believed.

"That's a very good point, Elise."

That very same day, we saw no less than seven trucks with quads and campers on our muddy road.

Three weeks later, my dad got a phone call. That night he came into my room. He kissed me on the forehead, the auburn stubble on his chin rubbing my skin, "I won't be home for supper tomorrow night."

"Where are you going?"

Dad sat on the edge of my bed and looked at me, debating his words. "Someone's broken

into the cabin. I have to go check it out."

My response was immediate. "Can I come?"

His response was also immediate. "No, Elise. It's a school day."

"But what if you get hurt, I could call for help. You need help fixing the cabin. I can help you. You can't go alone. That's just stupid." By now, I was out from under my covers, already gearing up for the expedition.

Dad sat there, looked around my room for a distraction or an answer, rubbed his tired face a couple of times, then sighed. "Fine. Leave your mother a note tomorrow morning saying you're having supper at a friend's house. We have to leave early. Be ready at five."

The front door of the cabin had been kicked in; the jam had been torn off and the door was dented. The early snowfall had blown in showing animal tracks. A window was broken, the beds had been turned over, and the wood stove was lying on its side. The cupboards were open with dishes and food strewn about the large kitchen /dining area. "I'm really sorry, Vic." The fish and wildlife officer named Terry said. The three of us stood in the middle of the cabin in our parkas and surveyed the mess. "I didn't stop by until Wednesday. I think they had been in on the weekend and then the animals got in." I felt violated and pissed all at the same time.

"Any news on the quads yet?" my father asked as he gently closed a cupboard.

Terry pulled a small notebook from inside his opened parka. "It's a good thing you registered them because," he flipped open the notebook, "the little one was seen in Edson. Guy tried to pawn it. The bigger one hasn't been seen, but the RCMP are on the lead from Edson. Probably the same guy."

"Did they wreck it?" I asked Terry. He's been the one who'd visited the most during the summer. He was a nice guy, about Dad's age with two boys, but they were much older than me and more interested in cars and girls than the forest.

Terry's eyes crinkled as he smiled at me. "I don't know, Elise. I hope not."

Terry left us to clean up the mess. We'd stopped at a lumberyard at one of the small towns on the way out and bought some plywood to board up the door and window.

We didn't get home until after eleven that night. The kitchen light was still on when we pulled up. Dad killed the engine on the rover and paused. "Go straight up to your room, okay Elise?"

On my way through the backyard, I noticed the curtains in Sebastian's window twitch.

I didn't need any further clues to tell me what was going on. My mother's voice rose up the stairs and to my ears under my bedcovers. "What on earth possessed you to take Elise out of school?"

I couldn't hear my father's voice. The door across the hall creaked; Sebastian was still awake.

"Imagine what the teachers think of us, pulling our daughter from school to go gallivanting about the countryside. And don't tell me you were fishing again, Victor. It's winter!"

A quiet knock upon my door. It opened. Sebatian's face peaked through. "Go away, Sebbie." I said through a slit in my blankets.

Sebatian stepped into my room. "Where did you go today, Elise?"

I pulled the blankets further over my head. "None of your business."

"Mom's really pissed you lied."

"So?"

My mother's voice rose up the stairs again. "Do you have any idea what you do to this family when you take off every weekend and come back smelly and dirty? The neighbours think I'm married to a caveman. You don't go to the charity meetings any more or play golf with Henry. Kim won't meet me for lunch any more; she thinks we're socializing with animals. And Joanne says you haven't called Marcel for months. What's wrong with you?"

Sebastian shuffled his feet along the carpet. "Can I come next time?"

"Piss off, Sebastian. Go back to bed."

Sebastian lingered as Mother took the final strip off Dad. "I know you don't care about your reputation, you never have. But you need to support this family, Victor. At least act as if you care about our well-being."

I heard Sebastian leave as my mother's angry steps sounded on the stairs.

I didn't see my father for nearly two weeks after that. He worked late, had business meetings, played squash on weekends.

One Saturday morning, I awoke to footsteps going down the stairs. I dressed quickly and followed. When I arrived in the garage, Dad was already under the Landrover draining the oil. "Can I help?"

Dad rolled out and the man I saw was suddenly ten-years older. His auburn hair was mixed with grey. I must have gasped because my father sat up and hugged me, "I missed you." I smelled his aftershave and the scent of pine and spruce on his fleece jacket. "Of course you can help. Hand me that rag."

We made it through that winter. Barely, it seems now.

By spring, I could tell Dad was up to something. I don't know how my mother didn't know. It was so obvious. I think now that maybe she didn't want to know.

One Tuesday night, I heard Dad come back. Only it wasn't the Mercedes he was parking in the garage, it was the Landrover. I slipped out of the house and met him inside the garage. He saw me and winked. "Doing anything Friday?"

Excitement shot up my body. "Nope," I beamed.

Friday didn't come soon enough. Dad was waiting outside my school, the overnight bag I'd left in my closet now safely stashed in the back of the Landrover next to a load of food and supplies.

Our lonely road was muddier than ever. Dad handled it very well. Perhaps too well. I watched as he maneuvered the Rover along the road. The Rover bounced in and out of the ruts, following tracks through puddles.

We pulled up to the cabin and I hopped out, stretching and rubbing my bruises. I stopped mis-stretch. The cabin had a new door, a heavy door with a lock. The window had been replaced. There was new siding on the cabin and quad shed. And the quad shed had a lock on it too.

I turned on my dad as he unloaded the back of the rover. "You've been coming here without me!"

Dad avoided my eyes, "I'm sorry. I wanted to surprise you."

I knew it was more than that, so much more. But it didn't matter. Not then, at that moment. I hugged him with the biggest hug I could muster. "Thank you. It looks really good."

He pulled back from the hug and smiled. He didn't look so old then, the moonlight shining on his rusted hair and his eyes glistening.

We ate beans and wieners and stayed up late telling stories over hot chocolate. While Dad had been sneaking out to the cabin, I'd been doing some research at school reading old urban legends and Indian myths. I would dream of running through the forest with the wolves and howling at the moon.

The next morning, I nearly jumped out of my cot and sleeping bag. Dad was already up, making coffee. "So, what's the plan for today? Hiking?"

My dad smirked, pouring two cups and adding milk to both. "Nah," he said, his back to me as I wiped my face of toothpaste. "I thought we'd dig out the maps and go quadding."

My heart skipped a beat. "But the quads....did we get them back?"

Dad continued to evade my look as he took his mug to the kitchen table and gazed out the patio doors to the pond. "Why don't you go look?"

I dumped my towel on the counter and raced out the cabin. The quad shed doors stood open. Inside were two brand new quads: a 300 for Dad and a new 150 for me. Mine had a winch.

That year we learned from our lessons. I enrolled in a gymnastics class on Friday nights and dance classes on Saturday and Sunday. I skipped all but once a month. Dad got a mobile phone for the Landrover and called Marcel on Saturday mornings. Once a month, we stayed in the city so Dad could play golf with Henry.

We also learned from our lessons in the bush. Our maps became extensive. We visited the forestry lookout towers atop the highest hills and eventually made it up passed treeline. By the end of the summer, we no longer needed our maps. The fish and wildlife guys gave us tips on how to lay corduroy over bad patches in the muskeg, where the old cabins and trails were, the back ways to the forestry towers.

This was our bliss for two summers. Winter was a mere blip in our countryside exploration.

The summer I turned twelve Mother found out about the cabin and the quads.

It was September. Maybe she'd been checking up on my classes, maybe she'd been checking into the family finances. I'll never know how, but she found out.

I didn't hear the confrontation. I know it happened because Dad disappeared for nearly a month after that. I waited in the garage at night until I grew too tired to wait any longer. I tried calling him at work; his receptionist, Lois, would only take my messages. Finally, I skipped school one day and took the bus downtown to his office.

Lois very nearly called my school when she saw me come through the office doors. "I want to see my dad." In all of my twelve years, I'd never been so serious or resolved. Lois stood up and walked back to my father's office. I followed.

I didn't recognize the man behind the desk. Lois left and I found myself looking at a grey stranger. There were dark bags under his eyes. He'd lost weight; his face was sallow and narrow. His hair was now almost completely grey. Even his suit was rumpled.

My father continued to peer at his computer screen, glasses perched at the end of his nose. It wasn't until I had approached his desk and muttered, "Dad?" that he finally broke his concentration.

He did a double-take in my direction and then everything he'd been trying so hard to maintain, so hard to force, finally melted in front of my eyes. "Hi, honey." He took his glasses off and looked at me.

"Hi, Daddy." My voice cracked.

"I'm sorry I haven't been home much." His voice was soft and apologetic.

I rounded his desk and hugged him. "I missed you."

"I missed you too." His words hushed into my hair.

"What happened?" I stood back and looked at him now; the grey stubble, the bloodshot eyes, the stained tie, the space between his neck and shirt collar.

"We can't go out any more."

I felt my feet root to the floor, my body becoming solid and un-movable. "Why?"

"The quads are gone." I continued to stand, boring my eyes into him, willing the truth to spring from his lips. "I can't go out any more, Elise. I've got a job to do."

"You're not happy, Daddy."

I felt a wall go up between my father and I then. It was as if the air changed. He picked up his glasses and placed them on his nose. "I have to work, Elise, and you have to get back to school." I remember the shock rearing up in my gut, throwing my heart against my ribs like my head against the door in the Landrover. "I'll have Lois call you a cab." He picked up the phone and spoke to Lois.

I saw my father only occasionally after that; at the dining table, from afar in his home office. We spoke even less.

The last time we spoke, it was in January. I was almost thirteen.

I was restless and was up late reading. I went down to the kitchen to make some hot chocolate when I saw the garage light on. I made two cups and put on my boots and coat.

Dad was hunched over the engine of the Landrover. He looked up as I came in. I handed him a cup and he smiled as he took it.

We stood, leaning against the counter in the garage, sipping our hot chocolate in silence for some time. Finally, he said, "I didn't sell the cabin."

A weight I didn't know I'd been carrying suddenly lifted from my chest. "I'm glad."

He drained his cup, picked up the crescent wrench and approached the Landrover again. He never got there. The wrench dropped to the cement floor. He clutched his left arm. His knees buckled and my dad sank to the floor.

I don't remember dropping my mug. I only remember my dad's head on my lap as he smiled at me and then was no longer there.

Chapter Five

Six Weeks in the Wilderness, Part I

"How do you feel about leading a large excavation?" Morris had asked me at my last performance evaluation.

"Sounds like a good experience."

Those were famous last words. They echoed in my head as I headed to the Fort McMurray Airport at 11am on a Sunday.

I'd agreed to lead a large excavation for three weeks. Three weeks of experience, then I'd be back doing my regular routine of pre-impact assessment jobs. It seemed like a good deal at the time.

This was a huge gig – HSAC was doing the pre-impact excavation for an open pit bitumen mine slated for construction next year. Russell, one of the folks from downstairs at HSAC, had done all the pre-impact assessment work last year. This year we'd be excavating all those sites he'd found.

I was the first permit holder in a series of three. I'd take the first eight sites, Scott would take the next eight, then Russell would take the last six. Russell and his second-in-command, Jacquie, would help Scott and me learn the ropes.

Needless to say, there was a deadline.

Russell, Jacquie, and I arrived in Fort Mac at 8am the day before. I was not a happy camper. Getting up at 4am does not agree with my constitution. Starbucks doesn't even open that early, not even at the airport. To top it off, it was Saturday. Little did I know that it would be the last weekend in a long while that I would see Calgary.

Apparently, we needed the whole day without the crew to get together supplies, trucks, and quads. A whole day. Even just the thought of having to spend the whole day doing logistics was an impending one. Either it was overkill or on the verge of mobilizing an army. For Pete's Sake, it was only ten people.

Famous last words.

We picked up our trucks, then headed to Wal-Mart after a lengthy breakfast of making lists and checking them twice.

"I never thought a cell phone would truly be useful," I told Jacquie as she, once again, phoned Russell who was on the other side of Wal-Mart. Russell had been working excavation in the oil sands for six years. I ended up with this project only because he couldn't hold a permit to dig; too many reports overdue to the government. Russell was a generous kind. I didn't know too many of the quicksand folks from downstairs, and if I did, I didn't know them well. Russell saved my ass with that Cold Lake job a month ago. That was pretty damn cool so I thought I'd repay the gesture and hold a permit for him. His generous nature was showing through as he agreed to tag along with me and my crew for the first few days to get us all acquainted with how things should run. "I'm going to help you, but you will be the permit holder and you will have the authority. We have to make that clear to the crew."

"Hey Russell." Jacquie said into the cell phone as she pushed around the first of our two shopping carts full of fire extinguishers, bungie cords, bug spray, mosquito coils, tarps, hand tools, and other miscellany. I was just having fun; it'd been a long time since I'd spent someone else's money so freely. "What size of totebox do we need? The big one, like a forearm wide by a whole arm long or a smaller one. Oh, here's one with a good clip to hold the lid on but it's small. We could use that for the tool kit." Jacquie passed the plastic box to me.

After Wal-Mart, I dropped $1600 on quad helmets for myself and the crew. Apparently, it was going to cost the same as outfitting a small army even if it wasn't one.

But standing there, at 11 am at the airport the next day, looking at ten fresh faces that June morning, made me think I was standing in front of a small army. Perhaps only a firing squad.

"Hi." My voice cracked. My palms were sweating. I probably had food between my teeth too. "I'm Elise. I'm your permit holder and team leader." They continued to stare blankly at me. Maybe only a few had worked in consulting during the summer. How many greenhorns was I getting? I couldn't remember. "Um, this is Russell." I motioned to Russell looking pristine in his NorthFace gear. How do people manage to maintain an appearance when they spend so much time in dirt? Then again, maybe the questions was, why bother? "He's worked up here for a few years so he'll be helping out for a few days. This is Jacquie." Jacquie was more my type of person. She'd cut off her hair, wore no make up, and appeared that morning, ready to go, in patched up army pants and a worn out T-shirt. Yup. It was only a matter of time before I cut my hair. It was my last hope that one day I would again return to the land of dead people. It was some sort of unconscious decision to make my hair a symbol of that hope. If I cut the red mop that currently hung down to my waist, I might as well slit my wrists. "Jacquie, also has been up here for a couple years and has lots of experience. She'll be the second crew lead. We're going straight to camp, unless anybody needs anything from town."

Famous last words.

After spending the next three hours between Wal-Mart, Marks Work Wearhouse, and Canadian Tire, we finally rounded everyone back up and started the hour and a half journey to camp with three trucks and fourteen quads. Russell had enough foresight to obtain an extra quad as a preventative measure against breakdowns.

It took two and a half hours to drive to the oilsands camp that would become home. Two and a half hours of winding forest road, idiotic truck drivers driving way too fast, and lots of roadkill. I actually wanted to get to camp after being on that road.

It wasn't until the next day that I began to appreciate that being a greenhorn wasn't restricted the archaeological part of the deal. "What do you mean we've only got six licensed drivers?" I asked Jacquie. "Don't you have to have a driver's license to drive a quad?"

Jacquie shook her head. "Nope. Only a quad helmet and supervision."

What was this world coming to? Now I was going to have to teach six people how to drive, forget about actually digging an excavation.

I'd forgotten I learned to ride a quad when I was 12 – much earlier than learning to drive. This could have also explained my current driving skills.

"We have to take everyone over to Manier's safety orientation training at the plant site," Russell reminded me. Right. Orientation. That shouldn't be too bad.

As we were loading everyone into the trucks to drive over to orientation, a tall, dark and moustached man approached us. "Shit," I mumbled. "First day at camp and already we're attracting every male in the place." Jacquie glanced my way and grinned.

"Are you here for the archlog….archolog…" Geez, the number of people that have a problem saying that one word.

Russell to the rescue. "Yes. We're here for the archaeological excavation."

"I'm Manier Oil's safety person, Gerry. You missed the safety meeting this morning."

My blood froze. Oh, shit. We'd messed up already. One day out and already I was demonstrating to my multi-million dollar client how unorganized I was.

Russell to the rescue again. "We weren't told that we had to attend the safety meetings."

"Yup. Every morning. We meet at 7am by the trailer." He motioned to the ATCO trailer off in the distance. "We'll see you tomorrow." He tipped his ball cap at us and got in his truck and left. Okay, so maybe he had every right not to be able to say "archaeological."

"So much for breakfast at 730," I muttered as we finally drove to Manier's operations plant for orientation. From camp, the plant was due west for 20 minutes down a gravel road. The forest was thick and pristine here – the aspen trees were old and tall; pine and spruce rose up straight into the canopy. Looking into the forest from the road, there was hardly any underbrush. It was a beautiful old growth forest and it was all going to become a crater next year.

Inside, we got everybody settled, with water and pencils and paper – never was I told that I would be turned into a babysitter and mom from an anthropologist – when the instructor arrived.

"Can I see everyone's H2S certificates please?"

Oh, fuck. Again. My crew exchanged blank looks with each other before finally turning their eyes upon my blank face. "Um, we weren't told to bring our H2S certs."

"Well, I need to see 'em before we can begin the course."

Six people whipped out their certificates. I had mine in the truck in my exploding safety wallet. Jacquie and Russell had theirs on them. That left four people. "Don't worry about it," the instructor said, "Bring 'em by later." My heart started beating for the second time that day. Would things ever get easier?

Not soon.

That afternoon was spent teaching everyone how to drive a quad. And that's when I found out that the lack of driver's license wasn't the problem. It was the lack of …I didn't know what, but people were freezing up whenever they came to a small log and had to jump it. God forbid if they had to turn too.

After learning how to ride a quad, suddenly city life ceased to stimulate me. When I wasn't out with my dad, I was spending time with country friends on their ranches and acreages. With my crew, I found myself facing a hard reality. These were city folk, born and bred. They didn't need a driver's license because they had public transit. Dirt bikes were non-existent because they weren't street legal, besides their best friend lived three doors down. Their forts weren't built in trees in the bush; they consisted of blankets thrown over a couple of lawn chairs in their postage stamp-sized yard.

I had my work cut out for me. I could feel my hair going gray. Not that I cared. Three weeks would not come too soon. But I hadn't thought of my family or my impeding financial doom all day. Seemed there were some benefits to working in the oilsands.

At 7am the next day, my crew and I were standing in a circle with at least twenty other people, all white males. Most were between 18 and 35 and surveyors. I was suddenly very protective of my predominantly female crew.

Gerry stood at the doorstep of the ATCO trailer, tipped back his ballcap, and began. "Good morning all. Since we have some new folks on site, we'll go over some stuff in more detail today. Consider this your call-in and overall tailgate safety meeting. You all sign in on the sheet that's being passed around. However, you should be doing your own safety meeting with your crews to cover any information that is specific to your duties during the day. I expect a copy of that meeting at the end of the day. I'll let these young folks explain to us what they do so that I don't make any mistakes." Gerry gestured toward us. I had to hand it to the guy. He very gracefully got out of saying 'archaeological' again.

I got a nudge in the side from Russell. "Um, right. We're archaeologists." A murmur of 'cool' wove around the circle with a few nods. Now wasn't the time to correct them. "Last year, Russell was up here and found a few sites. We're here now to excavate them. We are looking for evidence of old campsites, like stone tools, bone, and fire broken rock. We have eight sites to excavate over the next three weeks."

Gerry spoke up, "What does your usual day involve?"

I looked to Russell for help. He said, "We ride out to the site, dig and eat lunch there, ride back at night."

Gerry made a note. "Everyday, I want to know where you guys are and if you move. If you have a map of where all your sites are, I'd like a copy."

Russell and I nodded.

Gerry proceeded to tell us of Manier's safety policies and how he liked to run things. He was strict, but fair, something I had absolutely no problem with. Just as long as he was consistent and communicative, we'd get along just fine.

At 7:55am, the meeting adjourned. It felt like half the day had been wasted standing around. I followed Gerry into the trailer, took five minutes unlacing my steel-toed boots, then pulled out my map. Gerry scanned it, I showed him the sites – which he highlighted- then wrote on a big white board my name and the site name under the date. He was starting to remind me of Morris. I tried not to smile.

"Are you going to stick to your schedule?" he asked.

I shrugged, "I hope so. First time I've done this."

Gerry leaned back in his chair and appraised me. He didn't say anything for a minute or two and I let him have the time. Finally he took off his ball cap and set it on the desk and ran a hand through his thick brown hair. "Okay. Well, I won't keep you any longer. Any trouble or questions, just call." He plucked a small stack business cards from his desk and handed it to me.

We had to excavate 90 square metres over eight archaeological sites in three weeks. I hadn't created this schedule; it had been constructed by the powers that be. The powers that be hadn't included Morris. I'd been handed to another HSAC manager, one that did all the oilsands work. I hadn't worked with Michelle before and hadn't heard any-thing about her management style. The archaeologists who worked in the oilsands were always gone or always busy. I had no reason not to think the schedule wasn't well-thought out and possible. I had committed to three weeks, no more and no less. The first site was the biggest – 40 square metres. Once we'd finished this, it would be all downhill.

Did I mention famous last words?

After little ado, we all arrived at the site and dismounted our quads. We were atop a hill in the middle of undulating old growth forest. Not a soul around for miles. Beautiful.

Russell and a small crew had attempted winter excavation at this site. The one-metre by one-metre pits of the excavation weren't as square as they should have been, piles of half-burned brush dotted the perimeter of the excavation site, and there was garbage everywhere. "Looks like you guys just kind of abandoned the place," I said cava-lierly.

"It was minus 35 with three feet of snow when we finally called it quits."

Oh. Explained the garbage, though.

"We were using tiger torches to thaw out the ground so we could chisel it out, then campfires to thaw out the dirt enough to push through the screens. We were going through two to three packs of hand and foot warmers a day per person." I did a hasty calculation – about thirty packs a day – and my eyebrows rose at the expense. And the stupidity of it all. "We had flashlights hanging all over the place too to try to extend the day and get things done."

I considered how lucky I was at that moment, in the warm June daylight, even in the middle of nowhere. "Right. Listen up, everyone. Let's clean up this place. Get the garbage bags from the green Rubbermaid tote."

While I may like mud, I don't like messy. And just about every archaeologist I know has a seriously anal tendency toward details. I cringed when I had a closer look at the excavation pits. These walls weren't straight, the floors of the units weren't flat, and, as I found myself tipping my head sideways, the units didn't seem to be on a grid either.

A couple crew members looked at me and nudged Jacquie. "You okay?"

I snapped my head up. Now was not the time to breed animosity between the authority figures. "Oh yeah. Just trying to see the grid in my head."

Russell then piped up. "This where we put the baseline." He proceeded to find a couple nails with decaying flagging tape half-wedged into the ground south of the excavation units. The nails were there to demark a line from which the entire excavation grid could be based, in one metre intervals. Again I cringed. We couldn't base our excavation off a couple nails half-wedged into the ground.

That's when I decided to take Russell up on his advice at the airport that first day. It was time for Elise Marquette to take control. "Scott, I need more shovel tests of the area. We gotta figure out where this site ends so we can plan where to put new excavation pits. Jacquie, you and

Russell establish a baseline; make it at least fifteen metres long. Don't take the winter units into consideration; I want a true measurements from the baseline because that's what we'll be working off this year, not the winter units."

This series of statements should have worked. The crew scattered. Russell and Jacquie attempted to find more nails with flagging tape wedged in the dirt. After ten minutes, I looked around to find that nobody had really done anything.

I walked up to Scott at the edge of the clearing, "What seems to be the problem?"

Scott, a tall lanky guy who looked to be more at home in a computer lab than in the forest, looked at the faces of the crew then his fingers. "We're trying to figure out who goes where." I don't know how Scott landed this gig – he'd only been with HSAC a couple of months. He was fresh out of grad school. But apparently he had enough experience to appease the government and hold a permit.

I pointed to crew members – I hadn't yet learned all their names, "Leslie, Chad, and, sorry?, Vanessa, right. Pick up a shovel and a hand screen and go out with Scott that way," I pointed north, into the bush, "Dig shovel tests twice the width of your shovel and at least as deep as the blade of your shovel is long. I want shovel tests between five and ten metres apart. It should only take you a few hours to do the area."

The four seemed happy. They picked up their gear and nearly ran off into the forest.

I walked back to Russell and Jacquie. "How's it coming?"

"We haven't been able to find any more nails of the baseline."

"Set a new baseline as close to the nails you've got left over and re-set the datum. We need to start digging."

Jacquie nodded, again happy to have a concrete direction, but Russell persisted. I used the rest of the crew to organize the equipment into what I hoped would be an efficient system in a place away from the excavation units. Setting everything up was a matter of understanding and setting up the process of the excavation site: one person would dig out a one-metre unit in quadrants ten centimeters thick; a pit-partner would take the dirt from each quadrant of that individual one-metre unit and screen it. It was an efficient system that allowed the person digging to dig the entire one-metre unit down to sterile soil at about 40 centimetres below the surface whilst knowing the order in which they should dig their quadrants, and the person screening would like-wise screen all the dirt and know from which quadrant the dirt originated. There would be no confusion about who was screening whose dirt and where the dirt was from. It was a buddy-system that was simple in theory.

In theory.

We set up the screens in places around the excavation site where we figured that the screened dirt wouldn't get in everyone's way and far enough apart so that buckets of dirt from one unit wouldn't get co-mingled with dirt from other units. When we were done, Russell and Jacquie were done setting the baseline and laying out the grid. I turned to the seven crew members surrounding me. "We need a clean site. Take clippers and saws and clear out all the underbush. Make it look like you would live here."

I went out and visited Scott. Before I got to the four diggers, I heard, "And then Steve rolled over into the mud. He was totally covered!" Much laughing ensued.

When I arrived, everyone was over their shovel tests, but no one was actually investigating their dirt for artifacts.

"How's it going?" I asked Scott.

"Oh good," he said.

"How many you got so far?"

"Oh, four." I looked at my watch. In the hour since they started, four times that amount should have been dug. At least.

I turned and faced the rest of the diggers. "Okay, we've only got three hours to shovel test the whole site. I suggest less talking and more digging. We need at least 30 shovel tests in the area around the excavation site."

It was going to be a long three weeks.

I returned to the excavation site to find that Russell and Jacquie had finally pulled through. The grid was forming before my eyes. The baseline was clear line of nails with bright pink flagging tape hammered into the ground. One-metre intervals were indicated by more nails hammered into the ground, this time indicated by blue flagging tape. String was wrapped around and between nails to form one-metre by one-metre squares. And the crew was doing a good job clearing the site. I sat down and pulled out some graph paper and began to construct my maps of the site.

By 2pm, Scott and his team still hadn't finished shovel testing the site. They'd eaten lunch and were now slower than ever. I had the rest of the crew already digging their excavation units; their screening partners happily screening the dirt for artifacts. "Jacquie, can you watch over these guys?" I motioned to the excavation diggers. Jacquie nodded from her screen, dust clouding the sunlight. "Russell, let's go do some shovel testing."

Russell and I were on a mission. I don't know whether it was the look on our faces as we picked up shovels or the fact that we moved more dirt in five minutes that the others had moved in two hours, but the entire crew was watching us. In twenty minutes, we had dug four shovel tests and the excavation crew suddenly had a commentary going.

"Whoa, Russell, you better get your ass moving."

"Yeah, Elise is gaining fast."

"But the dirt's so hard over here."

"I see rocks in Elise's dirt and she's still motorin'."

Within two hours, Russell and I were drenched with sweat and happy. We'd discovered that the site was bigger than originally thought and extended to the southeast. All total, 56 shovel tests were dug; 24 of those were done by Russell and myself.

Russell and I high-fived each other and the excavation crew cheered. "Wow. I've never seen anybody dig like that," David said.

"That's the way it should be done," I said. I saw most of them smile and nod. I hoped that they also understood that I was willing to work hard, so I wanted them to work hard too.

It was four o'clock. Time to start packing up. "Liz," I said. "You're in charge of keeping the Rubbermaid totes organized. Tools in here; digging kit bags with the clipboards, trowels, baggies, and brushes in here; extra supplies for the kit bags here." Liz nodded, concentration on her face. I'd noticed how neat she kept her tools and notes while excavating. "Leslie, you are in charge of the safety muster point. Every morning put a fire extinguisher, the satellite phone, bear spray, and a first aid kit here. At night, gather it all up and put it away. Got it?" Leslie nodded and ran to retrieve the fire extinguisher and other pointless safety paraphenalia from a nearby tree. "Chad." Chad jumped up and saluted. "You are in charge of gathering lunches and putting them up a tree away from the bears." I got two thumbs up.

Russell piped up. "We need to cover the units in case it rains over night."

I nodded, "Everyone else, grab the tarps and spread them over the units. Cover things up and lock them down."

It was five o'clock by the time we mounted our quads and left the site. It was quarter to six when we got back to camp. We locked up the quads, threading a chain through the back and front racks, and headed for supper.

I'd only ever been to one other camp before, in British Columbia's northeast. It was dismal. Manier's camp, however, was a nice surprise. While it was still a series of ATCO trailers joined together, they were new and kept immaculate by the staff. My room had its own bathroom and a large wrap around desk. Quiet and cleanliness rules were strict; there was too much dirt and too many women in the oil industry now for slacking.

After pealing off my several sweaty and dirty layers, I tried to imagine what life in this place would be like after being here for three weeks. At the moment it was so new, it was difficult to see.

In many ways, I wasn't looking forward to supper. Stepping into a room full of rig-pigs wasn't something I dreamed about. It was, however, a re-occurring nightmare. I tied back my long wet hair, put on an oversized sweatshirt and stuffed my feet into a pair of old sneakers. I looked in the mirror one last time before leaving the safety of my room. There was nothing I could do about my turkey-shit green eyes, long red hair, nor 'peaches and cream' complexion – that was a plight of genetics and fresh air living. While most females tried to look good, or at least look female, I'd found ways since starting archaeology to downplay my femininity. The less I was perceived as a fragile female, the more respect I got. And less gawking. It wasn't that I had to do it to work with other archaeologists, it was because archaeology had predominantly oil and gas clients. I had to work with rig-pigs and they were a breed of macho, chest-beating males all to themselves. The more I could get said males to respond to my words instead of my breasts, the better off everyone was.

The dining room was large, fitting at least a dozen large round tables with the kitchen at the far end. My crew made it to supper by about 6:30, most with wet, clean hair. We fit all thirteen of us around one of the large circular tables. I was happy to find that no one was being excluded, that everyone was making an effort to be a team.

Russell, Jacquie and I converged on my room after supper. Russell showed me how to map out a schedule and how to track progress, and how to check the maps and artifact records for the day. We discussed crew and personalities and a few possible strategies for getting more dirt moved. "I leave the day after tomorrow," Russell reminded me. "But Jacquie will look after you."

By the time Russell and Jacquie left, it was 9:30. I was exhausted but pumped. It had been a 14-hour day. If I could get organized, I could get my day down to 12 hours and make the safety folks back home happy. It would also make me happy – three weeks of 14-hour days was not something I savoured. But it saved me thinking about my family and the domestic issues they wove. As I said, there were some benefits to working oilsands.

I plugged my cell phone in and noticed a message. I winced. But it wasn't from Theo or Sebbie. It was Gerry. I'd forgotten to check in with him. Shit. I called him, but his phone was off. I dug out the safety forms and put them by my door. I was not going to forget them tomorrow morning.

The next day found me and the crew fumbling for a routine. First, the quads needed gas. That took time and organization. Then we were halfway to the site before I remembered that I still had the safety forms from yesterday tucked in my survey vest. I escorted the crew to the site, then turned around and rode like a madwoman to make it up to Gerry. When I got back to the site, Leslie hadn't set up the muster point and the Rubbermaid totes were empty with equipment scattered everywhere. At breaktime, Chad remembered that his lunch was sitting in his room at camp. At eleven, I got a call from Erinson Power wondering when I'd be finished my report for the work I'd done last week.

Shit, I muttered. So much for getting my days down to 12 hours. The report was almost done, I just had to fix some errors Morris caught in his proofread. But that would require a clear head and some time.

We each gave Chad something from our lunches to make up for his lack. After lunch, Russell and I palavered to make sure I had a clear idea of what to do on the upcoming sites. "I have to be at the airport by seven, so we need to leave camp before three. Two-thirty would be best."

"But, it's only an hour drive," I said.

Jacquie shook her head, "Rush hour to Fort Mac starts at four. You need to beat it."

I looked across the site at my crew. It was difficult to tell at Day Two who was diligent and who wasn't, who was a digger and who wasn't. I didn't want to leave my crew, it wouldn't be a sound decision considering it was my crew and I needed to be there to ensure the work got done. But, if I sent Jacquie, I'd be completely alone if any questions came up regarding the excavation or artifacts. I took a risk. "Who's got their driver's license?" Three people put up their hands. With Russell gone, I'd be down to five licensed drivers; me, Jacquie, Chad, Scott and Ellen. Ellen was a good digger, Chad had note-taking and digging issues I wanted to pound out of him. "Scott, can you drive Russell to the airport tomorrow?"

Scott looked like a deer caught in headlights. "Okay," he gulped and nodded. He would be leading the crew after my three-week stint was up.

"You'll need to leave the site after you eat lunch tomorrow." Scott nodded again. I tried to reassure myself that this was a good idea, that I didn't need to do everything myself to get it done right. Yes, it was my permit, my responsibility, but things still needed to get done....somehow.

By the end of the day, we had six units open and none complete. Forty square metres seemed an eternity away. I stopped by Gerry's office after supper and took him the day's safety forms. "Are you still going to be at the same site tomorrow?" he asked.

"We'll be there for a while. Scott is driving Russell to the airport tomorrow. I'll get him to check in with you before and after."

Gerry nodded his understanding. On my way out, he threw me a chocolate bar. "You're doing okay," he said and leaned back in his chair.

I revised my estimate of Gerry – he was better than Morris.

I munched my chocolate bar back in my room while I finished the edits on my Erinson report. A few clicks later, I was sending it to my client. I waited. My computer chugged. The internet chugged. I dug the bags of today's artifacts out of my survey vest and started to double check the baggie contents to the record sheets.

My computer continued to chug.

By nine, my report still hadn't made it through the internet ether. I figured it was the size of the report; it wasn't huge but, the photos and maps could make a ten-page document seem big. I emailed Morris to explain the situation.

My computer chugged more.

Finally I grabbed my phone and walked out into the parking lot where I could get the best cell reception. "Hey, Morris. Sorry to call you at home, but I've got no internet at the moment." I told him about the report.

"Try again tomorrow." I was relieved to hear his support and not scramble to the client's ever-increasing demands. "While you're at it, I need you to file some paperwork on the bear incident you had in Grande Cache."

Ron had talked. Rat bastard.

"What kind of paperwork?" I asked.

Morris continued to humor me. "There was no injury, I take it."

"None."

"Near miss should suffice."

"Okay."

"Send it straight to Joe."

"Understood."

"Anything else I should know about?"

My mind whirled as I went through every project I'd done this year and what I'd correspondingly registered with Morris' photographic memory. "Nope. All is good."

"Okay. Play safe. I'll talk to you tomorrow."

I was glad I'd stayed behind with my crew the next day. A routine was beginning to take shape. This was also the day I began to find out who comprised my crew. The more time I spent with them, the less I worried about any potential situation between them and the horny, white male surveyors. Jacquie was committed to the excavation. Ellen, Scott, and Sharon were each married. Vanessa hated all men. Liz was too preoccupied with what she couldn't eat at camp and what she couldn't see in the forest. And Janet was too busy drawing in her notebook. She also had green hair. Apparently, the only ones I had to watch were David, who was flamboyantly gay, Leslie, a pretty brunette from Halifax, and Maggie, a chatty and hyper forestry dropout. As David and Leslie were reportedly in committed relationships, that left only Maggie to worry about.

On the other hand, in terms of work, there was more I had to worry about. Paul was too busy talking to notice anyone and anything but himself. It was becoming a chore to tell him to shut up and keep digging. I spent most of my time at the screen helping half the crew screen dirt the other half dug up. Instead of digging or screening, I needed to be double-checking the artifacts collected against the crew's notes and my maps. Checking this was a full-time job. But the diggers were out-pacing the screeners. My presence on the screen allowed the screeners to keep up with the diggers, but this compromised our bud-dy-system. We confused a couple of buckets of dirt but we eventually came up with a system to keep everyone busy and to know whose dirt was whose. We were all fairly impressed by our progress, not only in our little system, but also in our digging: we managed to finish five of the units from yesterday and start another four. Five down, thirty-five to go.

It was when I updated my schedule that night that I realized we weren't going to be done in three weeks. Michelle wanted an update so I emailed her the situation. I told her there was no way we could dig 90 units in three weeks; it was going to take that time just to dig our first site. Michelle needed to find someone else to take my place at the end of the three weeks and have them take over my permit. I had other work I had to do and clients that I needed to placate.

The internet was working tonight, so I also managed to send Morris my report. I split it up into parts to make sure it went through. I also mentioned to Morris the situation with the excavation schedule. I was really hoping Morris would have my back and sort things out with Michelle.

I ate supper, saw the crew in good spirits, then headed over to Gerry's trailer. I hadn't even sat down in the old sofa when he handed me a chocolate bar. "Who told you about my chocolate vice?" I finally asked.

He shrugged and for the first time, smiled. "I just guessed. I've got a daughter who loves chocolate." That spoke volumes about him. No wonder he was so strict about knowing about our every move – he was more protective of my crew than I was.

"Have you heard from Scott yet?"

He shook his head as he turned down the TV hanging in the corner of the trailer. A hunter was displaying his new rifle to the camera as his adolescent daughter looked on. "Russell stopped by to say goodbye."

I looked at my watch. It was past seven. Scott should have dropped Russell at the airport by five then been back by now. It was rush hour going into Fort Mac, not coming out.

Gerry gave me some TV commentary on the hunter, his rifle and his daughter -- reminded him of his daughter – then he scanned in my safety paperwork.

"Let me know when you hear from Scott, okay?" I nodded. "Ditto."

It took me until nine o'clock to finish checking the unit records against the artifacts. Between deciphering illegible handwriting, to deciphering the shorthand code individuals made up to note the number of chert, Beaver River Sandstone, quartz, or fire-broken rock they'd recovered and comparing it what they'd actually bagged and tagged, my head began to hurt. I made many mental notes on how to pound into Chad's head the importance of neat and accurate records. That boy was going to learn how to take notes and dig in a straight line even if it took me all summer. I'd even remembered to send in my safety paperwork on Ron's close call with a bear.

And by nine, Scott still hadn't called.

I looked at my phone. No calls missed. I walked down the hall and knocked on Jacquie's door. Ellen was propped up on Jacquie's bed in pajamas decorated with pink pigs, watching a movie. "Hey, have you heard from Scott?"

Jacquie shook her head then motioned me in. Her room smelled of clean dirt and Body Shop products. There were boxes, blank artifact records, paper and plastic bags littering her floor amongst clothing, equipment, boots, socks and a quad helmet. A Body Shop atomizer was hidden behind her computer on her desk. Jacquie ran a hand through her cropped hair as she checked her phone. "He should have been back by now. Did you ask him to stop for anything?"

"No. What do you suggest?" I looked around her room again, making sure I wasn't stepping on anything important.

"I was re-organizing," she said and looked at her watch again. "Have you talked to Gerry?"

"Not since seven. I'll call and see if he's heard anything."

Gerry picked up on the first ring. He hadn't heard from Scott. "We're going to go look for him," Jacquie said as I relayed the message from Gerry. I told Gerry this and gave him Jacquie's phone number. "Check in every half hour. I don't need three people missing."

"Do you need help?" Ellen asked.

"Can you go get your phone? We'll meet you outside." Ellen flapped down the hall in her over-sized pyjamas as Jacquie rummaged through the chaos of her room for her boots. I met her and Ellen outside in the parking lot. I gave Ellen Gerry's business card. "If we can't get through to Gerry or he can't get through to us, or if you see Scott, call."

Ellen nodded and dialed Gerry. Jacquie and I strode across the darkening parking lot. I was climbing into the truck, when I saw Jacquie pointing across the lot. I climbed back out and met her as we crossed to one of dozens of white pickup trucks. The lot was full of white pick-up trucks: all Fords, Chevs, and Dodges. We had three white trucks ourselves – two Fords and a Chev. They looked very similar. The one Jacquie had pointed out could have been mistaken for anyone else's white pick-up truck, except that it had pink flagging tape hanging from the antenna. It had been the crew's idea for quick and easy identification in the morning. And Jacquie was pointing to the third white pick-up with pink flagging tape.

I was instantly livid. I pinched the bridge of my nose and counted to ten. When I looked up, the sky was still red, so I recounted. I turned and headed back to camp. "Call Gerry. Tell him all is okay."

I strode passed a startled Ellen. I struggled with the laces on my boots. "What room is Scott in?" I asked as my last boot hit the floor.

"410," Jacquie said. I don't know if she was angry too and trying to keep it down like me, or frightened at what I might do to Scott. It had been a while since I'd been this angry. It'd been even longer since I'd been this angry at someone outside of my family.

My knuckles rapped on 410 and threatened to wake up everyone else in the hall. Apparently, I'd woken up Scott. He opened the door, flannel pajamas askew. "Forget something?" I asked, unable to contain my irritation any longer. I noticed that Jacquie had stopped a few paces down the hall, out of sight of Scott.

"I don't....," Scott began, but as he woke up, remembered. "Oh, no. I'm sorry. I'm so sorry. I got lost and then forgot...."

I raised my finger, rage threatening to well over my infantile walls of conformity and diplomacy, "Got've got a phone and a GPS. Don't do it again."

Again, Scott took the deer in headlights look, but was silent this time. Apparently, his wife hadn't yet trained him to check in. No. That was my job. Archaeologist, babysitter, mom, and wife.

Chapter Six

In Ireland

Unless you like meat and grease, there's not a lot going for English food.

I hadn't realized how much I liked fruit and veggies until, suddenly, there were none in sight. I poked at the mushy fried tomatoe on the plate of sausage, egg, black pudding, and beans all swimming in a plate of grease. I sliced the tomatoe into halves and put the first half in my mouth. I nearly gagged. I chased it with a mouthful of coffee and continued in that manner for the other half of the tomatoe and the beans. I got a couple bites of sausage in, but had to quit after that. When the waitress came back, she raised her eyebrows at my half-eaten breakfast. "Sorry," I said. "Jet lag. Could I have another coffee?"

It was the dead of winter in Windermere. I don't know what possessed me to fly half way across the world to vacation in the Lake District in winter. Some part of me thought that only Canada and Siberia really got winter in winter. I'd pictured the Lake District like I read it described in one of Beatrix Potter's stories. Or, William Wordsworth. Green hills, glistening lakes, trees dotting the landscape with stone fences. It was all fairly romantic, I have to admit. Just really far from the cold truth.

After this first breakfast, I resolved to find a grocery store. It'd been a long time since was last in the UK. My adventures of settling into life in Galway, Ireland were slowly coming back to me. For one, I'd forgotten that liquor was sold in grocery stores. Score one for Elise. I'd also forgotten that everything is sold in small quantities. A small bag of sugar for 92p was a good deal.

Doing my rounds about town, I shook my head as I listened to the voices. I was so far away from the Irish accent I'd grown to understand and love. The accent I heard around me in Windermere was something altogether different. I remember a family friend back in high school telling me the difference between the English accents and what they revealed about a person's social status. I was fascinated, of course, as only an anthropologist-in-the-making could be. Liverpool was a working city and had a 'poor' accent. The north was, well, it was the north, what else could you say? It definitely wasn't London. And Wales, well, that was the ends of the earth. Sounded like it too.

It was the same in Ireland; not so much with the social structure, but one could definitely be placed based on accent. My friend, Aideen, was ridiculed at her Dublin school for having a Meath accent. After having spent nearly a year there, I had been able tell the general region of where a person was raised. Even better was when I arrived at a hotel in Dublin to catch my flight back to Canada and the hotel attendant saying, "You have a fine Galway accent." No wonder no one could understand me when I got back to Calgary. I had become enculturated. Eat your heart out, Margaret Mead.

This time, ten years later, I hadn't come to Windermere to become enculturated. In fact, I don't know why I'd chosen the Lake District. I spent my days in Windermere reading, eating, walking, trying to keep warm, and eventually watching movies at the theatre next door to my flat. Funny how I had to go thousands of miles from home just to do those things I wanted to do at home. Was it my family I was escaping or work? I didn't know any more. I just knew I had to get away, far away. This was as far as my three months of banked time allowed.

I rode the boat cross Windermere Lake, went to a play in Kendal, visited Wordsworth's cottage. The highlight of my trip was attempting to take a sightseeing tour of the countryside west of Kendal. I was driving your standard UK tin-can car and regaining my memory of how to drive on the right side of the road. The Lake District is hilly. I hadn't appreciated how hilly until I tried to drive across country. My little car barely made it up the switchbacks. I decided to turn around when ice appeared on the road and I saw my life flash in front of my eyes. Leave it to me to find the most desolate and treacherous patch of road.

After two weeks in the Lake District, I was incredibly bored. And hungry.

When I landed in Dublin, my first words to Aideen were, "Feed me, please. I need good food."

Aideen smiled, holding me at arm's length, her blue Irish eyes sparkling under her black hair, "Ten years and you haven't changed."

"Sorry," I shrugged. "I feel like I haven't eaten since I left Canada." I looked at my friend again. "Actually, it looks like you've given up eating. You're too skinny."

Aideen took my suitcase and hooked her arm in mine, "It's the job. Those kids keep me running." Aideen was finishing her Master's in Education (after a two undergrad degrees in Biology and Organic Chemistry) and was teaching at a school in Longford.

Her arm was thin and angular against my muscular forearm. "How's the job?" I asked trying not to dwell on her frailty and my over-masculinity.

"Great. Stressful with school, but great." She let go of my arm and pulled the airport door open. I scooted through and grabbed my suitcase from her. She let go of the handle with reluctance.

"When are your exams?"

"June."

"What are you going to do when it's over?" Aideen reminded me of me trying to finish my seven years of undergrad – I was on overdrive, determined to finish. It took a trip to Ireland and a year of getting drunk to simmer me down.

Aideen grinned as she pulled out a set of car keys from her purse, "I'm going to read a novel."

We pulled out of the airport parking lot, gabbering on as if five years hadn't elapsed between our visits. I was breathing deeply between questions and expletives; I couldn't get over how good it felt to be back in Ireland. It was overcast, like much of my time in the Lake District, and humidity-laden cool, but it was as if my feet knew I was home. Like the first time I took the plane from London to Dublin, the sky had opened up and revealed a land of vivid green lushness. It truly was the Emerald Isle and it was again saving me from my life.

As Aideen and I drove through twilit Dublin, I remembered my bus rides from the B&B, going into the city centre trying to find a job, then a place to live. Job offers were numerous, accommodation wasn't. I'd tried the B&B owner's patience with unexpectedly extending my stay, trying to find permanent accommodation in Dublin. So, I left and went west to Galway. Within three days I had a job, within a week I had accommodation. It was kismet.

That's where I met Aideen. She was doing her undergrad in Galway, working at the pub part-time.

By spring, I'd acquired my Galway accent, was living with three Irish girls, and was getting along with my regulars at the pub. One night a couple men slid up to the bar to have the lamb stew. After many months of being immersed in the Irish climate, culture, and mystique, I was well on my way to becoming fully enculturated. I had yet to fully educate the staff on the differences between Americans and Canadians; the winter was devoid of tourists, so illustrating the distinction between the stereotypes was difficult. When the men came in, ate their stew, and talked, something piqued my interest. They sounded familiar, but I couldn't figure out what it was that made me feel warm and invited. During their hour or so of conversation and questions, the feeling nagged at me. Did I know them? Had I met them at a pub or a party one night? When they asked if the pub accepted Interac, I finally put it all together. They were Canadian, in fact from Alberta. I hadn't heard the Canadian accent for so long I couldn't place it. After they paid and left, I reflected on what made me feel so warm in their presence – they felt and sounded like home.

I managed to find that feeling, not as strong, meeting up with other Canadians as I traveled throughout Europe that year and later. However, nothing equaled the warmth those two men radiated.

I felt it again now, being in Dublin again after ten years. This was home. I'd felt a kinship with Ireland at first sight. It wasn't a home second to Alberta; it was just another home, of equal rating. The Alberta forest had become my home after many years spent there with my father. The forest knew me and I knew it. Perhaps this is why I gravitated towards doing boreal forest archaeology; nobody else wanted to do it and I loved the forest. Ireland knew me too. I knew the feel of the ground, knew the smells, knew the sounds. Outside the forest, outside Ireland, I felt awkward, stumbling over my own feet, pushing against forces unseen and untouchable. Here, everything flowed with a grace that made my heart weep with relief.

Here, everything fit.

Darkness descended as Aideen wound the car through County Meath's roads. We were going to spend the night at her parents' place. Her boyfriend, Eamon, was waiting there for us. Ten years ago, Aideen had invited me to spend a few days in County Meath. I'd had quit the pub and was looking forward to seeing a bit of the country before I was obliged to return to my life, and family, in Canada. Those few days at her parents' house were glorious. Fields of grass and hay. An abandoned castle. Biking along gravel roads. Visiting Newgrange. Shopping in Dublin. This time around, I had three days in Ireland; I could only hope for another visit as wonderful.

Aideen's parents had already gone to bed. The house was quiet. Eamon, just as tall as I remembered, poked his head out from the kitchen door. "Have you eaten?" he asked. Both Aideen and I were famished and Eamon quickly made up the best meal I'd had in weeks: soup and ham and cheese sandwiches, with tea and biscuits. I went to bed contented.

The next day, Eamon took the bus back to Longford. "Sorry," he apologized the next morning. "I have to be back at work Monday morning. It was great to see you again. I'll see you on Monday when you come round."

"You've got a good man there," I mentioned to Aideen later as we strolled down a path next to the river. "I still can't believe it's been ten years."

Aideen picked up a stick and swatted nearby grasses. Her complexion, that translucent Irish white, had picked up a bit of colour during our walk and made me feel less like a bronze Hercules from North America. "God, yeah. Ten years. Doesn't feel like it. Feels like our trip to Tokyo was just last year." Aideen and Eamon had gone to Tokyo to spread their wings and teach English for a year.

"Are you two going to get married?" Again, I was attempting to push away a feeling of being something other than a normal woman.

Aideen nodded and threw the stick into the dense undergrowth, "Oh, probably. When I'm done school and things calm down."

"Will things calm down?" In that respect, Aideen was too much like me; things just never seemed to calm down enough to live life.

Sitting in Windermere, I began to see that unless I took action, my life would pass me by, completely unlived and unnoticed. I was essentially on call for my job May through December – I had to leave at a moment's notice to go to the remote reaches of the wilderness. I couldn't commit to further education, or even an intimate relationship because, when I wasn't on call, I was completely exhausted from being on call for eight months. In Windermere, I began to see the leaves on the trees and not resent the fact that they were obscuring my view of the topography; I wandered aimlessly instead of taking aim and finishing in record time; I began to look at men for their smiles and not for their potential to hold a shovel.

Aideen and I spent the day wandering the countryside, visiting small towns, a local war museum, and small churches. We had no destination in mind; our only objective was to wander, talk, and be together.

On Monday, we headed to her home in Longford. She showed me her school and the town, then we curled up on her sofa, using the TV to prompt conversation. Eamon arrived after work with curry take-away then we all fit on the sofa and talked into the small hours of the morning.

The next day, Aideen and I headed back to Dublin. I was to leave the next morning, so we would again spend the night with her parents. We met up with her sister, who was taking Literature at Trinity College. Mary showed us around campus, the Books of the Kells, and ended with the bookstore. "I know I can leave you here and not feel like I'm abandoning you," Mary said as she hugged me and turned toward class.

Aideen and I fell into an old habit, quickly losing sight of each other in amongst the bookshelves. I was trying not to think of leaving the next morning: I was stacking book upon book into my arms, while in my mind, daring airport personnel to tell me my luggage was overweight.

As I rounded the bookshelf corner, my shoulder bag strap caught on the corner and brought a display shelf of books toppling down.

"Shit."

I dropped the armload of books I was carrying onto the floor and began to reassemble the display before guilt, embarrassment, or a manager could find me.

A silky, male voice from beside said, "In Ireland, we say 'shite'."

I cringed. I didn't want to cringe, but embarrassment had found me. Maybe even a manager. He was being overly nice about it – an Irish thing to do – but I still felt bad. Maybe I was being too Canadian.

I was attempting to pile the books on the now-broken display and it wasn't working. I was frustrated and embarrassed. He, whoever he was, had bent down and was piling the fallen books onto the lower shelf, out of the way.

I didn't want to look at him either; I didn't want to put a face to the source of my embarrassment. But I turned anyway. He had blond hair and blue eyes; an uncommon phenotype in Ireland. He was wearing a suit. Did store managers wear suits?

I continued to fumble with the display when the whole thing col-lapsed again. "Fuck. Um, sorry."

He laughed and drew the newly fallen books towards him and piled them onto the lower shelf with the others. "It's okay. We swear over here too." He picked up my books and moved to put them with the fallen display books.

"Actually, those are mine," I said.

He picked up the books and stood. He was tall and lean. And despite not wanting to look at him, there was really nowhere else to look. He was casually put together: the suit fell gracefully from broad shoulders; the burgundy tie was loosened; his hair was gently tussled; his fingers were long and nimble; his cheeks formed apples as he smiled. He reminded me of David Tennent's Dr. Who and I didn't know why. I wanted to look to see if he was wearing sneakers but I couldn't tear my eyes from his face.

"You like dead people," he said as he handed my books to me.

"They're easier to deal with than the live ones." As soon as I said, I regretted it. "Sorry, nothing personal."

He laughed again. It was a hearty sound, like it had been cooped up too long. "I know exactly what you mean." And that's when he looked at me and the world stopped.

Yeah, it'd been a long time since I'd been attracted to a man, even longer since I'd been in a relationship. It wasn't just because of my job: things had just seemed to cumulate into a long abstinence. Between being jaded, being too busy, and just not being motivated any more, I'd stopped looking.

He held his hand out to me, "Gavin Cleary. Archaeologist."

I was stunned. I'd traveled halfway around the world only to stumble into yet another archaeologist. It seemed to be my plight. I knew that my frizzy hair was escaping its ponytail tie too.

"Elise Marquette." We shook hands. Mine was already sweating. His was warm and firm. Dear God, did he know how appealing he was? He had a beautiful smile and he could have definitely held shovel.

"Are you a student here?" Gavin's blue eyes glanced at my books again.

I snorted. "I wish." Geez, I was such a moron. Why couldn't I at least act civilised? He probably thought I was American.

"Dead people are just a hobby then?"

Usually I sighed at this line of conversation. Once I said my profession, people generally were enraptured and thought archaeology was the coolest job ever. After the first couple of times trying to set people right, I eventually gave up. I endeavored to avoid the topic of profession or lack thereof. "I'm a physical anthropologist; I do archaeology to pay the bills."

If I didn't know better, I could have sworn I saw wheels start to turn in Gavin Cleary's head. His eyebrows rose. "There's a place where you can pay the bills doing archaeology? Do you have a grant from National Geographic?"

It was my turn to laugh. "It would be my dream to work in the Rift Valley with the Leakeys, but no. I'm merely a Consulting Archaeologist in Alberta."

"I kind of figured you weren't American." Now I was officially in love.

"And you? An archaeologist in a suit. I never thought I'd see that."

He smiled and perhaps even blushed. "I'm a lecturer here. I have an impression to maintain."

Gavin Cleary had stunned me into silence again. My friend, Aideen, choose that moment to come around the corner, "Elise, there you are. Are you done?"

I recovered my senses. "Yeah, I just have to pay for these. It was nice to meet you," I held out my hand again to Gavin.

"Actually, I'm done here if you and your friend want to join me for a lunch. I just came in to order some course materials."

Aideen must have noticed my face, or my lack of words. She became a godsend and filled the void, "It's about time for some food," she looked at me again to gain a sense of what I wanted. "Sure. We have time."

I nodded, too shocked at my good fortune.

Gavin Cleary followed us up to the cashier exchanging idle chatter with Aideen. Aideen wasn't completely subtle. She'd accurately sensed my feelings and was grilling the gorgeous lecturer standing beside me.

I honestly didn't know what to think. When I'd lived in Ireland ten years previous and worked with Aideen at the pub, I'd learned that Irish men were just plain nice. That's the way they were. While working at the pub, I saw many, many occurrences of strong Irish women walking all over their nice Irish boyfriends. It was eerily like back home. But unlike back home, these same Irish men were very charming. Even if they had a girlfriend, they'd talk up a girl, buy her a pint or sit and talk for an hour or two. I'd been caught in this little trap a couple times ten years ago. I would get all flattered when some Irish guy sat and chatted with me then be disappointed when he let slip a story about his girlfriend. By the third time, I'd learned it was just the Irish way. And after my trip to the continent, discovered that this was fairly common in Europe. However, Irish men made it into a fine art.

I didn't know what to make of Gavin Cleary.

Was I becoming old and skeptical?

He held the door open as Aideen and I exited the bookstore onto Trinity College's stone-cobbled campus. Chivalrous too. He must be a serial killer, I thought. Nobody could be this perfect.

We walked and talked. Aideen fishing and digging into Gavin's life and me tagging along nodding and smiling at Gavin's comments. We ended up a couple blocks from the college at a small eatery. Gavin insisted on buying us lunch. As much as I didn't like being taken care of, Aideen was beating me down: she hadn't let me pay for anything except my books since I'd arrived three days earlier.

During lunch I learned that Gavin was trying to get on the Dakhleh Oasis team. His specialty was Roman Archaeology. "It's a well-run, well-funded operation that's been going on for years," he said. He told stories of Roman battles and conquests in northern Africa, funerary rights, and festivals to celebrate the seasons. I know he was delving into the dead because of my own interests; Aideen knew my morbid predilections and humored me. I was riveted.

"Oh, Elise," Aideen looked at her watch. "We need to go."

I met Gavin's eyes. "Sorry, we have tickets to the Body World exhibition."

"Dead people," he nodded and smiled.

Gavin walked us across O'Connell Bridge and down the street to the exhibition. He then surprised me by walking up to the ticket booth. He walked back, me staring at him, and shrugged. "I had to ask, but they're sold out." Gavin held out his hand. I held mine out too and he shook it.

"Here." Aideen's voice descended between us.

Gavin broke our connection and looked at Aideen's hand. In it, she held out her ticket. "Here. Meet me back in the restaurant."

"But, Aideen..." I began, but she thrust it into Gavin's hand.

Aideen turned on that gorgeous bright smile, blue eyes glistening, "I needed to do some shopping anyway." She leaned in and kissed my cheek quickly before striding away, my shopping bags in her hand. I was left, my mouth opening and closing like fish out of water. Or, a reluctant archaeologist out of her depth.

"Shall we?" Gavin held out his arm. He was smiling, eyebrows raised expectantly.

I stood rooted, willing myself to the do the one thing in my life that I knew was right, the one thing that I knew would make me happy. If only for a few moments, an hour. Outside of work, away from my family, devoid of any financial decision or obligation, this time and place with this man was completely free of how screwed up my life really was. In typical Irish fashion, Ireland had presented me with a mystical moment, freeing me of reality.

After all this time, fighting for my own way, my own stretch of happiness, why did I have such a difficult time when that stretch concerned relationships? Fighting in school was easy: I worked harder, got better marks, got scholarships. Fighting at work was easy: I worked harder, got done projects sooner, under budget, and with better results. Fighting with my family was easy too: I just stopped talking to them when they pissed me off. Sooner or later, one of them called and we'd start all over again. But, fighting for happiness in a relationship? Well first, one had to get a relationship...

I had suspicions regarding my self-esteem; I wasn't completely ignorant of my own psychology and what my familial upbringing may have incurred. But to think that I didn't feel myself worthy of a relationship seemed so far out of whack. Now, with Gavin Cleary standing, smiling at me, waiting and wanting, I had to wonder. What *was* holding me back?

It was with this question that my hand began to move. It had a life outside my own and reached out to wind around Gavin Cleary's arm. My body moved then too, catching up with my disembodied arm, and finally I stood next to Gavin. My mind, however, was still catching up. Slowly it moved closer, reveling in the journey my body took next to Gavin: I could smell his aftershave and the way it mingled with scent of laundry soap in his clothes; feel the heat from his body and how the cool air threatened to seep between us; then, the rough weave of his jacket upon my fingertips. Finally, I looked up, his blue eyes and blond stubble directly in front of my eyes.

"Grand," he said led me into the exhibition.

It took until we were halfway through the exhibition. Then, I fell into place. I was happily sated; I had an intelligent, witty, beautiful man at my side and dead people all around me. Morbid, but my truth, nonetheless. And Gavin accepted me, wholly. I hadn't been able to say anything to unhinge him; not my fascination with funerary rights and how and where people were buried and treated their dead, not how I stuck my nose nearly into the exhibits to examine just how the muscles attached to the bones, and not how I asked point blank why he consented to being an over-educated labourer.

"I can't help it," he grinned and shrugged from behind an encased infant's brain, "I love it. I love the mystery, the puzzle, the challenge.

"It's not the labour – of that, I have no love lost – it's about holding the past in my hands and divining the lives of those people. It's about telling a story of people who can no longer speak. If I could do it without the digging, I would. But dirt tells a story too, an integral one that needs to be considered in the story."

If he had been my prof, I would have never left school.

We spoke the same language. I felt the exact same way about a person's body; what did the person eat, how did they make their way in life, who did they love and support, how did they die. It was all the same -- a personal connection to people of the past.

An hour and a half later, we stood outside. "I am taking a drive out to the Burin tomorrow to have a look at a site for my class. I could use some company. Interested?"

The world fell out from beneath my feet. "I can't. I'm leaving tomorrow."

Was there disappointment in his eyes? I couldn't tell. I was too disappointed to read him. All I knew at that moment was that I wanted to remember his face. I wanted to remember him as completely and wholly as he was standing there in front of me.

"I have kept you from your friend too long. Please thank her for the ticket. It was very generous of her." He fished into his jacket pocket and pulled out a twenty Euro note and a rumpled business card. Dr. Gavin Cleary. Trinity College Dublin. "Please keep in touch," he said as he took my hand. He didn't shake it, merely held on. I didn't want to let go. "I'd really like to hear how you're doing."

In an act of desperation, I retrieved my hand and dug around in my bag. I managed to find an old card from my graduate days. The email was a personal one, but the phone number was for Simon Fraser University.

We bid farewell, the printing on his card already fading in my sweating and tightly-clenched palm.

Aideen was waiting in the restaurant, a pint of lager in front of her. I slid into the booth opposite her. Aideen pulled her eyes from one of the books I'd bought at Trinity College and gazed at me. "So, are you still leaving tomorrow?"

"What do you think?" I was suddenly miserable. Aideen had astutely summed up my life in one question.

"You don't have to. You can change your flight. I'm not due back at school until next week and frankly, I've got some studying to do for exams."

I plunked my head down on my folded arms on the table. "Why did he have to be so perfect, Aideen? Why?"

A pint of Guinness appeared before me. "Drink, Elise."

But the stout didn't tempt me, "I don't want to drink. I want answers, Aideen. Why is my life so fucked up?"

Aideen leaned across the table then, eyes blazing and her cheeks flush with alcohol, "If it's fucked up, then un-fuck it."

I picked up the Guinness and downed half it in one gulp. I hadn't tasted its creamy texture or the fullness in my mouth. I just needed its anesthetic. Two hours later, I'd had three Guinness and was pining for sleep.

I still wanted to find out if Gavin was wearing sneakers.

Chapter Seven

Six Weeks in the Wilderness, Part II

"**I**f you don't sit your ass down in that seat, I'll staple it down," I yelled as Chad drove by standing on the footpetals of his quad.

Week Three saw my crew and I approaching Site #6 out of eight sites. I had three days left before we all headed back to Calgary for a week off. We were behind schedule. Big time.

I had agreed to work three weeks on this excavation. I had my own projects. These two thoughts pervaded my every waking moment. I had an agreement with HSAC. A sick feeling in my stomach told me that that agreement would be broken, and not by me.

My weekly timesheets averaged 90 to 100 hours for each week. Temperatures had reached + 30 degrees Celsius. We were all so hot and tired we'd started singing show tunes to ward off the delusions. We couldn't work more or faster.

I still hadn't heard from Michelle regarding the schedule. I'd send her several emails by this point, all without a single reply. How could a manager avoid her subordinates? How could I update her if she didn't talk to me? I was copying Morris and the owner of HSAC, Tim Bowden, on every email I sent to Michelle. I was at my wit's end. None of HSAC's management responded, except Morris and he only said, "We'll talk when you get back." I was getting pissed and, unfortunately, I'd forgotten to unlock the caps lock on my keyboard while composing my last email. I was getting to know Michelle's management style and I didn't like it.

Gerry couldn't get a hold of us during the beginning of Week Two because we were at a new site without cell reception. At two o'clock we had a pair of surveyors arrive at the site in all their muskeg-soaked glory to make sure we were alright. When Gerry later asked if we had two-way radios, I had to break it to him that management didn't see the value in it when we already had a sat phone and cell phones. "However," I said, "If the client wants us to have radios, then we'll get them." Gerry, the intelligent man that he was, got the hint and two days later, Jacquie drove into Fort Mac to pick up a couple sets of two-way radios. As I said, I liked Gerry.

Then Gerry wanted some of the maps I had. "Print me off another copy," he said. I had to break it to him again when I said we don't have a scanner or a printer. As before, he paused, looking at me. I could see the wheels turning in his head – they had turned the same way in my head several times over the past couple of weeks.

Half way into Week Two, Michelle emailed to say that Maggie was to be sent home to Calgary and that a replacement would be coming the day after. Michelle effectively screwed me out of two days digging time with that little maneuver. I lost Jacquie driving to Fort Mac twice in two days instead of having her dig. Jacquie was a good digger. Her two-day absence meant we would be about five units behind. That's a lot, especially when you're digging a twenty-unit site. Four schedule days at one site turned into six actual days. Michelle apparently didn't know how much time was lost whenever we had to do a run into Fort Mac. "Oh, she knows," Jacquie said when I ranted to her over the screen. "It isn't like Russell and I haven't told her several times."

Maggie had been replaced by Nicolas, an archaeology student so green, he didn't even know how to hold a shovel. More digging time lost. I'd also shipped Paul, the "Talker," home, but I suspected I wasn't losing any digging time with that one.

On the brighter side of things, while Jacquie was living up to her position as my Number One, Ellen had become my Number Two. What Jacquie couldn't or didn't have time to do, Ellen effortlessly took on. As well, Chad's notes and digging had improved dramatically, and my crew, overall, was congealing nicely as a team. If only I could get Chad to sit down while he drove.

The point remained: I had an agreement with HSAC and I wanted to stick to it. However, I now had an ulterior motive: I wanted off this project not only on principle, but because the whole set-up was just stupid.

The two-way radio clipped to my vest squawked, "Elise, have you seen Vanessa yet?"

I turned from raging at Chad's lack of quad safety, back to the patch of muskeg we were trying to cross. The peat quivered as a quad spun its wheels somewhere in the tamarack and stunted black spruce. "No," I toggled my radio then peeled off my helmet and listened. "She's stuck."

I followed the mucked up quad path down the slight embankment and sighed as my boots, once again, sunk into the muskeg. I felt the water flow through the laces of my boots and up around my ankles. So much for a dry-boots day, I thought. And so much for waterproofing my boots.

I hopped through the bush and muskeg as best I could, trying to use clumps of grass and spindly tree roots to keep me from sinking in knee-deep or further.

Vanessa was rocking her quad side to side, like I taught her, but she had her throttle to the max. The quad roared and steamed poured out the exhaust behind her. "Stop!" I yelled above the racket and motioned to cut the throttle.

Vanessa sank back to her seat, panting. "I tried rocking just like you said, but it just sunk right in."

I walked around her quad, surveying the situation. I was now soaked up to my thighs, the muskeg sucking noisily at my every step. Jacquie appeared from the other direction, muskeg sucking at her boots. "Fun!" she said. Jacquie had developed a reputation of getting stuck and it wasn't because she tried to avoid it. It didn't matter how hard I tried to impress upon everyone that we would have to use these trails all summer. Some people just loved the adrenaline of getting stuck.

"Okay, Vanessa. Have you used a winch before?" Beneath the green goggles, Vanessa's eyes grew. The quad helmet shook side to side. "It's okay. That's what Jacquie and I are here for. There's nothing to worry about."

Jacquie moved behind me and scouted for a suitable tree. "See this button here?" I tapped a small box on Vanessa's handlebars, "This is the winch control." I grabbed a hold of the winch hook and pulled while pushing the button. The winch motor ground slowly and the cable unwound. "This is out, this is in. Got it?" Vanessa nodded.

I continued to pull the winch hook as Vanessa depressed the button. Jacquie had picked out a small spruce tree the size of my arm. Outside of mosquitoes, not much else thrived in muskeg.

I reached the tree and I motioned to Vanessa to keep unwinding the cable. Jacquie and I tied the cable around the tree, motioned to Vanessa to take up the slack, then we hopped back through the muskeg to Vanessa. "Jacquie and I will be pushing behind you. Steer toward the tree. Let the winch pull you out. NO THROTTLE, okay?"

Again, Vanessa nodded, wide-eyed.

Jacquie and I took up position behind the stuck quad. "Okay, Vanessa, push the winch button."

Jacquie and I dug our boots into what little there was in the muskeg. Jacquie was now soaked up to her upper thigh, I was nearly up to my underwear. There's nothing worse than trying to work all day with wet underwear. Even if it was sunny.

We felt the quad slowly begin its trek out of the hole. Vanessa felt this and stood up to rock the quad again. I grabbed the back of her pants and thrust her butt back down in the seat. "Don't stress the cable; it could break."

Jacquie and I continued to lean into the back of the quad when it finally lurched out of the hole. Jacquie and I fell to our hands into the muskeg, both smiling. Jacquie jumped up to high-five Vanessa. "Great work! Wahoo!"

Jacquie unhooked the cable as I plodded through the spindly spruce trees trying to find another path across the muskeg easy enough for my naïve crew to negotiate. I got back to Vanessa. "I want you to follow me out. Are you in second gear?" She nodded. "Good. Remember don't stop and don't floor it. Just nice and steady, okay?"

Vanessa made it through, to much cheering from the crew. Well, I thought as I got back on my quad, that was getting into the site. Getting back out was a whole other story. Our hour travel time to the sites was growing everyday. We'd wasted an hour on the muskeg. No wonder we were behind schedule.

We got to the new site and began to unpack our gear. Ellen sided up to me. She hadn't been stuck, but muskeg splattered her pants and the back of her plaid shirt. "Elise, I need to talk with you."

Okay. This was new. I nodded and we rounded my quad, our backs to the crew. "What's up?"

"We've got a female problem. Liz's tampon is stuck."

I paused as I translated this statement. It was no surprise that Ellen was telling me this and not Liz. Ellen had become the liaison between me, Jacquie, and the rest of the crew. I was beginning to appreciate what it was like to be management and not know what was really going on with your employees. I hadn't the foggiest idea what my crew thought or did most of the time.

I nodded. I didn't need details, I just knew that this was a situation that required getting two members out of the bush and to Fort Mac. "Do you feel comfortable taking her into Fort Mac?"

"No problem. How are you going to get everyone back to camp?"

"I'll figure something out. Two trips maybe." I dug my truck keys out of my pants pocket. "Call me when you to town. Stash your quads behind the bush pile and we'll lock them up tonight. I'll follow you to the muskeg. Use the new path." With Ellen and Jacquie, everything was so easy. I didn't have to specify little things like leaving the quad keys in the quads and that I'd be down to two trucks for ten people, they just knew.

Our site was far enough from camp that we now drove the trucks to where we stashed and locked up our quads every night. Problem was we had so many people we need all three trucks.

Jacquie got the crew set up while I followed Ellen and Liz to the muskeg patch. Liz was very subdued, but I didn't pay her any mind. I just squeezed her shoulder before she took off across the muskeg.

When I got back, the crew was already at work and David was off singing his pee song in the forest. There were a variety of ways people conquered their fear of bears while in the forest. Of the different ways the crew humoured my maternal paranoia of keeping tabs on everyone at all times, David's pee song was the most enjoyable.

Jacquie looked up from rummaging in one of the toteboxes. She was looking past me, "What's up?" I asked unable to figure out what she was looking at.

She didn't answer, but shock was slowly working its way across her face.

"What?" The panic in my chest was rising. I had visions of Ellen being pulled over because her license had expired, that Liz would have to be flown home because she had toxic shock syndrome, that Jacquie just remembered about her own tampon. Considering all that I'd had to pull myself and my crew through in the past three weeks, I was on high alert every hour of every day.

Jacquie pointed at the tree behind me. "Look." I spun and stared at the trees. It took a second before it registered. By the time I'd figured it out, the rest of the crew had too.

"Eew!"

"Oh, my God. Yuck!"

"Holy shit!"

It was caterpillar season. Blackness seemed to encompass the white aspen trees and the blackness moved. I looked up. It was June and there was virtually no leafy canopy. A caterpillar fell from its heights and hit my face. Good thing I didn't have my mouth open. Jacquie screamed. I shook it off.

A good thirty minutes was spent taking pictures and grossing out each other by picking up mounds of caterpillars.

Eventually, we pounded brightly flagged nails into the ground for our baseline and grid, like the six sites before. Today's topic of conversation was religion. Sort of.

"Jesus was totally a vampire," David said as he wound up the tape measure.

"Nuh, uh," Janet said, her green braided hair flying as she tied flagging tape to spikes, "Jesus was a zombie. He was totally night of the living dead."

"But he had the charm of a vampire," David purred. "How else did he get so many converts, darling?"

"And he rose from the dead," Chad added.

"But what about sex?" Sharon asked. "Jesus was chaste."

"Yeah and Mary Magdalene was my mother," David retorted.

I had to admit that David kept things interesting. I never had to worry about morale with David around. I had begun to think that every excavation needed a token gay guy.

"Elise," Jacquie called from the equipment area, "You're phone's ringing." After walking around the site, staring at our cell phone screens, Jacquie and I'd found the only place for cell reception. If it hadn't been a "safety issue" to not have cell reception, I would have happily stuffed the thing in my pocket and forgotten about it. As it was, we'd put the equipment and the shelter where there was reception and I'd laid my phone on top of one of the totes.

I ran back and answered. "Hi Elise, this is Joe. I need you to fill out an incident report on the bear you encountered in Grande Cache." I didn't feel like telling him it hadn't been just one bear.

"There was no injury and no medical aid given."

"Doesn't matter," Joe said. "Any bear encounter is an incident. I need those safety forms as soon as possible."

"I can do them tonight."

"Can't you do them by the end of day?" This was typical. Too bad it wasn't just my clients that didn't understand what being out in the field meant.

"Joe, I am in the field. I don't get back to camp until 6pm. You will get safety paperwork tonight IF the internet is working."

Joe signed off and I called Morris. "Morris, what's this about the Grande Cache bear thing being an incident?"

"I wasn't aware of anything changing," I could hear Morris' brows furrowing. I told him about Joe's phone call. "I'll talk to Joe."

I hung up. I was just walking back to help lay in the grid when my phone rang again. It was going to be one of those days.

"Elise, mom is in the hospital again." Fuck. Even hundreds of miles away, my family still managed to find and pester me.

"That's nice." I started to pace but remembered the sweet spot of cell reception.

"Don't be snide," Sebastian said. He was keeping it together today. I was proud of him.

"What's it this time? A brain tumor?"

Sebastian sighed. "She's not reacting well to the chem and rad. We're going to the hospital tonight. I'll pick you up at five."

"You can try, but I'm not home. I'm in Fort Mac."

"Oh." He was about as bad as our mother when it came to appreciating what I did. "When can you come home?"

"I'm not coming home. I'm working."

"I'll phone your boss and say it's an emergency."

"Don't. Even. Think. About it." The crew behind me had become very quiet. "I will be home in three days. If mom isn't out of the hospital by then, I'll think about a visit."

"Three days?" I could hear victory in Sebastian's voice.

"I said I'd think about it." I snapped my cell phone shut and seriously considered turning it off.

By lunchtime, we'd laid the grid and begun digging. Ellen had called saying they were waiting in Fort Mac's emergency. Morris called after lunch. "Tell me what happened with the bear."

I told him, excluding the mother and second cub. I wanted to keep this simple. "When did any encounter with a bear become an incident?"

"I don't know. I'll go talk to Joe."

Great. I was in the middle of a safety paperwork catastrophe with a side of familial politics and all I had was a phone in the bush.

"Elise!" A voice screamed from the forest.

My heart skipped. It was an easy dive into panic.

David was emerging from another of his pee breaks, waving his arms. "What?" Jacquie was beside me, breathless.

"I saw bear poo!" He pointed back into the bush.

I just about fainted from relief. "Jesus Christ, David! Can you be any more melodramatic?"

David peered at me, all innocent and wide-eyed. "Maybe."

I took a swat at him as he giggled and pranced over to his unit. Jacquie and I investigated. The bear scat was a couple days old. Lots of berries. "Are the bear bangers still in the totes?" I asked. A bear banger was essentially a noise-maker or a cap gun that came in various shapes and sizes. We had a gun-shaped one and a pen-shaped one, both using the same types of caps. Jacquie and I loaded each and put them at our muster point.

Jacquie double-checked that everyone had their bear spray close by. I pulled out my phone to call Gerry when I realized I'd taken it with me, out of the reception sweet spot.

There was one missed call. And a text.

Great. I could already hear the disappointment in Theo's voice.

But the voicemail wasn't from Theo. And it wasn't Morris or Joe.

My knees turned to jelly when I heard the Irish accent. "Um, hello Elise. This Gavin Cleary from Trinity College Dublin. We met a few months ago, while you were in Dublin. I don't know if you rem ember.....um, I lecture at the college...we went to the BodyWorlds exhibition, I offered to show you the Burin. Anyway, I was hoping to talk to you....I hope this is a good number to reach you; I got it from the signature of your email. Could you please ring me back at 095633421? Thank you."

"Paper. Paper! I need paper. Shit!" I spun around looking for my notebook and pen. Jacquie dropped the kit bags she was organizing and flipped open a new notebook. I replayed the message and wrote down the number. I began to dial, but then couldn't remember the country code for Ireland. "Shit!" And by the time we'd get to camp at night, it'd be too late to call. "Shit! Shit!"

My phone rang again. "Oh, now what?" I answered.

"Elise? Elise Marquette?" Great. Maybe I should just shoot myself now to save stuffing my other foot in my mouth.

"Sorry. Yes, this is Elise."

"Hi, Elise. This is Mark Van Gutten from the Historic Branch. I got your report on the Arctic Power transmission line through the Peace River valley." I remembered asking him about this report a couple months ago, before I went to Grande Cache. It was a big report. I had recommended that the proposed development could proceed because it was far enough away not to impact the nearby historic resources. No further assessment was recommended. I had wanted give my client an update on when the governmental clearance paperwork would be issued. "I'm going to want backhoe testing along the transmission line. When can you do it?"

My mind tripped. More assessment. I stumbled over the fact that Mark didn't agree with my recommendations, and instead saw the benefits of the situation: this was another reason to keep me from coming back up here. "I'm currently in the field, but I'll be back in Calgary next week."

"Can you do revisions on this report instead of writing a new one?" Mark asked.

"Sure, can you extend my permit from last year, or do you need a new one?"

"I'll need a new one." Again, more paperwork was needed and I was out in the middle of the bush with only a phone. "But, I'll let the director know it's coming and we'll push it through. How are things going out there?"

"Um," I stumbled. How did he know where I was and what I was doing? His area was the west not the north. "It's going all right."

"Make sure you dig big blocks of units instead of just single units all around the place." I agreed. "Keep me updated, Elise. I'd really like to hear what you find. Don't let the mosquitoes or the strange immigrant riggers get to you."

I hung up and looked at my phone, bewildered. I'd only met Mark once at the Historic Branch. Our communication was limited to how he wanted my methods to be formatted in my reports and what to do about the recommendations I'd made. He was nice enough, but what this was getting a little personal. Then I realized I'd just volunteered to work on my federally required days-off. Great. Yeah, I should have just shot myself. I needed sleep. I called Morris once again to tell him to expect my signed permit application for the Peace River valley in the fax the next morning. He'd have to send it in for me.

Ellen returned with Liz at nearly eight that night. Morris hadn't called back. Neither had Joe or Theo. It was then that I remembered I had an unread text on my phone. My Irish friend, Aideen, had finished her teaching exams and was offered a job in Athlone. She was finally free. I was glad one of us was.

The crew was revived as we landed in Calgary three days later. I dumped my stuff in the hallway of my apartment, showered, then went to the bank.

The young man behind the desk couldn't have been more than 25 years old. He peered at the computer screen and the two lines of data on it: my banking information.

"You have a credit card with $17,228 balance and a chequing account with $128."

"There abouts." His numbers were three weeks old. My credit card was now up to $24,981 because of being in the field for three weeks and my chequing account was at $930 because I hadn't needed groceries or gas for three weeks.

"Do you own your home?"

"No."

"Do you own a vehicle?"

"Yup. It's an '92 Toyota Tercel." He hummed and made a note.

"Do you have an RRSP?"

"Nope."

"Any stock, bonds, or mutual funds?"

"Nope."

"And how much do you need?"

"$50,000." My palms were beginning to sweat.

The financial advisor finally turned to me. "I'm sorry, Elise. You just don't have enough credit history and assets for us to lend you $50,000.

If you can find someone to co-sign for you, though, we might be able to work something out. Someone who owns their own home."

Not only could I count the number of friends I had in Calgary on one hand, not one of them owned their own home. That's the pitfall of being an academic for so long; all your friends are in the same boat as you and are scattered across the country or further.

Outside and rejected, I realized I hadn't told him about my dad's cabin. I don't know why. It would have been logical to tell him. But there was something in me that refused to use my father's memory as leverage for a bank loan. Tack it up to emotions and familial paranoia, perhaps.

I went home, to bed, and surfaced at the office two days later.

Morris and I each had a coffee in hand when we entered Michelle's cramped office downstairs. I had made a list of what we'd accomplished and what needed to be done. While we'd only finished six of eight of the sites outlined in my permit, most of them also needed to be expanded. My permit wasn't even close to being complete.

"Is it possible to transfer my sites to Scott's permit?" I asked.

"No. Not possible." Michelle said through lipstick-coated, pursed lips.

"Is it possible for someone else to take over my permit?" I tried again.

"No."

I was exhausted. The two days rest I got on the weekend had only brought me back to the living without the energy to actually function. I was having a hard time making sense of which end of the phone to speak into. "Michelle, I agreed to work this excavation for three weeks.

It's going to take longer than three weeks. I have other projects, my own clients."

"What are you recommending at the sites?" Michelle asked.

"An additional ten square metres of excavation on each site except number 1 and 4; I want another thirty metres at those two."

"Why?"

"We found a decent variety of artifacts which tended to concentrate around tree roots and there are more trees opportunely placed at these sites."

"No wonder you're behind schedule – you shouldn't be digging up trees. Dig around them."

I was stunned. Michelle had pretty much said, 'don't do good archaeology.' My blood began to shift from its sloggy hibernation in my veins, but not quickly enough.

Silence descended over the three of us. Michelle's words hung in the air. Beside me, I couldn't tell what Morris thought of Michelle's comment.

Finally, the silence broke. "This needs to be done," Michelle said, her glossy brunette bob flashing in the sunlight as she shook her head. "I've talked to Morris. He can get Frank and Ida to work any projects coming in and to handle your clients until you're back."

Morris was being very quiet. "I got a call from the Historic Branch last week. Mark wants me to backhoe test in the Peace River valley ASAP. I can't go this week because technically I shouldn't even be here, at the office working."

Morris took a sip of his coffee before answering. "How long will it take?"

"A couple of days. Then I have to revise my report and resubmit."

Michelle interjected, "We can send the crew back up and you a few days later. Jacquie can get them working." I stared at Michelle's red lips and posh hairstyle and wondered at the last time she'd worked in the field, on a large excavation.

That's when my blood finally reached its boiling point.

"Do you know how much digging time we lose every time we have to run into Fort Mac? I lose two people for half a day. That's a two-unit-per-day loss. I agreed to work for three weeks up there, but every time you mess around with my crew, I lose time, so don't say I'm not trying hard enough to make the schedule work, or that we aren't digging fast enough, or that we're not digging in the right spots. I'm working my ass off, doing the best archaeology I know how to do, and you're jerking me around."

I was standing. Michelle and Morris were staring. My empty coffee cup hung limply from my hand. "Two weeks. That's all I'm giving you. In two weeks, I'm on a flight back to Calgary. Take it or leave it."

Morris sipped his coffee. Michelle woke from her shock and nodded. "Okay. We can do that."

"Good," I sputtered.

"Good," Michelle nodded to Morris.

"Good," Morris muttered.

I don't remember coming back to my desk. I don't remember going home. Even if I did, I was too tired to care. I unplugged my home phone, turned off my cell, and cratered. I have no doubt my family was pissed at me. But they didn't show up at my door and neither did the cops, so it couldn't have been that bad.

I flew to Grande Prairie four days later. I had a backhoe operator meeting me that afternoon in the Peace River valley. Arctic Power was putting a transmission line through the valley linking the Town of Peace River to the north and Grande Prairie to the south. Apparently, Peace River routinely experienced brown and blackouts so a new source of electricity was needed.

Mark and Historic Branch of the government were making a fuss because the Peace River Valley contained some of the oldest Fur Trade Period posts in the province. Of course Arctic Power wanted to put their transmission line right through prime Historical territory -- it was Murphy's Law. This was big time Canadian history at my fingertips. Too bad I was too tired to care. Too bad there were no bones involved.

I drove from Grande Prairie to the Peace River in about an hour. This was good time considering they were still doing construction on the Dunvegan Bridge: they'd only been at the construction for at least two years now. I peeled off the main highway before hitting the town of Peace River, and took an industrial road down into the river valley. The Peace River Valley was steep, deep, and wide. The river embankment was also steep: a three- to five-metre high embankment separating the river from the 500 metre to one kilometer wide floodplain. The floodplain upon which Arctic Power wanted to put their transmission line was flat, heavily cultivated or disturbed in some areas. Further back from the river, the floodplain gave way to valley walls that, in some places, rose at a nearly seventy-degree angle. I know. I've climbed them. In 30-degree heat.

The floodplain was where the Hudson's Bay Company, the Northwest Company, and maybe even a couple of independent folks had placed their Fur Trade Period posts. And where people chose to build a post or, later, a town, usually started out as a precontact campsite for

First Nations' folks. It's a continuity thing; once a good place to camp, always a good place to camp.

There was very little to indicate the area was an Historical Point of Interest, except for the provincial sign. Beneath the surface, however, lay some of the province's oldest Fur Trade Period cultural artifacts. The issue here, for Arctic Power, was whether or not they were going to be impacting any of those buried Fur Trade Period posts and artifacts. They'd attempted to placate the government -- and the historians and First Nations folks -- by moving the transmission line as close to the river, and as far from where the posts were recorded, as possible.

However, the government wanted proof that nothing would impacted. I needed to give them that proof.

My backhoe operator was waiting at the end of the road. He was a young twenty-something guy named John dressed in jeans, Superman T-shirt, and a red ball cap. John walked with me down to the embankment of the Peace River and I told him what I wanted. "You see those survey stakes?" I pointed to wooden stakes painted with neon orange paint. "That's where they're going to put the transmission line. I need you to dig me trenches along this embankment and up to those stakes so that I can see if there's any archaeological stuff imbedded in the floodplain. I'm looking for bones, stone tools, charcoal, and anything from the Fur Trade, like old lumber and metal cans."

John unloaded the small backhoe and, after a bit of difficulty getting the backhoe positioned along the uneven and steep embankment, we began.

Twenty-five backhoe tests and a day later, I was satisfied that the Historic Branch of the government would be satisfied. I had found nothing except a few metal cans and glass bottles on the surface of the embankment. Nothing suggesting that a Fur Trade or archaeological site would be impacted by Arctic Power's development. I was confident that I could easily get Arctic Power the clearance they needed to build their transmission line; I wasn't so confident I would have to time to write the report to recommend clearance.

I had tried to convince Morris to let me fly home, but Michelle had already booked me on a flight across the province, from Grande Prairie to Fort Mac. Unfortunately, it went through Edmonton and took six hours. So much for saving time. I didn't think I could be more exhausted when Chad picked me up at the Fort Mac airport. "Can we please stop for chocolate and coffee?" I asked. Chad nodded meekly and peered at me. I must have looked bad. Geez, I'm dead on my feet and crabby with management. How am I supposed to lead a crew through the wilds of Fort Mac and negotiate the dangers of quads, bears, and twenty-something angst?

To top things off, I'd been too tired to remember to call Gavin Cleary back. A reminder of this hit at the most inopportune times, like when I was on a plane over Slave Lake, or in the bottom of the Peace River valley where there was less cell reception than Grande Cache. I never seemed to remember to call him when I was near a working phone and could look up the country code for Ireland.

When I got to my room at Manier's camp, I sunk to the floor and cried. Things just couldn't be any worse. I couldn't get a bank loan and get out from under my family's thumb. I couldn't stand up for myself and win out over people who just haven't got a clue. I couldn't even find the time and energy to call Gavin Cleary back and have the smallest nugget of hope in my life. To be back in my room at camp broke my heart.

I had tried my best and failed. Again.

My presence the next morning was greeted enthusiastically by the crew. I, however, was still bleary eyed from crying myself to sleep the night before. Gerry, the clever man he was, must have sensed something was wrong and cut short his welcome speech during the safety meeting.

The days had been sunny and bright while I'd been away. The puddles had dried up. The caterpillars had vanished. Even the muskeg was more manageable.

"We've split the crew into two groups to gain some speed," Jacquie told me before we headed our separate ways. Jacquie took a small crew of four to a site east of us. Ellen and five others came with me to finish at the caterpillar site.

As my small crew flitted about in their units, I dug out my maps and attempted to organize myself again after nearly two weeks away. A shadow fell across my notebook. I didn't have time to look up before Ellen put a handful of miniature chocolate bars on my notebook. "Take your time," she said. "We can manage." Ellen smiled, her green eyes twinkling, and left to organize the troops.

I nearly burst out crying again. Just when you are so sure, so absolutely positive that life sucks serious shit, someone comes along to prove you wrong. I don't know which I hated more – life or being proven wrong.

Ellen further surprised me the next morning by pulling out a book on the drive to the quads. "I thought you could use a little diversion from life." She showed me the cover of the book. A scantily clad woman clung to an equally scantily clad man.

"Smut?" I said. "Are you kidding me? I don't do smut."

Sharon and Vanessa sitting in the back agreed with me. "It's too early in the morning for smut," Vanessa said.

Ellen smirked, "Everyone can use a little smut. Even this early." Then she began to read. I swear that drive to the quads was the shortest drive ever. Sharon and Vanessa couldn't wait to get back to the truck at the end of the day. We managed to entice David and he appeared in our truck that night for another segment of smutty reading.

Contrary to what I had expected, the following two weeks were the easiest two weeks I've ever spent in the bush. The crew was a well-oiled machine. I didn't have to tell them what to do any more, or even how to do it. I practically glowed the first time I looked up from my maps to see they'd already packed up the gear and were ready to leave for camp on time. I didn't need to screen to keep their digging speed up. I was able to check the artifacts against everyone's records while at the site. I was finally down to 12 hours a day. Joe would have been pleased. However, I still had my report on the Peace River valley to revise.

And I was still pissed that I'd been maneuvered into coming back up here again.

I phoned Morris while the crew was digging. "Morris, why didn't you have my back at the meeting with Michelle?" It was a good day. The sky was blue. The crew was happy. I was well-rested, relatively speaking.

"It's Michelle's project. I can't tell her how to run her projects."

I understood this, but I didn't like it. Morris was my supervisor. Where did I stand if I didn't have the support of my supervisor, especially in a precarious job like this? "Well, between you and me, Morris. I'm not working for Michelle again."

"I can understand that."

It was then that I had to wonder if Morris had let me jump into this just to see if I'd float. He more than likely had known the situation, but hadn't said anything to pre-empt my acceptance of this project. In fact, he'd acted in a very un-Morris like way.

"Morris, why am I on this project?"

"Because Russell's behind on his reporting and can't hold any permits."

I rubbed my forehead and tucked errant strands of hair behind my ear. "No, no. Why was I approached?"

Again there was no hesitation from Morris, "You said during your evaluation you wanted to try large excavations."

"Am I just some big social experiment to you? Throw me into these situations to see if I sink or swim?"

Morris chuckled, his veneer finally cracking. "It'll be nice to have someone upstairs with excavation experience."

"Thank you for finally telling me the truth." I slipped a mini chocolate bar into my mouth and picked up my clipboard of maps again. "I'm going to need a week off after I get back."

"Maybe eventually. Michelle wants an interim permit report for the excavations sent to the government to recommend more excavation. The interim report needs to be approved by the government ASAP so that any additional excavation can be completed this fall and on your permit."

Suddenly the chocolate bar didn't taste so good. "And Michelle couldn't tell me this because?"

"That's her department."

I had yet to figure out if my phone call to Morris was a good idea. "Well, I guess I'm going to need two weeks off then."

"I'll see what I can do."

The next week it rained. Archaeology in the rain isn't nice. Archaeologists in the rain are even worse. The dirt turned to mud. The mud was the consistency and colour of babyshit. It was gross. I was frustrated. The crew was frustrated. Despite Jacquie's unrelenting duty to get the job done at any cost, I pulled rank and brought the crew in. We cleaned artifacts for two days. I even managed to revise my Peace River report.

When the skies cleared, we only had a day left before we headed back to Calgary. Jacquie and I decided that instead of digging, we'd use the day for housework. Half the crew had been about to start a new site; starting a new site just to leave it for a week wasn't a good idea. The other site would be too wet to dig. We had half the equipment at camp. Now was a good time to take stock of what we had, what we needed, and what needed replacing. A check of the working order of the trucks, quads, and trailers was in order too. Gerry would be pleased.

I assigned people to trucks, quads, trailers and equipment, and armed them with checklists and clipboards. We laid all the equipment and supplies out on the double-axle trailers in the camp parking lot. Pens, baggies, hammers, spikes, string, levels, trowels, clipboards, etc. were sorted neatly into piles and counted. Crew members walked around trucks and quads, checking tire pressure, oil, and general maintenance.

That's when we discovered that a couple fire extinguishers had exploded in their boxes. That's also when we discovered that the bear spray had done the same.

"Water! I need some water, quick!" Ellen came running. I pulled my jug from the back pocket of my survey vest. Ellen grabbed it and ran to the far end of the trailer. I followed.

Bear spray is the same as mace or pepper spray. It contains capsicum, a derivative of cayenne pepper. It hurts when you get it in your eyes. Really, really hurts.

Liz was in the fetal position. She was struggling against David and Janet holding her hands behind her back. They were reassuring her at the same time. Ellen ran up, "Hold your head back, Liz. Liz!" Liz was moaning and crying. "Liz, listen to me. Hold your head back."

David and Janet coaxed Liz's head back and Ellen drenched Liz's eyes. "What happened?" I asked.

"Bear spray," Ellen said.

"David, Janet. Get her into camp and under a shower. Don't let her touch anything." I turned to Ellen who handed back my empty water jug. "Where's it from?"

I followed Ellen back along the trailer. "It was a spare one in the box." The cardboard box had been stored in the box of one of the trucks and was drenched from the rain. "Shit. Okay, listen up everyone. We've got a bear spray leak. Nobody touch their faces. Go to camp, change your clothes, wash your hands and face, then come back."

I glanced around the piles of supplies along the trailer. I scooped up a couple boxes of latex gloves, a small carton of masks, and a couple unopened boxes of safety glasses.

I turned to Ellen, "We need warm soapy water. Can you go to the kitchen and ask for a couple buckets?"

Ellen was off and running. The crew slowly returned and Jacquie was bringing some more gloves and glasses she'd stashed in her room.

It took the rest of the day and couple more minor incidents of bear spray contamination before we got the supplies clean, sorted and organized.

The crew would be returning to camp in a week to start digging on the sites under Scott's permit. Mine were finished. While Morris was doing his best to keep me from going insane, I was now under no delusions that I could wriggle out of my permit duties. Michelle had effectively stapled eight sites to my butt and now six of those sites needed further excavation. It was my responsibility to make sure those sites were excavated properly.

I would be coming back before the field season was out. The length of time, however, was something I was hoping to negotiate. I was hoping that the crew and the way I'd trained them over the past two months would save me a lot of hassle.

Chapter Eight

Here Be Dragons

Oyen? Where the hell was Oyen, anyway?

"Oh shit."

It was all I could say when I'd looked at the wall map in the office and discovered I was being sent to the ends of the earth. That was what the Saskatchewan border was to forest-dwelling me. Little did I know that dragons still existed.

"Geez, Elise," Cam said, sipping his coffee from behind me. "Sucks to be you."

I pulled my eyes from the wall map and took what I thought may be my last look at Cam, the office, and civilization, "Yeah, it does. Think nice thoughts of me when I'm gone."

Cam smiled that side smirk of his, making his freckles condense on the one side of his face, "Only if you do the same for me. I'm helping Frank with the arky portion." He nodded at Frank's messy and vacant desk. Frank had been gone since early June.

It had taken me a week of 10-12 hours days of solid writing, but I managed to finish the interim report on the excavation of my eight sites. Then I'd taken a couple days off while it went through Michelle's audit process. It had been submitted to the Historic Branch this morning. I still hadn't finished up the report from the fieldwork Cam and I did in May or Erinson Power's Cold Lake report. It was mid-July. And now I was being sent to Oyen. This was how it went: fieldwork in the summer, reports in the winter.

"Yeah, well at least you guys aren't camping," I said as I regained my seat at my desk.

Cam leaned against the wall. "What do you mean? *Camping* camping?"

I sighed again. "Yup. Tent and all."

"Cool," Cam beamed. "Just like in the old days." I growled.

"You camp?" Cam continued to sip his coffee. He was one of those irritating outdoorsey types. Probably used a Coleman stove on his balcony every weekend just to keep his skills fresh.

"Nope." I tapped at various keys on my keyboard hoping the letters were forming into words that would help the Cold Lake report make sense.

Out of the corner of my eye, I could see Cam's eyebrow crease. "Then why'd you sign up for this gig?"

I looked at the goobledy-gook I'd just written and tried to figure out what the hell I was trying to write. "Believe it or not, I didn't have a choice on this one."

"Is HSAC supplying tents?"

"Nope. I'm camping because I can't stand the thought of being coped up in an RV with four of my colleagues for two weeks. The tent was my idea."

"Are you sure that isn't the other way around, Elise."

"Oh, yuk, yuk, yuk." And slammed the backspace button with verve until the line was clear again.

"RVs, huh?"

"Yup."

Cam straightened and gulped the last of his coffee. "I got a great four-man tent you can use."

"That would be really great, Cam." I didn't know if I was relieved or not. I was kind of planning on buying a $200 tent and billing it back to the company. But, maybe that would be pushing things.

"I can bring it in tomorrow. If you need any camping equipment, let me know. I've got lots."

"Thanks, Cam." Thankfully we had someone else cooking for us. I couldn't remember how to work a Coleman stove.

Cam left and I tried for the rest of the day to write a report and not think of my life coming to a tortured halt at the ends of the earth.

I decided I didn't like Oyen. Frankly, there wasn't much to like. It was two Chinese restaurants, a Super 8, and a gas station. The gas station had the best food.

Safety training was in the pipeline construction camp next to the Super 8. You know you've got a big pipeline operation going on when the construction camp is larger than the town.

Our first day was going to be safety training with the First Nations participants. I'd forgotten I worked on this very same pipeline the year before in Manitoba. They were actually constructing out there; the construction wasn't due to start in Alberta until next year. When I arrived at the construction site in Manitoba, I was surprised to find that most of the guys were from Alberta. We struck up easy conversation while the pipeline was trenched through an archaeological site.

My previous experience on the project meant I didn't have to do the training again. This is why I'd been volunteered for this gig. Once our training was over, I couldn't help but ask the safety coordinator, "Hey, I worked in Manitoba last year. Are any of the guys from there here?"

"Oh yeah," the safety coordinator said. She was bleach-blonde with too much make-up and long, fake nails. "They're over on mile 52. You guys are going to be working mile 32 and down."

I was disappointed. No small talk with the Alberta riggers. That would have been the closest I'd get to decent, from-the-hip conversation. I was now stuck with the cultural facilitators. No archaeologists out here.

Other than my safety training, I was still having problems figuring out why I pulled "cultural facilitator" duty. "You said you wanted to try new things," Morris said when I asked him.

"But not in Saskatchewan!" It was a poor rebuttal, I admit. Oyen wasn't quite in Saskatchewan.

I felt I was getting pretty good at the archaeology game over the past few years -- reading survey plans instead of academic journal articles, looking at the landscapes instead of crime scenes, looking for stone artifacts instead of bone. I'd never worked on a Traditional Land Use study. From what I'd heard, it was just following around First Nation's participants and recording whatever they said was important. Okay,

I could do that. Frankly, I thought it would be nice change from archaeology. Sometimes, all those stone artifacts could be a bit much.

I stepped out of the safety trailer and was face to face with Joanna, the lead cultural facilitator, in all her blonde, push-up bra glory. "Anything I should know about?"

"Um, no. Just asking about some of the guys I met last year, that's all."

Joanna jammed a pencil into her notebook. "We're here to work, Elise, not socialize." She walked off to round up the rest of our teammates.

I frowned and shook my head.

Morris had sent me on this project with the explicit direction, "Be good."

"I can do that," I countered.

"Prove it," he said.

That night we slept in the Super 8. It would be the last good night's sleep I would have for two weeks.

It was July 20th. The field season was in full swing, but here I was, on the Plains instead of the forest.

So there's the Saskatchewan border, I thought as sweat began to trickle down my back. Christ, could my job put me in a place more desolate? Why on earth would there be artifacts out here?

It's all hills, grass, gophers and barbed wire. It all looked the same.

I was in the middle of bald-ass nowhere.

Heat waves flickered off the baked hills while clouds begin to accumulate in the overly ripe sky. It was only 10am. Would my sunblock last until lunch? To make matters worse, Hadden Oil had some seriously strict safety policies. We had to wear hardhats, safety glasses and vests and steel-toed boots while on the project. Yup. Gets pretty damn dangerous on the prairies.

I put the finishing touches on my sketch map, put the UTM coordinate at the top of the page with the participants' names and the date. Medicine. That was all I could call the plants that they told me to record. They wouldn't tell me what it was or what it was for. Just record it. The previous pipeline was about 50 metres to the east; these medicine plants would be impacted by the new pipeline that would parallel the old. The participants wanted to come back in the fall and harvest these plants before the new pipeline was constructed.

I recorded it all and slipped my notebook into the back pocket of my survey vest.

I scratched under my hardhat and took stock of where the First Nations participants were. They hadn't moved from the clump of plants. They were huddled together and talking amongst themselves in Cree. Maggie, the hyper forestry drop-out who had been stolen from my Fort Mac excavation, was now my co-worker. She looked on from the sidelines. It was obvious we were the outsiders here.

I decided I had time to apply another layer of chemical refuge on the skin not protected by what would soon be sweat-drenched clothing.

I slipped off my vest and retrieved the bottle of 50 SPF from the back pocket. I had just pulled up the flap of the pocket when my eyes drifted to something white to my right.

It was a bone.

My heart skipped a beat. The sunblock was completely forgotten as I scrambled to get it into my hands. I knelt over it, running my fingers over its porous structure. It was weathered – dark on the underside, bleached and feathered on the top. I spun it, looking at the features. That it wasn't human didn't matter. It was bone, bison or cow, sitting on the Plains, being munched on by scavengers, waiting for me to find it.

A shadow fell over the bone. "Whatcha got?" It was Leon, a First Nation participant from Hobbema. Leon was what he liked to call an FBI, a "full-blooded Indian." He wore a ball cap with his long hair in twin braids. I felt privileged that he'd told me a couple stories of attending the reserve schools. Pretty harsh stuff. There were some days I really hated being white.

I held up the left proximal tibia to him. "It's a bone." I couldn't help but beam. I must have looked like an idiot, fondling a bone and smiling. Leon eyed me before taking the bone in his leathery hands and rolling it around.

"Yes. It is a bone."

"It's a proximal left tibia. Cow or bison." Leon continued to stare at me. "Ah, that's the part of the leg just below the knee." I illustrated with my own proximal left tibia. "And you can tell it's a left because the articulation is bigger on the left side, see?" I was standing now, pointing at the smoothed dipped surface.

Henry was beside Leon now, as well as Max and Kevin. Leon stared at me for one last moment, perhaps contemplating the heat of the sun on my very white skin.

At last he, too, smiled. "Elise found a bone," he said and passed it around. "This here is a bison bone, from this part of the leg." Leon motioned to his left shin.

I couldn't have loved him more at that moment.

"Elise!" I turned, startled out of my reverie. Joanna was marching up the hillside toward us. She was sweating profusely; her blush and lipstick looked heavy on her glistening face. "Why don't you have your vest and hard hat on?"

"I found a bone."

"Is it archaeological?"

"Probably not..." I attempted.

"Do the participants think it's important?"

"I don't think so."

"Then what are you doing?" It was then that I could have sworn I saw steam coming from Joanna's ears. If it hadn't been for the shock of her reaction, I would have laughed. Hard.

"Excuse me?"

"You are supposed to be doing a job, Elise." It was then that I noticed all the participants had vanished. Leon was nearly up the next hill. How did they do that?

"I was. I am."

"Then get your vest and hat on and catch up to the participants."

I threw on my vest and hat and stumbled down the hill. Best behavior, I thought to myself. By the time I caught up to the participants, the sky was no longer red and I wasn't gritting my teeth.

Morris was no doubt counting the days until I burst. I wondered if there was a betting pool going on back at the office regarding how long

I would last. Or maybe Morris was merely still playing out his social experiment with me.

By lunchtime, I had come to no new conclusions.

By Day Three, I was exhausted. Heat-exhausted, that is.

I was collapsing into my sleeping bag by 7pm, waking twice to trudge down to the outhouse, and then up at 6am. For three mornings in a row, I was thirsty when I awoke.

When I fell asleep at lunch, I wasn't surprised. Actually it was kind of nice. However, I was slightly embarrassed when I awoke and had to wipe drool off my chin.

That night, I was cornered in the RV when I stopped in to recharge my cell phone. Joanna had just brushed her hair and reapplied a fresh coat of "Passion Plum" lipgloss. "I know you're new at this, Elise, but you're being extremely unprofessional."

"Excuse me?" I was in shock again. I was too tired to be angry. Hell, I was so tired that even with a road map I wouldn't have been able find my anger.

Joanna continued, flipping her flaxen hair to the side. "You should be setting an example for Oliver and Maggie. You are representing HSAC here."

I blinked and tried to regain some sense. I didn't work. "Joanna, I have heat exhaustion. I warned you all about this before we got out here. I do my best to avoid it, but it happens. What do you expect me to do? I'm human. And a red head." Okay, maybe I did have some anger hiding out in my eyelids.

"You need to drink more water."

At that moment, the RV shook violently as someone came up the steps. "Water doesn't do a damn thing." Oliver opened the door and walked in without a glance in our direction and headed to the bathroom. I took that opportunity. "I'm just a grunt on this project. I knew that when I signed up. You want your team to follow an example, then you set one." I flipped my braid back over my shoulder and left the RV, cell phone in hand.

I phoned Morris. After the automated voice stopped, I said, "Morris, it's Elise. This isn't working. There seems to be some sort of personality conflict between Joanna and myself. I need to get out of here." I wondered who just won the office pool.

Unprofessional, huh?

Armed with four hours of sleep and my last chocolate bar, I approach Maggie. "Hey Maggie, you want to help me do a check of the trucks?"

Maggie stared at me. I had baffled her. That was a first. During her time with me up in Fort Mac, she would whither under my glare. Maybe I was confusing her. "Um, okay." She grabbed her safety clipboard and followed me to the first truck.

Maggie was a good sort. Always trying to please everyone. I felt bad whenever I'd chewed her out at the excavation. She was a good digger when she wanted to be, just really hyper and talkative. Those large brown eyes looked at me now, pleading not to ream her out.

We popped the hood and I climbed up on the radiator to reach the oil dipstick. "Oh, that's where that is," Maggie said.

Wow, I thought. These trucks were running all day and they hadn't been checked for oil all summer. Then I thought 'Wow' again as I realized Maggie was yet another city folk person out in the wilderness.

I taught 'Fluids Check 101' to Maggie while we surveyed all the trucks. Two trucks were low on oil, three needed brake fluid, and one of the tires was getting bald. I told Maggie to make a note of it and to look into getting it all rectified.

My mistake was not explicitly stating that she go directly to Joanna to ask permission to think or act on her own. This mistake came back to bite me in the ass at the end of the day.

"Elise, can I talk to you?" Joanna said as she walked by my truck.

Oh, what now? Instead of saying it, I nodded and followed Joanna around the back of the truck. I should have just given up and blown up at her right then and there. Hell, Morris had already won whatever bet he'd had with himself or the office. What did I have to lose? But I promised him. So I followed Joanna.

Oliver was filling the trucks up with gas and the First Nations participants were raiding the gas station of all their pizzas and hot dogs. I was envious. "Who's in charge of this project?"

I frowned. It was becoming a permanent expression on my face. "You, of course."

"Then why did you authorize Maggie to go and buy oil and a new tire?"

"I didn't."

"She said you told her to go buy oil and a new tire."

I rolled my eyes – it was an involuntary reaction. "We did a safety check this morning – the one that's supposed to be done *every* morning," I said, trying to pull some of the venom out of my voice, "The trucks are in need of maintenance. Are you faulting me for discovering that you haven't been doing your safety checks or for Maggie acting on her own?"

"I am the supervisor for this project. Don't forget it." She walked off and I was left swearing at the tailgate of the truck.

That night, Morris called me from home. "What's going on, Elise?"

"Are you betting on me to lose my temper and throttling her? Is this another one of your social experiments?"

"Elise." Morris' voice was calm. "What's been happening?"

"How the fuck should I know? Joanna's got something big up her ass and she's taking out some serious shit on me." At that moment, I didn't care how lucky I was that I could talk to my supervisor like that.

"Okay. Explain to me what's been going on." I did my best to recap the major events in my heat-exhausted and stress-laden life in the past few days.

I could hear Morris pulling at what hair was left around his ears. "Yeah, sounds like a personality conflict. There's not much you can do."

"Can you get me out of here?"

"Not really. Can you finish the shift?" My mind reeled at the thought of spending another week under Joanna's unbalanced, tyrannical rule. "Okay. Look, Elise. Stay out of her way and don't be alone with her. We need this project. We can't afford to upset anyone."

"Are you sure there isn't an office pool going on me?"

Morris managed to chuckle. "I'm sure. But if there was, I'd put money on you." I had to hand it to the man. He knew what to say to get me to do things.

However, I was not looking forward to stuffing my pride. Even if Morris didn't have money riding on me.

On Day Eight and I swore it got hotter. But, unfortunately, I was getting used to it. I was no longer collapsing into my sleeping bag after supper. In fact, I was barely sleeping.

I hate camping. Too much noise. Goddamn birds chirping at 4am. Coyotes howling in the night. Wind in the bloody trees. Ugh. It was just too much.

Then there were the bladder breaks at midnight and 3am. I'd spent too much time in the field. This was what women do in the field when they work with men; they hold it. I was only 32 years old and my bladder was already smaller than an anorexic pea. Usually it wasn't a problem. Usually I was the permit holder, the one in charge; I took pee breaks in towns whenever I wanted. I've been known to drive a couple miles just to use a decent restroom. But now I wasn't in charge. I was working in the middle of the bald-ass prairie with a bunch of strange old men and nowhere to pee. Not to mention that if I took five minutes away from my participant-watching duties, Joanna would hunt me down and tear another strip off my raw and sunburned neck. So, there I was, every cold night, twice a night, unzipping my tent to walk down the dark roads of the campground to the outhouse and empty out the 4 litres of Gatorade that I'd drunk the day before. What used to be a two-minute flutter in a good night's sleep in a hotel room, was now ten-minute break that seriously shook up my REM cycle.

I had sunblock all over my face when Maggie came up to me. "Do you have a skirt?" she asked.

I snorted, then when she didn't laugh, I finished rubbing in my sunblock. "Why on earth would I bring a skirt on a job? I haven't own a skirt since my mother tried to make me into a girly-girl in grade three."

"They want to have a pipe ceremony," Maggie jerked her head to the group of participants in palaver around a bush. "They say there's strong medicine here."

I grumbled. Morris' words in my head – be good. Why didn't I go to the University of Toronto to study Old World Archaeology? I could have been in Turkey right now looking at bones and coins instead of at the ends of the earth looking for rocks and medicinal plants. Hell, I'd even take pottery at this point. Maybe a nice burial urn...."Do I have to be present?"

"It would be disrespectful to not attend."

I grumbled again. Grumbling had become a part of my daily vocabulary. And since there wasn't a Tim Horton's within fifty miles, there was nothing to bring my grumbling down to a mumbling level. "And I suppose that I need to wear a skirt to attend."

Maggie nodded. I grumbled again, notes of feministic reforms and patriarchal bullshit flitting out from between my lips. "Can I symbolically wear a skirt?"

"What do you mean?"

"I mean does it actually have to be a skirt, or can I wear something that represents a skirt and, therefore, my femininity?"

Maggie smiled then, perhaps seeing an out for herself and other female members of our troupe. "I'll go ask."

A moment later she returned, her heavy steel-toed boots making the dry grass crackle. "A substitute would be acceptable."

I nodded and gulped my Gatorade.

After lunch, we went back to camp to perform the pipe ceremony. I wrapped a couple long-sleeved shirts around my waist and was walking to the picnic tables and the assembled First Nation's participants, when Joanna and her bouncing boobs, cut me off. "Look, Elise, I know you don't want to be here, but can you at least try to do your job."

I was reminded of those black and white movies where the femme fatale walks in and brings nothing but trouble. Joanna was a woman with a martyr complex and stress steaming from her ears. She also wore enough make-up to be in one of those old movies. Too bad she didn't have the industrial-strength underwear to go along with it.

I stopped and nearly choked on the Gatorade that was midway down my throat. "Excuse me?"

"Fine. Look. You're going into Wainwright to pick up some supplies."

I managed to shake off the shock, "Is this all because nobody told me to bring a skirt?"

"It's because of your attitude, Elise. It sucks."

Again, I was stunned. Where the hell was all this coming from? I'd been on my best behaviour since coming out to this god-forsaken land, better since talking to Morris, and, for me, three days without so much as a sarcastic comment was something that would make my mother kneel down in church.

"Sorry, Joanna. I'm only doing the best I can do with what I was given. If I'm not doing my job maybe you should have explained my duties better." Three days without sarcasm was a stretch.

"Your duties were explained very well. You're just choosing not to follow them. I'm sick of trying to explain your actions to the participants. Here's the list." She thrust a torn piece of paper at me.

Explaining my actions? What actions? All I'd done that day was drive, walk, make notes, walk, and drive some more. "Aren't the participants going to wonder why the whole team isn't participating in the pipe ceremony?"

"We need supplies. You are going to Wainwright." Wow. Nothing like an inferiority complex to top off the list of neuroses, I thought.

I nodded and stripped the shirts dangling from my waist. I wasn't team leader on this project, I reminded myself, and I wasn't the one who had to contend with the participants. But, for once, I also hadn't done a single thing to deserve Joanna's hot-headed criticism. I jumped in one of the trucks, and cranked up the AC for hour-long drive to Wainwright. I plugged in my iPod, chose some Irish music and cranked it up. I needed to compensate for the four hours of pow-wow music everyday.

During the drive, I started to think maybe I should do something to get Joanna going, to deserve my punishment. If only to keep my own sanity. However, Morris' words held me back. God, that man was good at his job. And sometimes I hated him for it.

It had taken me only an hour or so to find everything on the list. Instead of heading back to camp, I called into the office to find out where the arky crew with Cam and Frank was working. They were doing an excavation not far from Wainwright, on the same project, only farther up the pipeline. I thought Frank was quite lucky. He was picked to do the excavation and was racking in the artifacts. Ah, to stay in one place for a period of time and work with the same group of people. How nice. Suddenly, my excavation time in Fort Mac didn't seem so bad.

I picked my way through the soft patches on the truck trail and finally made it to the site. Frank, one of my fellow attic-rats, was there waiting for me in his survey vest, checked shirt, and torn jeans.

"Hey, how's it going?" He held out his hand for me.

I looked at his outstretched hand, "What's this? We've only be been working in the attic for what, three years."

Frank turned sheepish and dropped his hand, "Sorry, Elise. Too many school groups and executives coming around for tours lately."

"Hey, that's cool."

"Not when they keep falling into the excavation units." Frank motioned me toward the footpath and began explaining the layout of the site. "This is where the bison pound was. Found a lot of bone here. Took a while to dig an excavation unit." I started to salivate. Bone. Even if it was only bison bone.

He motioned to the shallow gully we were passing through. "On top is where we are currently digging. It's a campsite with lots of artifacts and pottery."

"Pottery? You found pottery in Alberta?"

"Yeah. Here I'll show you." He dug some plastic bags with index cards from inside of his survey vest and handed them to me. I didn't dare open the bags because inside was some of the crudest and smallest pieces of pottery I'd ever seen. I was afraid that just handling the bags would make the pottery crumble.

"That is totally cool." I handed them back and looked around before we ascended to the campsite portion of the site. He was digging just west of an area where there were pipeline scars and signs for no less than four pipelines. "There's an awful lot of development around here."

"Tell me about it. We had to go through a lot of red tape to dig below 30 centimetres out here."

"Did you tell them you were using trowels?"

"Didn't matter. They still wanted the paperwork. And I had to personally explain what we were doing to five engineers and a couple project managers in a conference call one day. They just didn't seem to get that to do an archaeological excavation we had to dig."

Atop the campsite site, the excavation was in full swing. Power screens and backdirt piles dotted the periphery while people stood in or around their units. It was a nice spot all in all. An open aspen stand overlooking the shallow gully to the west and the river floodplain to the east. "Hey, Elise." I heard my name yelled and I turned. Cam was striding up the path in all his plaid and freckled glory.

"So, what are you finding?" I walked off with Cam as Frank attended to a question from one of the excavation units.

"Oh, you know. The usual out here. We got some really nice projectile points. Lots of 'em. Did Frank tell you about the pottery?"

I nodded. "Yeah, that's pretty cool. I didn't even know what I was looking for until he showed me. We haven't found any firepits yet. Frank is pretty disappointed."

"It's only a matter of time." Frank returned so I followed him out. I noticed a lot of familiar faces digging in the excavation units. I was glad that there was work for at least some students. "How many units have you dug?"

"We're up to 36 square meters now. I want another 40." I was impressed. Frank had been here for two months and in that time had dug less than I had in five weeks in Fort Mac.

"Do you think you'll get it?"

"If we find a firepit, I'll get it. Otherwise, I'll have to beg and plead."

"But what about the pottery?"

"Apparently the Historic Branch doesn't think too much of the pottery. They want a firepit." I grumbled.

We returned to the power screens and I thanked Frank for the tour before heading back to the truck.

On the way back to camp, I did a re-evaluation of the situation. It dawned on me that I wasn't answering to the client, for once, or the government. This time I was answering to the First Nations' participants. And everything was fine between me and the participants. I figured that out about halfway into my drive back to camp. I consequently sorted out my perspective and then felt much better. I wasn't stuffing my work ethic for Joanna any more. I was drawing the line at that.

I got back to camp about six, just in time for supper.

Joanna stormed up to me. "Where were you?"

I stopped. Between the emotional trauma that morning and my newly sorted perspective, my shock didn't last long. "I was in Wainwright. Picking up supplies. Remember?"

"What took you so long?"

"It was a long list."

She must have seen that my line had been drawn. Frankly, I didn't think I could draw a line without swearing.

Joanna narrowed her eyes. "Bring the supplies to the RV after supper. And the receipts." I could have sworn I saw steam erupting from her ears again as she walked away.

I nearly laughed.

I sat down next to Leon. "Elise," he said before he'd finished chewing. "You were missed at the ceremony."

"Yeah, sorry about that. I had some errands to run in Wainwright. I apologize. I wanted to be there."

"We said a special prayer for you at the ceremony. Hope you had a safe trip." Sometimes I didn't know what to make of these guys. Just when you are sure that they're just a bunch of old farts walking around the Plains telling dirty jokes and chewing their tobacco, they pull out some sentimental crap and blow you away because they really mean it. Leon's comment had hit the open gap that Joanna's turmoil had caused and I didn't know whether to laugh or cry.

I nodded and stuffed some moose sausage in my mouth.

I put the plastic bags full of supplies on the RV floor. "Can I have the receipts, please?" Joanna held out her hand, lacquered nails waving at me. Jenny sat, glasses pushed up her nose, in her pyjamas, and stared at her laptop. Maggie sat at another laptop but her eyes flickered between me and Joanna and her fingers fidgeted with a lock of hair. Oliver sat at his laptop oblivious, head bobbing along to the music in his headphones. Cords and paperwork were strewn over every available piece of counter and floor space. And management wondered why I didn't want to room in the RV.

"Why?" I knew the real reason she wanted them. She wanted to see if I'd bought anything illicit which I would then submit for reimbursement under the project name. God forbid I would buy a Tim Horton's double-double while working on her precious project.

She sighed dramatically, "So they can be submitted."

"Thanks," I said, "I'll do it myself."

"Don't you want your money back?"

"Like I said, I'll do it myself when I get back to the office."

Joanna rose then. "Elise, can I talk to you a minute?"

Oh great. Here we go. "Actually, I got some office stuff to do."

"This won't talk long." I could see Joanna's temperature begin to rise.

"Then we can talk here. What did you want?"

She fidgeted, then bit the bullet. I didn't know if my respect for her rose because she actually had the guts (or stupidity) to say it in front of the others, or if my respect dropped off the scale because of what she said. "Did you say something to the participants this morning?"

"I talk to them everyday. I have to. It's part of my job."

Joanna rolled her eyes. "That's not what I mean. They seem to be under the impression that this is your project."

I laughed then. I couldn't help it. "I don't know where they got that idea."

"Well, I just want to make sure that you understand that this is my project, not yours. Don't undermine me."

No, Joanna, you're doing a good enough job at that already, I nearly said. I really wanted to say it. Instead, I merely said, "Right-O, Capitain." I did a mock salute, spun on my heel, and exited the RV. Morris would have been proud. Maybe.

Would that be enough to send her over the top? Who knew? I was just getting sick of putting up with a 'leader' with an inferiority complex.

Just when I thought I couldn't sleep less, it started to get cold. It was freezing outside. Typical desert-type climate; scorching during the day and freezing at night. The tent and sleeping bag weren't enough to keep the cold from waking me at 2am and keeping me awake. Just when I thought my mood couldn't be fouler, the lack of sleep was beating me down to primal levels. I was getting ready to a do some sort of chimpanzee dance on someone's head and then slap them in face with my sweat-drenched Tilley hat.

Tension was thick the next day. Cut-it-with-a-knife-thick. I could sense the other team members looking at me and Joanna and wondering who would blow first. How long would the proverbial knife last before getting dull? Would I soon need a blowtorch? The temptation to taunt fate and Joanna was growing stronger and I was in the right mood to act that day. Our relationship was already beyond being salvageable. So, I thought, why not regain some dignity in the process?

After breakfast, the drizzle started. As we drove toward the pipeline, it turned into a downpour. We stopped for gas. Joanna came up to the window of my truck. "We're not going out today. It's flooding where we'd be working."

Usually I liked rain. I loved Irish rain. But working in rain was just nasty. I've done survey in it and remembered trying to excavate in Fort Mac in the rain.

We went back to camp and dropped off the participants. They scurried off to their RVs looking forward to their satellites TVs. Must be nice.

"Elise, you and Oliver will be servicing the equipment. Oliver is in charge." Nothing like being blunt about it.

"Aye, aye, Capitain."

It turned out to be an enjoyable day. The skies cleared and the sun reappeared. Oliver was good to work with. He was a nose-to-the-grindstone kinda guy with ethics. Didn't find many of those nowadays.

After checking the fluids on each truck, checking to make sure we had enough water and bags for medicinal plants for the participants, we had eaten up about four hours.

"Thanks for helping me out, Elise. Usually this would take me all day to do."

"You would do all this by yourself?" Now Joanna was just irking me.

He nodded, his mop of dark hair bobbing down over his eyes. "It's great that you know so much about trucks too. That really helps. Your dad a mechanic or something?"

"No. I've just had to work my way out of some tight spots working up north. But I did learn some things from my dad."

"Hey, we should watch a movie tonight. I'll hook up my laptop. We never get a chance to talk and have some fun."

I snickered at that. "Are you sure Joanna would allow that?"

He didn't shutter or hesitate. What surprised me was that he took my comment in stride. "We'll watch it after supper. I think we still have some whiskey in the cupboard too. That'll be good."

We wiped the oil and grease off our hands and walked back to the RV.

I managed to stay out of Joanna's way for the rest of the day, citing other project obligations. I took my laptop to my tent and pittered away the afternoon trying to write reports.

Oliver had apparently spread the word before supper. Movie night. The air in the RV had changed considerably. Maggie was already into the whiskey when I made my appearance. "Hurry up and shower, Elise. I want to watch the movie."

I glanced the far end of the RV. Joanna was nowhere in sight.

I took my shower and when I re-entered, Jenny held out a tin cup with whiskey. "To yet another shift on the pipeline!" We knocked our cups together. Maggie was dancing to some music blaring over the RVs speakers.

"Start up the movie, Ollie. Let's get this party started!"

It was the best time I'd had on the project. It didn't take much whiskey to get my head spinning. Thankfully, I didn't have to go anywhere and I was looking forward to sleeping well that night.

Maggie's hearing apparently became impaired while drinking. Watching the movie was difficult. "What did he say? Why's he doing that?"

"Maggie," Oliver said, "He just said he needs to go protect her. Listen to the movie for Pete's Sake."

"I *am* listening." She was beginning to slur. I was beginning to like Maggie. "Hey, did you guys hear what happened to Bill at the Pow-Wow last night?"

Suddenly Maggie had Jenny's complete attention. "Bill went to a Pow-Wow last night? No wonder he looked so tired today. Where was it?"

I was having a hard enough time following the movie plot. Now I was completely lost. And drunk.

"North Battleford. He stubbed his toe while he was dancing. It turned black and blue. He showed me. I was really gross."

It took until about halfway through the movie before Joanna showed up, took a seat, and settled in like it was the most natural thing in the world. In all honesty, I was glad she'd caved in. While I was all for pushing for a goal, sometimes you just had to go with the flow.

How long could someone be a bitch? I don't know, but it seemed Joanna was going for gold.

The next day, it was clear and sunny. I'd slept a sound, whiskey-induced sleep and had a supply of candy in my survey vest. Things were looking okay.

Then Joanna pulled me aside. "I know you haven't wanted to be here. You won't be coming back next shift. I just talked to management."

Oh boy, was she lucky I was in a good mood.

"Look, Joanna. It's no secret that I prefer bones to rocks and dead people to living, but I chose to be out here. You're the one with her knickers in a knot. Besides, you're not kicking me off this project. I spoke to management on Day Two. You've done nothing but treat me like crap. Since you want this project so much, you can have it all to yourself. I choose not to come back."

Joanna was the one to look stunned this time. I'd taken away her final glory -- dumping me. And I finally felt like I'd done something right on this project.

She left me alone then. Hell, if I'd known she'd have done that, I would have told her off on Day Two. Suddenly she was asking for my opinion on maps and access into areas. It was a real shocker. However, it didn't gain her any respect from me. She'd already blown it in my books.

The next few days were practically blissful. Joanna treated me as if I was an equal. And, since I now had nearly two weeks under my belt, I almost felt I knew what I was doing.

But, I was still counting down the days. I was shell-shocked and sure that Joanna was going to blow again. I couldn't take any more of her borderline-personality-flipping. The field season was beginning to gang up on me and it was only July. Usually it took until September before I felt the symptoms. It was going to take another trip to Ireland for me to recover. Unfortunately, I couldn't look forward to vacation time until after Christmas.

Around two o'clock, we discovered a flat tire on one of the trucks. It was the same bald one Maggie and I had identified a couple weeks ago. There was no spare. We weren't going anywhere. The problem was getting the truck out of the bald-ass middle of nowhere and into a town to fix it. The strategy had been to drive to the beginning of the assessment area, park two trucks, then drive another around to the end of the assessment area. The First Nations participants would walk the assessment area, from the parked two trucks to the one, then we'd ferry them back to the beginning. The other two trucks were four miles away.

The wind was coming up in a way that made my Alberta skin crawl. "Elise, can you and Oliver go get the other trucks? We'll get the tire off this truck in the meantime."

Oliver and I started to hike. I looked up at the sky and I nudged Oliver, "Look."

We looked at the north together. The clouds coming in weren't just black; they were green and spooky. "Doesn't look good."

I shook my head. The wind was becoming fierce. This year's tillage and topsoil was sandblasting my face. Suddenly the requisite safety glasses weren't so cumbersome.

"How much further?"

Oliver pulled out his GPS. "We're almost there. Over the next hill."

"I'll race you," I said and started off, the fear of what those clouds were bringing in quickened my pace.

By the time we made it back to the trucks, I was drenched and dirty. The dust stuck to my sweaty sunblock-coated skin. I looked in the rearview mirror and wish I hadn't. The safety glasses and hardhat had only made the sandblasting more comical.

We drove out of the field and made for the road, me following Oliver, the navigator. Oliver had all the maps and was in charge of getting us to and from the pipeline everyday. He was the only one who knew where we were and where we were going. Without Oliver, we'd all be seriously lost. Without Oliver, I think I would have been clinically insane by now.

Five minutes later, we were on the highway. I thought we were home free. I was getting anxious about those clouds. The wind was still rising. Eddies were traveling across the fields and foreshadowing what was to come.

Then the highway traffic came to a sudden stand still. There were cars, truck, tractors, and semis as far as I could see down the highway. Oliver got out of his truck and walked up the shoulder to see what was going on. I pulled out my cell phone and took another look at those clouds. The wind was now howling. The call went to voicemail. They can't hear the phone, I thought.

"Joanna, it's Elise. We are at the highway but I think there's been an accident. The traffic's backed up. We're going to be a while."

I phoned Maggie. She picked up. "I can't hear you," she yelled back.

"It's Elise. We're going to be late. Traffic accident."

"It's getting......dy. Lots o....st. Hurry."

Shit. I had people stranded and an incoming tornado. I started scanning the shoulder for a way around the traffic. There were cultivated fields all around us. Barbed wire fence went on for miles.

My phone rang. "Hello. Um, this is Gavin Cleary. We met at Trinity College in Dublin a few months ago."

Fuck.

"Hi, Gavin." Wind howled around the truck and found me out. I tried to curve my body around my three-inch phone. "It's good to hear from you. Unfortunately, this isn't a good time."

"Why.....back...from.....while......" Then my phone went dead.

"NO!" I screamed into the wind. I was in motion to throw my phone onto the yellow centerline of the highway when Oliver appeared.

"Yeah, it's an accident. Semi's in the ditch. We're just gonna have to wait."

Double shit. "Is there another way around?"

Oliver shook his head and dove back to his truck. He returned with a folded map; it must have been several feet across when unfolded because, when folded, it was a couple inches thick. It was an air photo composite with the pipeline plan overlaid; phone numbers and coordinates were scribbled all over it. "This is where we'd parked this morning and this is where Joanna and the gang are." I noted the highlighted road we taken in this morning and taken out just now. We'd already walked about five miles that day. "This is where we're heading to pick them up." Oliver's finger pointed to a well site near Joanna's present location. The access road to the well site was just up ahead. "We can't make the participants walk back the way we came. We have to go in and pick them up."

Shit. I took another look at the sky. A tumbleweed bounced across the field.

"Traffic's starting to move."

Relief swept over me. We passed the semi. No accident damage. Looked like it was blown off the road.

Shit, I thought again.

I peeled off the highway following Oliver onto the gravel road. By the time we saw our group, the sun was behind the clouds and things were getting dark really fast.

I can honestly say I've never seen a tire changed as quickly. Leave it to an impending tornado to speed things up. We loaded the participants and all our gear from the other truck and peeled out of there. "Holy cow, Elise. You could use a bath," Leon snickered as we got back to the highway.

"You have no idea, Leon. Bubbles and all."

We stopped for gas at our usual station in Oyen. Joanna walked over to Oliver and I. "The campground just called. They just rescued your tent. Trees are falling down everywhere. I think we should stay here and see if we can wait it out."

For once, I had to agree with Joanna.

The restaurant attached to the gas station seemed like civilized heaven after spending a week in a tent. They had a TV too. I couldn't keep my eyes off it. There was a newsflash ribbon streaming across the bottom of the screen. Tornado touched down in Provost. Provost was 15 minutes away from us. Yup, Joanna had made a good call. Maybe it was a good thing the tire had blown. It was definitely a good thing that I was going home the next day.

Chapter Nine

Burned

Cows don't like orange snow fencing. However, they do like big, white pick-up trucks.

"Hey Ida," I called across the excavation site. "You might want to get some pictures of this, for insurance purposes. Just so they know that we didn't do it." I remembered my own fight with the rental company over covering the shot-out windshield of my truck a couple months back.

We'd been informed that there'd be a bull in the mix. We, however, hadn't been told of the bull's apparent predilections.

The truck continued to rock and gyrate as the bull rubbed himself on it. I heard the side view mirror snap back into place. Ida moved around to a strategic position and snapped a picture on her phone. "There's bull snot all over the side of the truck," she said. "But he seems docile enough."

The cows, and the bull, moved on as the heat rolled in. The day before it had risen to 30 degrees; it would easily reach that today. At one-thirty, waves of heat were rolling off the grazed land next to our site. I was afraid I would start dancing around the site singing show tunes. Again. Amazing how the heat can affect some people.

I smiled when I thought of my crew in Fort Mac. They were a good bunch, if talkative.

Edmonton was a far cry from Fort McMurray, and thankfully a jump and a half away from the bald-ass prairie of Oyen. The accommodation was better too. The first night out, my face was sore from grinning. Nothing like two TVs and a hotel suite to cure a person of any past woes.

But that was two days ago.

Now it was just hot. I was Canadian born and bred, and proudly so. I found winter much easier to take. I discovered a long time ago that pretty much anything above 22 degrees Celsius and I was a continuous mess of sweat. I still didn't think I was recovered from Oyen. Waking up in the morning with sweat-soaked sheets and no one beside me wasn't really the best way to start the day.

Speaking of waking up with no one beside me, I had finally managed to call Dr. Gavin Cleary when I was last in Calgary. I left a message with his secretary, or the secretary at the department office. From experience, I didn't trust secretaries, so I followed up with an email to no avail. My Irish friends were notorious for not returning emails, or, if they did, it was several months after the fact. I don't know why I was expecting anything different from Gavin Cleary.

Morris had made good on his desire to have more attic-rats with excavation experience. Ida, a fellow attic-rat, had a small but good crew; two First Nations participants, Clive and Cecilia, and one seasoned digger, George. I was pleasantly impressed by them all. At first. Clive could dig like he was born doing it and George's records were like mini-novels on each unit. Despite the heat, that made me smile. One less thing to worry about. Now if we could just keep the cows from falling into the excavation pits. And despite the amazing effort it took to lug the steel menagerie of the power screen into the truck and then out into the field, it wasn't that loud. Not really. It released my back from the effort of digging. As Indiana Jones said, "It's not the age, it's the mileage." Besides, I was out here primarily to teach Ida how to lead an excavation. It astounded me how valuable five weeks of hard-won experience can be to others.

We'd erected the orange snow fence late yesterday afternoon to keep out the cows. It only had to last the couple days we were digging. We had 10 units to dig. This would be a piece of cake.

The crew had made jokes while erecting the snow fence. "We should get some hot dogs. Stick them on the rebar and they'd cook from the inside." Yup, hot.

Between Oyen and this Edmonton stint, I had managed to pound out both the report from May and the Cold Lake report. Thankfully, I hadn't found any archaeological sites while in Cold Lake; that was an easy report to write. But finding the right words to delicately and diplomatically skirt the fact that I'd found a dead guy off the pipeline in May, especially when I was still heat-exhausted, sleep-deprived, and bitchy with my family? Well, that took a bit of skill I was not too sure I had. It's not that the government needed to know about the dead guy; they just needed to know why I hadn't yet finished the historical assessment. I wrote the report anyway and threw it on Morris' desk with a post-it note stating, "Review if you dare." Diplomacy was Morris' forte and admittedly I had begun to rely upon his talents. Perhaps a bit too much.

After that, Morris had managed to secure me a whopping four days of downtime. During which I did three weeks of laundry, shopped for items that could no longer be washed or otherwise salvaged, went to another bank and got the same response regarding my need for a $50,000 loan, then scoured my address book for anyone I could think of who would either lend me the money or co-sign a loan. Of the three names I came up with, only one was in the province: my friend, Kara in Edmonton. So, it may have been fortuitous that the next job I pulled was in Edmonton.

On my fifth day off, Morris called at 9:21am. "Ida needs some help." I'm sure he'd been itching for two hours to call me.

This was Ida's project, but she'd never run an excavation. I was freshly sprung from Oyen and the pipeline circus. I was happy to help, but out in the field again, with my brain only loosely tied on, I had to wonder if I should be there. I stood at that noisy power screen, pounding dirt through the mesh, looking for artifacts and I had flashes of what life should be, could be. By two in the afternoon, my legs were sore and my feet ached and I wondered how long I could last; at the screen, at the job, at this fight with my family, at this fight to find happiness. I didn't know anything but the fight. I'd been doing it for so long. I didn't know anything else. Was I creating my own fight? Could I be happy with my job, with my family, with my life if I stopped fighting?

Not bloody likely.

Besides, this Edmonton gig was an easy one: it wasn't mine, I was only screening, and we lived in civilized comfort. I had next to nothing to worry about. Next to nothing except my fried brain. I had another handful of days off in sight and a ticket to the Calgary Folk Festival tucked securely in my wallet. I just had to make it until then.

On Day Three, a pack of visiting First Nation Elders, client representatives, and project managers descended upon the site. The Elders wanted to have a pipe ceremony. Nothing like management and a pipe ceremony to put a crimp in the digging schedule.

As at Oyen, the women – Ida, me, and Cecilia – were requested to wear skirts. We peeled off our long-sleeved shirts, lathered the sunscreen onto our now bare shoulders, and made symbolic skirts. We women were not offered the pipe. Don't get me wrong: I don't smoke and, frankly, I don't know what I would have done if I had been offered the pipe. Could I refuse? Probably not. It was the principle of inequality that had me bristling, as usual. I'd discovered during my limited discussions with Leon in Oyen that there were some First Nations women that were pipe holders; that in some groups, women were considered as or more powerful than men. I appreciate the functional sexual differentiation of anatomy, I just didn't understand when one was considered better than the other. I understood when this inherent differentiation was manifested as complementary structures within cultures: for example, because hunting is a little more difficult with a kid strapped to your back, women instead gathered the food while the men hunted. One wasn't better than the other; both activities were essential. I got that. It's when status and ego were layered atop these inherent differences that things got whacked. Instead of participating in the pipe ceremony – doing another, complementary activity within the ceremony -- we women were made to watch from the sidelines, as the men sat and smoked away. To me, it was a clear demonstration that women weren't considered equal. It was an infuriating yet humiliating experience all at the same time. Especially considering that this was Ida's project.

When the pipe ceremony was done, the client's Project Managers brought out bag lunches for the Elders. They sat around the site and ate. The rest of us had eaten at lunch so we sat around and waited for them to finish eating.

The number one rule of excavation (other than the standard rules of archaeology, like don't get separated from your lunch) is don't eat in the excavation grid. It risks contamination of any artifacts or soil samples that might be taken.

And that's exactly where the Elders were eating.

Admittedly, the units made a nice seat. The excavated blocks were the right height for sitting with your feet on the floor of the unit.

Ida sided up to me. "What do I say? I can't let them eat there."

"I don't know," I wiped the back of my neck with my shirt collar. "Why don't you just explain to them why you need them to move?"

Ida looked at me then contemplated. "Yeah. You're right, Elise." She took a deep breath and walked over to the group. I saw her bow toward them, gesture then tightly grasp her own hands. The Project Managers stood immediately. The Elders followed.

Way to go, Ida, I thought and smiled to myself.

It took an hour for the Elders to finish their lunch and let us resume our digging. I tacked up the two hours of lost digging in my head along with all the other injustices I was beginning to hang up in my imaginary closet.

As it was, we quit early from the heat. If you're working all the time, you don't notice the heat as much. It's when you stop then try to start again that it really hits.

That night, I was awoken by a storm. At midnight, I looked out at the street across from the hotel. It looked like a news video clip from a hurricane; trees were being whipped around and rain was coming down in sheets. The next morning it was beautifully cool. Trees had been ripped down and branches littered the streets of Edmonton. An apartment complex opposite the hotel had lost most of its shingles.

Seven am was a glorious time and I felt invigorated. I was itching to dig. In retrospect, I just wanted to be finished.

The storm was not confined to that night. At 1100, I looked over my shoulder and saw a black wall of clouds coming in from the west. "Ida, we should consider sealing up the site." So instead of lunch, we scurried around in the gale force winds and tried to lay tarps over the units. It was another short day; now we were running out of time and budget.

It was Sunday. Back at the hotel room, I assessed my options. I'd already emailed Gavin Cleary – no response yet. I wasn't tired – a nap was out. Yet, I didn't have enough energy or brainpower to put together a coherent sentence. Michelle had emailed me her edits on my Fort Mac interim letter, but I just couldn't look at them. I also didn't have a requisite punching bag upon which to take out my frustrations as I attended to the edits. Oh, to be restless and brain-dead.

That's when I called Kara. "I'm in Edmonton. What are you doing?"

"I was on my way to do some shopping. Wanna come?"

I was showered and out the door in ten minutes. Kara and I had roomed together while she was doing her undergrad in Environmental Science and I was doing my MA in Anthropology at Simon Fraser University. After a few years of working, Kara was now in Edmonton doing an M.Sc. in Renewable Resources and Reclamation at the University of Alberta. It was an easy friendship, especially since Kara was nearly my ethical double. She was a country girl from BC; hardworking, fair, with a backbone of common sense and wit. The day went fast and easy, ducking in and out of shops in South Edmonton Common.

It took until the end of the day before she finally asked, "So, you wanna tell me what's wrong?"

I rubbed my eyes and looked at the construction on 29th street. "How do you afford school?"

"Student loans and parents."

"I thought you owned your house."

"Nah," Kara switched lanes and passed a slow-moving pick-up truck. "They bought it for me and I'm paying them rent to pay for the mortgage. I'll get it when I'm done school." I turned back to looking out the window at the traffic. So much for asking Kara to co-sign a loan for me. I could feel Kara looking at me. "What else?"

I shook my head, appreciating her directness. "I don't know," I finally said. "I'm just so tired."

"Ah," Kara smiled as she wove in and out of traffic, "You just need to get laid."

If only it had been that simple. "I'm exhausted, Kara. I don't know what I need any more."

At the red light, Kara turned and looked at me. I knew I looked like shit. I was bleached out and burned out and ten pounds of restaurant food overweight. "You need another job, Elise."

Was that it? Was it that simple? But it wasn't simple. Once an archaeologist, always an archaeologist. There was no upward mobility. You moved from one company to another, always doing the same thing, never progressing, never developing as a professional or an indi-vidual. The only way you moved up in the world was by doing a Ph.D. And frankly, I just didn't have the funds or the patience for that.

"And you need to get laid," Kara tacked on as the light turned green.

Three days later, we finished digging. Clive had begun to show his colours as an alcoholic, George's back was acting up from digging through hard packed clay, and Cecilia was too busy chatting with Clive to dig. We were lucky to finish when we did.

The opening day of the Calgary Folk Festival, I found myself walking the sterile halls of Foothills Hospital. What can I say? I'm a glutton.

Had Sebastian finally got to me? It had taken 32 years, if he had.

"Hi Mother," I said as I walked into the four-bed room. The TV was on and mother was in possession of the remote control. She probably slept with it.

Her hair (she still had it) was curled and styled. Her rouge was on and perfect. Only her clothes and jewellery were missing. She was the only woman I knew who could make a hospital gown look like more than just green cotton. "Oh, Elise. Took you long enough to visit me."

I slid into the chair next to the bed. "I've been working." Mother looked me up and down. "Yes, I can see that." She turned back to the soap opera. "Where were you this time?"

"Edmonton."

"Did you find many...," she waved a hand, "artifacts?"

I registered my shock at her question and attempted to take it in stride. "No. Not as many as we wanted."

She humphed and returned her attention to the TV. "Theo and Ashley came by yesterday to see me." Mother smiled. "I like Ashely. Such a nice girl." At this, Mother finally turned back to me, then, seeing me instead of Ashley, paled and turned back to her fantasy world.

"Yes, maybe she has a sister we could marry to Sebastian."

Mother continued her brown-eyed stare on *The Young and the Restless* but waved her hand at me. "Sebastian is already married and he doesn't need to be married again. Twice is quite enough. He's had a rough time. Trisha will serve him well."

"Yes. Serve him, she does."

Now, I got an index finger. "Don't start, Elise. Fate has not been kind to Sebastian. He just doesn't have Theo's luck with women."

"Yes. Poor Sebastian. Lucky Theo."

Mother's shoulders sunk, "Why do you even bother coming around, Elise, if you're going to be like this?" She finally turned to meet my eye and, for an instant, I felt guilty. I saw the tubes coming out of her arm and I winced.

I swallowed. Then shrugged. "This is who I am, Mother. You know that."

Mother swallowed this, perhaps for the first time in her life. "You always were one to yourself."

"Is that what Dad said?" I don't know why I said it. It was unkind.

Mother turned on me then, as I knew she would, and threw her words at me, "No, Elise. He didn't say that. He never said anything except that you were his little doll. That's all he said." Her voice died as the TV paused before commercials, and the room was thrown into silence.

A nurse bustled by in the hall. IV stands squealed by the door. Electric monitors beeped.

I finally rose from the chair. "I hope they're treating you well, Mother." Then I left.

I found myself on a road I'd nearly forgotten. I had only ever been a passenger on this road and, until now, hadn't fully appreciated the challenge of the drive. Especially in my little Tercel. It didn't matter, though. I could get stuck out here and not care. Not now.

It had taken me nearly four hours. I wasn't really thinking, just driving. I hadn't realized where I was until I recognized the little general store. It was the last stop before the real forest began.

It was nearly eight by the time I turned onto the road to the cabin. It was overgrown. I was relieved. I was even more relieved when I saw the cabin had been unmolested. It was well-hidden under the years of growth.

After Dad died, the lawyer had taken me aside and told me the cabin was mine. I hadn't been out there since I was last out with Dad. It just hadn't occurred to me to come out here without him; it was our place.

I fiddled with my keys and finally recovered the one that fit the cabin door. I beat a path through the brush to the door and, with a bit of effort and shoulder, I managed to open it. It was beyond musty and mice had found a way in, a long time ago.

I opened the patio door and the windows then surveyed the interns. There was rodent dung in the corners of the one room cabin and boxes of cereal had been pulled from the cupboards and torn to shreds on the floor. Dad's sleeping bag had been reduced to tatters on the threadbare cot. A half-filled can of Mountain Dew sat on the counter where he'd set it nineteen years ago. I dug around under the sink and found a bottle of bleach and a bucket. I started the stove and boiled some water from the pond.

After I was done, I stepped back to take in the cleaned and repaired room. Something just wasn't right. I had thrown out my Dad's cot and sleeping bag, emptied out the majority of the cupboards and patched up the hole in the floor with some spare wood and nails from the shed. I spied the Mountain Dew can sitting on the old laminate table. I'd moved it during my cleaning spree, but not thrown it out. I emptied it outside then set it back on the counter where I'd first found it. Better.

I retreated back to the car. I dug around in my trunk and pulled my trusty winter driving survival kit and sleeping bag. I was putting my feet up on the deck nursing a cup of hot chocolate made from pond water and nineteen year old canned hot chocolate when the sun begun to set. A loon called out as the moon rose, glowing on the pond water.

Never in a million years would I sell this place. Nor would I tell Theo about it. And I was still conflicted about telling the bank about it, if only to save my own neck.

I drove back on Saturday morning well aware that I'd given up a the better part of a weekend of the Folk Festival. Instead of mulling over the waste of a hundred dollar ticket, my mind was otherwise occupied. Was this all my father's fault, instilling this jealously of me in my mother? Or, was it his fault that he'd instilled the pursuit of happiness in me? Was it his fault at all? Maybe it was just me and my personality and had nothing at all to do with my father. I didn't know any more. No matter which way I tried to make sense of it, it never did. Thirty-two years of history rehashed in my brain during the five-hour drive back to Calgary. I went to bed that night with no answers.

I called Kara the next day. "Okay, how do I go about getting a life?" It was Sunday. I had one day of the Folk Festival left. I'd woken early to secure a good, shaded seat down at the park.

Kara's voice was muffled by sleep. "I didn't say you needed a life, I said you needed to get laid."

"Yeah, well. That's not going to happen."

I heard Kara shuffle, then a cupboard bang shut. She was up and making coffee. "Fine. Then go out. I thought you didn't have time for a life."

"I don't."

"Then why are asking how to do it?"

"Because I have to do something. My life sucks. Maybe if I had something to do outside of work, maybe I'd be happier."

Kara mulled this over as she ran the water, turned on pot and unloaded the dishwasher. I knew her morning routine well. "Okay. I see your argument."

"So, how do I do it?" Now I was starting my kitchen cleaning routine.

"What do you mean, 'how do you do it?' You just go out." I heard the garbage can lid shut.

"Where? How? I mean, how do you meet guys?"

"Are you serious?"

"Kara, between eight years of university and four years of consulting archaeology, I haven't had the time or the energy. The last time I went on a date was in my early days of undergrad, the last time I kissed a guy was when I was drunk in Ireland ten years ago. I'm kind of out of the loop."

"Point taken." The coffee maker beeped and I heard her pouring herself a cup. My coffee maker wasn't as quick. "Okay. Do you have internet at home?"

"It's too expensive."

"God. Are you sure you're not Scottish?" She took a swig of coffee as my maker beeped.

"The library has free internet."

"Whatever. Look up speed-dating."

I nearly choked on my fresh coffee. "Are you kidding me?"

"No. It's easy, it's gets you of the house to meet new people, and there's no commitment."

I simmered as I topped up my coffee. "Have you done it?"

"Couple times. I do it for kicks."

"For kicks."

"Yeah. Like I said, there's no commitment."

"Geez, are you sure your name isn't Samantha Jones? I want a life, not sex."

"What you need is sex to show you what you want in life," Kara corrected me. "Let me know how it goes."

We signed off and I gathered up my Festival gear. Apparently, I had a date with the library before the visiting the Folk Festival.

Monday morning I was back at my desk. I had indulged my dear friend Kara and registered on a website called Playing for Singles Inc. Just my luck, they were having another event the next night, 'Making Sushi.' I liked sushi, didn't own a sushi knife, but it was a meal, so I figured what the hell. No commitment, right?

I was already anxious. I tried to drown myself in work. It wasn't difficult.

At 10:04am, I received an email from the Historic Branch. Mark van Gutten had rejected my Artic Power report.

My mind vaulted from rage to confusion to frustration. I read the comments on the review, but couldn't decipher them through the haze of red.

I went for a coffee.

When I got back, I barged into Morris' office. "Morris, this is stupid and uncalled for." Morris continued to check his email as the sun reflected off his desk directly into my eyes. I strode over and pulled down a blind. "I wrote a good report and went back out to do his stupid backhoe testing. Most of what he's citing as inadequacies are things over and above what we normally include in a report. AND my client is going to think I'm an idiot. Mark didn't mention any of this when I last talked to him." Morris clicked his mouse and finally turned to me. "Sixty-three review comments, Morris. Sixty-three. What the hell? My report was more than adequate."

"I know it was." Morris finally said, as he took off his bifocals and placed them on his desk. "Bring me the comments and the report."

I ran across the top floor to my desk and pulled the report and comments, already printed, off my desk. Ida looked up from writing her excavation report to raise her eyebrows at me. I slapped the paperwork onto Morris' desk then returned to the revisions on my Fort Mac interim letter.

I had to wait until after two that afternoon before Morris appeared at my desk. He pulled up a chair and took off his bifocals. This wasn't good.

"There are a number of typos that Mark picked up that I didn't. I'm sorry. However, there are a large number of things that he is requiring that aren't reported as a normal standard of practice. Did he mention any of this to you prior to submitting this report?"

I shook my head. "No, Morris. I was really good on this one. I was thorough and I was in constant communication with Mark. I also printed off everything that I got from both the client and Mark; I put it all in the file. I know this is a big project. I wanted everything on paper."

Morris nodded and returned his bifocals to his face. "Then I suggest calling Mark and clarifying each of these comments." I began to object – I didn't think I could hold my temper that long and I didn't think it would get me anywhere – but Morris continued. "I suggest a phone call for two reasons: I think you should try talking because there maybe a breakdown in communication between you two on paper; and, I think having a witness to the phone call would be a good idea."

"Witness?"

"You can do the phone call in my office, on speaker phone."

In that moment, Morris redeemed himself.

We went over each of the sixty-three comments and figured out how to address each. For the most part, the comments centred around just a couple major points. Barring a clarification phone call, I could submit a revision of the report.

That night I had dreams of Mark turning into a fanged, leathery monster. I am pleased to report that I slayed said monster. However, I woke up sweating and couldn't get back to sleep. So much for my victorious slaying.

Morris and I cloistered ourselves in his office first thing.

Within the first two minutes, Mark ceased to be the fanged monster I imagined. "All I really want is a professionally surveyed map of the area."

I frowned. Sixty-three points of revision and all Mark really wanted was a map? It was only 9:23am but I could have used a stiff drink. And a couple of extra-strength ibuprofen.

I got a nudge from Morris. He was nodding. "We can do that," I spoke to the speakerphone. Morris scratched on a notepad and shifted it to me. "I need to submit a scope change and reasons to my client before I can go back out with surveyors and put together your map." Morris continued to write. I read it out loud before comprehending what Morris was asking. "It might be useful for you and the client to accompany me to make that everything you need is on the map and accurate."

Mark's voice sounded like he was smiling. "I can do that. Let me know what your schedule is and we can meet out there with the Arctic Power representative. I think he lives in Peace River."

We signed off and reality sank in. "You want me to meet up with Mark out there?"

Morris regained his chair behind his desk. "This way you can avoid any further miscommunication. You can talk to him, face-to-face, and get exactly what he wants. Then the client can also witness why they need to pay the extra costs and that you're not an idiot. I'm doing you a favour, Elise."

Yeah. Some favour.

The sushi restaurant was identified by a red dragon. No sign. Just a dragon. I should have know right then and there. No wait. I should have known before I left my apartment.

My evening had started with me trying on everything in my closet. Not because I was trying to find the right outfit; I was just trying to find an outfit that fit. I had gained weight since starting archaeology. And, because I'd been so stressed lately, I'd gained even more. The gym workout of my school years had been dumped for overtime at work. My work clothes fit, but I didn't think wearing torn cargo pants and a stained T-shirt was conducive to first dates, despite what Kara had to say about men.

I was stuck with a pair of black track pants and a second-hand men's collared shirt I'd planned to take out on my next field project. At least I was clean.

The event was to take place in a sectioned off area of the sparsely populated Red Dragon restaurant. We were organized around four tables under the pretext of learning how to make sushi. There were no knives. A sushi chef stood at the front of the room. I was one of eight women. There were eight men. This was definitely planned. I struggled to decide which was worse, pissing off my family or being here.

First came the saki. Thankfully. However, it was only a thimble full. Then came the box of questions.

"What's your worst memory of childhood?" Darren held up the strip of paper as he read it out to our table. Darren was a 20-something exec with his own golf cart and natural gas fireplace. I learned this within 30 seconds of meeting him. Thankfully, he was squat and balding with acne scars. Not that I was into golf carts.

The woman sitting beside me wore a fitted black dress. She had streaks in her blonde hair and her nails had a French manicure. She would have of reminded me of Ashley if she hadn't been trying so hard. I picked at the dirt beneath my fingernails as Denise addressed the question, "My worst memory of childhood was when my mom made me wear this hideous sequins dress to my grade six piano recital. She'd read that all girls my age loved sequins. I hated it. The audience thought I was going to play showtunes instead of Chopin."

The table laughed.

I put a smile on my face.

Louis, sitting across from me, was tall and wore a white shirt. I couldn't see anything more because the women were strategically placed in the light, the men in the dark. Louis had a nose, hair and a nice voice. He asked, "So, did you blow the socks off the audience with your performance instead?"

Denise shook her head, white teeth shining in the lamplight, "No, I'd stunned them into silence with my sequins."

Again the table laughed.

I wanted more saki.

"Elise, how about you?" Fuck. How could I tell them that my life had turned to shit once my father died? I was thirteen and suddenly alone in a family of four. My brothers were obsessed with school, my mother with her charity groups. They found camaraderie over their obsessions. I was just mad dad died and left me with a bunch of people who cared more about money and networking than asking how my day was.

"Nothing." I said. "I have no bad memories of my childhood. All was great."

The table was in awe. Then the men stood and switched with another table. The night of musical-chair-sushi was in progress.

I was glad to finally have some sushi to stuff in my mouth. I was also glad that everyone else's mouths were stuffed. I looked at the clock. Five after eight. I was starving and one roll of sushi wouldn't be enough. Neither was the one small thimble of saki they were serving us every hour.

Louis had been replaced by an eighteen year old sales rep from Cannon named Carl. He was nice enough, but I was beginning to feel really old. I couldn't keep up with his sports talk.

Apparently, Carl and another guy at the table, Terry, were in the same soccer league. For singles. Yeah, I was really out of the loop. Kara would have words with me later.

At long last, the final switch took place and Carl and Terry were replaced with Brian and Patrick. Patrick, to my relief, was older than 22. In fact, he was older than 30. And in the dim light, that made him look pretty good.

With sushi eaten, three thimbles of saki drunk, and no men reliably observed, I was more than ready to leave. I had managed to avoid telling anyone I was an archaeologist and I was very proud of that. I thought I might be able to end the night on a good note and leave early. However, we had one more task to do.

Our host, Maxine of Playing for Singles Inc., stood and grinned. "Under your placemats, you'll find a list of guys, if you are girls, and girls, if you are guys. Write yes or no beside the three names you'd like to contact. We'll do the rest." She smiled as if she'd just granted us the very gracious gift of dreams on high.

I cringed. What ever happened to the 'no commitment' thing Kara promised?

Patrick and Brian were the last names I remembered, so I wrote 'yes' beside their names and Terry of the soccer league for singles. Then I bolted. On the way home, I picked up a burger and fries. Then had a long hot bath.

The next day at work, I made the mistake of checking my email. I had three new messages. Terry said I sounded "cool" and thought I might like to come out for a soccer game. I deleted his message.

Brian's message was full of spelling mistakes and didn't even address me. It was probably a form email sent from his Blackberry. I deleted his message too.

Patrick's message was formal and invited me out to a coffee at Chapters. I forwarded the email to Kara who – also being a Blackberry addict -- promptly emailed me back: DO IT!

I emailed Patrick back and said that Sunday night at Chapters would be good. I would meet him there.

Then, as usual, shit hit the fan. I never did meet Patrick.

Chapter Ten

Looking for Bones

I t was one of those times I wished I hadn't answered my phone. I should have been grateful; at least Teresa, our receptionist, kept the outside folks outside. We were located in downtown Calgary, after all.

"Elise, there's someone at the front to see you." Granted, I had visions of Gavin Cleary flying a few thousand miles to see me. I wasn't prepared for my brother sitting in the lobby.

"What are you doing here?"

Sebastian uncrossed his legs, stood, and buttoned his suit jacket. "Can we go for a walk or a coffee?" He didn't look good. He had bags under his eyes and his skin was paler than usual. I nodded and pushed open the front door.

"There's a Starbucks around the corner."

Sebastian stopped once we were outside. "Elise, can we just talk for a minute?"

"What do you want to talk about?" The sun was beating down. I wished I'd brought my sunglasses so at least I didn't have to look my brother in the eyes. "This isn't about mom, is it? I went in and saw her a couple of weeks ago."

"No, it's not about mom. And she told me you dropped by. Thanks. I know you did it for me." It was Sebastian's turn to avoid my eyes. We stood silent and awkward for a moment. I could see that Sebbie was working up to something, so I waited. "I just," he started, then looked at me, hard. "Are you happy, Elise?"

I wanted to make light of it, as usual, but his tone was knocking me off guard. This was very un-Sebastian-like. I shrugged. "I've got a job, a roof over my head, and I can pay my bills."

"No," he took a pace up to me and dug into the words again, "are you happy?"

I shrugged again. "No, not really."

Sebastian's blue eyes flashed, "Then why do you stay?"

He was being way too intense to be the middle kid. Maybe he was taking lessons from Theo. "Sebbie, what's this about?"

His hands found my arms and startled me. "Elise, I need to know. Why do you stay?"

"I don't know. I don't think I've really got a choice. It's either this or Starbucks. Not much else someone with my education can do."

Sebastian let go of my arms and ran a hand through his hair. For the first time in my life, Sebastian was scaring me. There was a look about him – desperation. He was pacing when I caught his arm. "What's this about? What's going on?"

"Trisha's having an affair." I could see the terror in his eyes. "Elise, why didn't she tell me she doesn't love me? Why does she stay if she's not happy?"

Oh god. This was so not my forte. "It is possible for someone to love more than one person, Sebbie. She probably still loves you, but maybe she's going through a stressful period or something." He was shaking his head and pacing again. "Have you talked to her about it?"

"No. I just found out."

"You told Theo?" Again, he shook his head.

"Do you still love Trisha?"

He rubbed the back of his neck, "Yeah, I think so. I just don't..... why is this happening again?"

"You should talk to her."

"But I just don't understand. You're a woman..." Sebastian pleaded.

I grabbed his arms and held him in front of me. "Sebastian, you need to talk to Trisha. Now." He was losing it and fast. "This has nothing to do with being a woman, Sebastian. She's a person like anyone else." Like his first wife, Laura. "If you want to continue to love Trisha and save your marriage, you need to get a hold of yourself and talk to Trisha ASAP, understand?"

Sebastian nodded.

"How's mom?"

Sebastian nodded, still reeling but regaining some control. "She's okay. They're trying a different approach. Doc says she's doing well."

"Yeah, well that's mom. She won't die until she's good and ready." This made Sebastian chuckle and I was glad. "Go drag Trisha from work, take her home and talk. Talk until you get things sorted out."

Sebastian breathed in a deep breath and nodded. "Okay."

As he started to walk away, I called back to him, "How did you know I was in the office today?"

"I called the front desk." Great. My family is stalking me.

I made it back to my desk, coffee in hand, just in time for our resident palaeontologist, Wilson Burnst, to pounce. "My assistant just broke her arm. I need a replacement. Morris suggested I ask you. Are you available to go out to the South Saskatchewan River on the weekend?"

Morris' definition of 'available' differed from mine. I was trying to find time to re-write my Peace River report, go back to Peace River to meet Mark Van Gutten and Erinson Power, and to go back up north to finish the additional excavation to my sites. To Morris, that meant I was available. Bastard.

An amazing thing happened. I'd finally made it to Saskatchewan. Barely. Oyen was a few kilometres west of the Saskatchewan border, still in Alberta; Burstall is just a few kilometers east.

And, just this side of the border, another amazing thing happened. I saw a rancher, under 40 years old, on a horse. He was hot. He waved. Besides the grill-your-own-steak in the Steak Pit in small–town Patricia, gorgeous ranchers were definitely a reason to revisit this desolate landscape.

That's when I remembered I forgotten to email Patrick to cancel our coffee at Chapters on Sunday night. Shit. I was once again going to the Land of No Internet and I didn't have his phone number. I don't know why I bothered to try.

The couple of phone calls from Gavin Cleary this summer had sparked something in me. It was something I hadn't felt probably since undergrad because, since then, I had given up. Every time I tried to get out, meet people, do something with my life, it took so much effort and usually blew up in my face. With Gavin it had just been so easy. And Kara, admittedly, had me thinking about my life all over again. She had that affect. Maybe she was right, maybe I should quit trying, quit closing off, start grabbing opportunities when they appeared. And then with Sebastian's recent soap opera, it all had me wondering: if I wasn't happy, why wasn't I doing something about it? I'd always said it was because I just didn't have the energy, but I wasn't even looking for opportunity any more. It was one thing to be tired and not have the energy to take advantage of an opportunity; it was another not to be open to opportunities. I had ceased to be open a long time ago, both to men and other jobs. I'd given up. I'd succumbed to my unhappiness. It was all pretty sad.

Gavin was an opportunity that been smack in my face. I'd seen it, but was too stunned to do anything about it.

It was then, on that drive to Saskatchewan, that I figured that maybe I should do something about not being happy. Maybe I should at least *look* for an opportunity to be happy. After all, I hadn't given up all hope, had I?

During this little excursion to Saskatchewan, I was a palaeontology assistant, devoid of all my usual permit-holding responsibility, and lovin' it. That was, of course, after filling out all the 'safety' paperwork back at the office. This excursion was for the pipeline I'd worked on in Oyen, and they knew 'safety' like nobody. But it was all good because, since I'd left the office, I'd had nothing to worry about. Nothing. Ah, to be able to walk erect around the countryside without 40 pounds of safety equipment and several tons of responsibility weighing me down. I'd even 'forgotten' my cell phone at home.

The best part was we were looking for dinosaur bones. At last a job looking for bones!

Maybe Morris wasn't such a bastard after all.

Wilson and I had a good chat on the six-hour drive to Burstall and continued our bonding experience that started three years ago on one of my first projects: I could drive a quad and he couldn't; I don't mind driving a three-quarter ton with a trailer-load of quads on the back and he did. I had immediately earned his respect.

Wilson was 46 and lived alone save for his pet iguana, Lucas, and a few other assorted reptile and amphibious friends. I was still trying to keep up with all their names despite repeated stories around the lunch table at work. He was strange and eccentric but in a good way. His only real quirk was that he lived for his job.

I managed to resist for an hour. Then I finally caved in and told him about my previous year's visit to the Creation Science Museum in Big Valley, the heart of Alberta's own bible belt. I knew that the driving conversation would be set once I'd started the topic and Wilson didn't fail to disappoint. The only person more adamant about the theory of evolution than a physical anthropologist (and possibly a biologist) is a palaeontologist.

"It's really not worth seeing, Will. They've no argument. All they do is slam evolution, thinking that if they debunk it, people will automatically defer to Creationism."

"How far is Big Valley from here?" The SUV swerved as Wilson fumbled around looking for the road map.

"Will, hands on the wheel. I'll look for it, but I know for a fact, it's a long way from here."

Wilson pushed his wire-framed glasses back up his nose. "Mmm, maybe we can catch it on the way back."

I sighed as I pulled out the road map from the stack of paperwork on the dashboard, "I told you, it's not worth it. It's six bucks just to look at a Greek relief of a dinosaur and Henry the Eighth's descent from Adam and Eve."

"They've got a picture of a dinosaur?" The SUV again swerved.

"Wilson! Geez, you're making me dizzy." I flipped open the road map and counted off the kilometres. "It's about 45 minutes north of Drumheller."

Wilson beamed and cranked the AC, "Oh heck, Elise. We can do that."

If I hadn't seen it, I wouldn't have believed it. There was a town smaller and flatter than Oyen. Burstall had two restaurants and one gas station. The post office doubled as the Sears catalogue office. The gas station was the local coffee shop and it came complete with fishing gear, hunting supplies, pet food, and fireworks. The houses surrounding the gas station and post office cum Sears catalogue office were surrounded by cultivated fields. It was like Burstall got caught up in a Wizard of Oz-like tornado and was plunked down in a field in the middle of nowhere.

Maybe it was the same tornado that had hit Provost a few weeks ago.

Wilson and I started our rotation between the two restaurants that night. With a choice between burgers, pizza, and steak, I chose perogies. It's no wonder I couldn't fit into my nice clothes any more.

Over the course of my four field days with Wilson, I discovered something I didn't know about him. Palaeontologists like hills. However, unlike archaeologists, who like the tops of hills, palaeontologists, instead, like the sides of hills. Wilson was part goat.

I was struggling to climb up the hill while looking for dinosaur bone eroding out of the stratigraphy when I began to see the pros of being an archaeologist: I looked the top of hills, I had a shovel (aka balancing stick, weapon, machete); I generally wasn't concerned with steep river valleys, but rather the tops of them.

After those three points, I couldn't think of any more positive aspects about my job. Palaeontologists had it pretty good. They didn't work in rain or snow (it was too slick – remember the sides of hills thing), they didn't have to work with First Nations participants, and they were always looking for bone.

Ah, the things you learn AFTER eight years of university education.

I finally got to the top of the hill and the screaming wind threw my Tilley hat off my head and my eyelashes into my eyeballs. I flung myself against the hillside to avoid being thrown off the hill altogether and managed to land on a clump of cacti. I didn't care; I was too terrified of being blown off the hill. Caring about the cacti spines up and down my legs came later in the bathtub. Wilson, meanwhile, was jogging along the top of the hill.

Wilson stopped abruptly after I hauled my windblown ass and punctured legs atop the high hill. I then saw his boots in front of me. When I looked, Wilson was holding out his cell phone to me, "Phone call."

Shit, my family had found me.

I reluctantly put the phone to my ear. "Hey Elise, it's Maggie. How you doing?"

I began to breathe again. "I'm okay. Where are you?" I tugged at my hat string, tightening like a garrote around my throat.

"The other side of the river."

I turned around and looked at the west side of the South Saskatchewan River. A group of high vis-vest clad people were mulling about. I waved. Several waved back.

Apparently, Joanna and the Traditional Land Use Study group had found me. Thankfully the South Saskatchewan River separated us.

"When did you get here?" I asked.

"Just now," Maggie said, giggling and trying to carry on half a conversation beside the phone. "We watched you and Wilson climb up that small mountain. Leon and Henry had binoculars. Um, Elise, I think there might be a few marriage proposals coming your way."

Oh god. I had ungracefully displayed my butt to the river valley and a bunch of old FBIs. "Yeah, that's probably why Wilson climbed up so fast."

"He's amazing."

"Yeah, and part goat. Stay cool, Maggie." I handed the phone back to Wilson who inquired after a palaeontological sight on the other side of the river. He was fiercely protective of the sites and didn't want anyone pillaging them before he got a decent sample for the Tyrell Museum. "I can let you know where the site is when we're over there. I need to collect a representative sample for the Tyrell first. THEN, I can show the participants where the site is and they can collect whatever they want."

I could barely walk back to the truck. I had blisters on my sides of my feet. Wilson chose to tell me at the end of that first day that he generally didn't wear steel-toed boots; he wore regular hikers. Steel-toed boots weren't meant for side-scaping.

Note to the archaeologist for next time.

The third day was a long one; we could go home on the fourth day if we finished on the third. I was still having flashes of that hot rancher on his horse. I hadn't sung any show tunes, but that rancher was definitely foremost in my heat-baked mind. Yup, just looking for opportunity.

Despite the presence of scorpions (witnessed on Day One), plus 30-degree weather (the first two days), wind gusting to 30 knots (the last two days), this was the best time I'd had had in a long while: I was looking for bone. Granted it was a few million years and a few species beyond my area of expertise, but I was looking for bone and bone was always good.

The sun was sinking and Wilson wanted to finish assessing one last area.

"Can you go look at those outcrops over there?"

I headed off, the sun at my back.

My foot stopped in mid-air. What came out of my mouth was unintelligible, but not inaudible. "Nalh." I recoiled and looked toward Wilson. I hadn't gone far. Wilson was already looking back at me.

I pointed. "Snake," then pulled my hands close and shrunk away.

"Is it a rattler?" Wilson asked. Despite my rising fear, I could see the excitement dancing in his eyes.

I held my hands up about a foot apart, "It's about this big."

"Is it a baby rattler?"

"It's a snake." My hands shot into my pockets. The blood was slowly beginning to come back to my head from my legs.

Wilson arrived, camera in hand. "Oh, it's just a baby. It's a bull snake."

"What does that mean?" I was a forest girl, not a prairie girl.

Wilson started to snap shots of the motionless snake. "It doesn't have a rattler."

"Do they bite?" I found some courage and stepped closer.

"They're not venomous." Wilson laid his rock hammer next to the snake and snapped more shots. Then he stroked the snake's tail. The snake moved. I retreated, thanking my steel-toed boots.

After Wilson tormented the baby snake some more, we moved on and continued to survey the eroding bedrock for fossils and dinosaur bones.

A few minutes later, Wilson let loose an unintelligible yelp. "Elise, come here."

Too many times that summer, a yelp meant pain or I-need-help-before-I-sink-into-the-muskeg-forever. I began to run. Wilson was motionless. I got within about twenty feet then called, "What's up?"

"I've found a baby rattler." I skidded to a halt. I would take David's "bear-poo" squeal over this any day.

I approached cautiously. Wilson had stopped a good four feet from the snake. The snake was clearly visible against the bedrock. My bull snake had been mere inches away from his foot in the grass. This snake, however, began to move.

Wilson fumbled to pull his camera out of its case. The scale bar flew out. I reached for it. "Don't move. You'll scare it." Wilson said.

Wilson crept up to the snake while I stayed behind and secured the scale bar.

The snake began to rattle. It was a hissing sound. I knew that sound would haunt me.

Wilson took his shots then returned to pick up the scale bar. "It wouldn't be nice to be bitten by a baby one. They don't know how to control their venom. When they bite, they give it their all instead of just enough to kill a mouse." Wilson put his camera away. "I'll be okay. You can go look at that outcrop there."

I glanced across the grassy hillside and took a deep breath. Right. I prayed my steel-toed boots would finally prove useful on this trip. But I really hoped not to test them.

When I returned to Calgary, windburned and parched, Morris announced that I had one week to schedule a trip to Peace River to meet Mark van Gutten and the Arctic Power representative, before I was to head back Fort Mac to finish my excavations. He also tacked on an oilsands job for good measure. Thank you, Morris.

Things managed to work out that both Mark and my client were available and able to meet me in Peace River. I didn't know if that was good or bad. It was kind of eerie, really. I wasn't looking forward to this meeting. I viewed as going into the lion's den. And having the schedule line up so well with both Mark and my client, well, that just got me all geared up for another shit-storm. Despite appearing confrontational, especially with my family, I generally didn't go looking for conflicts. They just always seemed to find me. And there were always signs.

For instance, when Sebastian showed up at the office a week ago, I didn't know I wasn't supposed to talk to my own brother. When I arrived home and turned on my cell phone, it had two messages. The first was from Sebastian – Trisha wanted a divorce. The second was from Theo. Apparently, I was not supposed to give out marital advice. I called Theo and left a message on his home phone, just because I knew he wasn't home and that I'd be able to spout my two cents in peace. My luck didn't hold out. Theo called me at work the next day. Thankfully, both Ida and Frank weren't in the office. I hope that Morris didn't think any worse of me for what I yelled into the phone that day.

"You shouldn't have told him to talk her out of it," Theo began.

"I didn't. I told him to talk to her. Period. Communication is a good thing."

"You should have stayed out of it. Now we won't have a strong case."

"Sebbie was distraught."

"It would have been better to hire a private investigator and get some evidence against her."

"Could you stop being a lawyer? This is your brother!"

"And they're married. She's entitled to half, unless she's deemed unfit."

"You are such an asshole! She's a person, so is Sebbie and all you can think about is money."

"Get off your moral high horse, Elise. Stop giving out advice on things you know nothing about and stay out of Sebastian's business."

"Then stay out of mine, butt-kissing cocksucker!" I slammed the phone down and headed down the street for my consolation fluffy five-dollar coffee.

I was very happy to be leaving for Grande Prairie and working in a river valley with no cell phone reception. I wasn't looking forward to defending myself against Mark. Driving there, I envisioned every possible scenario in my confrontation.

I couldn't have possibly foreseen what actually happened.

It had to happen sooner or later. Being out in the bush with anyone brings up strange topics of conversation. Sex, religion, politics, spirituality, you name it. I'd seen it with my Fort Mac crew. But it wasn't too often I did fieldwork with a couple of single men close to my age. Usually, the men were at least ten years younger or had wives. Or, if I was very lucky, gay.

It was just a matter of time before something happened. The odds were against it. And apparently both Mark and Brandon of Arctic Power knew about those odds.

First, it was a competition to see who could keep up with the other as we climbed up and down the embankment. Repeatedly.

"You see this soil here?" Mark pointed out, perched a metre above the river and two metres below the top of the embankment, "This is the layer I'm interested in. This is the layer in which the historic sites are located. You can see if better from down here."

Brandon and I descended the embankment to join him.

Then Brandon scurried back up the top. "Where is the nearest location of an historic site in relation to that soil layer?"

Mark and I pulled ourselves up the embankment. Me, not as quickly.

Mark walked away from the embankment, along the floodplain, and eye-balled a location. "About here." I tried to remember where he eye-balled that location – it was all grasses, shrubs, and bush.

Then Brandon scurried down the embankment, "How do you know this soil is the same as up there?"

Mark slid down the embankment to join Brandon. I decided I wasn't going to play this game any more. Besides, I was pretty sure I wasn't competing with anyone here.

After a bit, the surveyors showed up. Two more young guys. When it rains it pours. Then suddenly I was wanted everywhere. "Elise," Mark called from a clump of bushes, "you'd better come see this depression. It might be a garbage pit."

In the bushes, alone with Mark, he seized the opportunity. "So, Elise, have you got a boyfriend?"

I belched a laugh. I couldn't help it. I was in shock. I was ready to fight for my professional competency and here was Mark making a pass at me.

I finally found my voice, "I don't have time." Was this an opportunity? Should I take Kara's advice? I didn't think I was up to 'jumping his bones,' but my eyes were open.

Mark wasn't all that bad looking. He was tall-ish, with blond hair and brown eyes. All in all, he was a well-kept, middle-aged divorcee with a son and alimony. He wasn't the hot rancher in Saskatchewan and he wasn't Dr. Gavin Cleary. As we walked to the first of the historic sites he wanted the surveyors to map the next day, I had to wonder if, at three post-secondary degrees and 32 years of age, this was all I was going to get -- an archaeologist with their own archaeology.

Then Brandon called, "Elise, can you come explain to these guys what you need to see on the map?"

I explained to the two surveyors that I wanted them to flag the right-of-way at 50 metre intervals and make sure that it accurate according to Brandon's latest maps. I turned to leave when I found Brandon keeping pace. "Are you up to Peace River that much?"

I was desperately close to screaming at the sky just then. "I can be up as much as five times a year or not at all. It depends on the year."

"Keeps it diverse and different." His dark eyebrows rose suggestively under his wide-brimmed hat. "You go down to Drumheller much?"

Oh, great. "Not much there to interest me."

"You don't like the big stuff?"

I had to stuff my foot in my mouth almost literally to keep from exploding. Then I breathed. I actually was looking forward to getting back to the one-on-one awkward conversation with Mark. "I'm an archaeologist, Brandon. Think Indiana Jones. Drumheller is for palaeontologists. For them, think Jurassic Park."

While his brain screwed that one in, I left him standing and broached the bushes where Mark was blundering around.

It took Mark maybe five minutes and some physical manoeuvring through the dense brush toward me to pick up where he left off. "I know what you mean about not having any time," Mark retorted, continuing to push through the bush, looking for tin cans and bricks in the leaf litter. "I once dated this girl for five years. I think the only reason we stayed together that long was because we never saw each other."

I pulled my legs over some deadfall. "I understand that having a re-lationship with an archaeologist would be a good thing -- they under-stand your lifestyle." I said, "But then again, you'd never have anything to talk about besides archaeology because that's all you do." I'd been to enough archaeology parties to meet the spouses of the people I worked with: they were all archaeologists at competing archaeology companies or academic archaeologists. And all they talked about was work.

Ten minutes later, Brandon called me back out of the bushes. I was getting more scraps and bruises from entering and exiting the bush than I was trolling around inside it with Mark. "I'm done here with the surveyors. They've got what they need from me. You around for dinner tonight? We could go over some future plans."

Oh god. Morris would kill me if he found out I'd turned down possible work. But then I would kill myself if I had to withstand any more thinly-veiled sexual innuendos.

"Sorry, Brandon. Mark wants notes of what we talked about today. I need to draw them up tonight."

I felt bad. It would have been nice to have dinner with someone, and someone other than an archaeology assistant. And Brandon did look slightly down-trodden. "I'll catch you next time, okay?" I tacked on.

He instantly brightened. I really didn't want to know what dreams he was bound to have that night.

And, once again, I began to wonder if I was ever going to have a life outside of my job, outside of archaeology. Even finding time to volunteer with local Search and Rescue groups to help look for human remains was difficult; calls like I got from Mikey a few months ago were incredibly rare. I couldn't imagine being in a relationship; I didn't know how people like Ida did it. Her boyfriend of eight years was a computer programmer. How did they cope with her essentially being gone for six months out of the year? How would kids fit into the picture?

It's no wonder I had fits of hormonal angst. Maybe Kara was right. Maybe I did need to get laid. No commitment. There was opportunity and then there was opportunity.

Brandon left and I returned to Mark, to help look for depressions and historic debris for the surveyors to add to their map.

"Where'd you do your undergrad, Elise?" As it turned out, Mark was born in Vancouver and had also done his undergrad studies at Simon Fraser University. The conversation then turned to comparing notes of our time spent at the SFU. We'd both visited the same coffeeshop and pub, five years apart. Mark discovered that campus hadn't changed much in the time since I'd been there.

We continued snaking our way under willows and deadfall. I suddenly became very conscious of every move Mark made, every step he took, and every glance he threw my way. At one point, I stumbled over a branch and he caught my arm. I got butterflies in my stomach. I couldn't believe I was doing this, forget contemplating it.

Eventually we finished our assessment of the bushes and joined the surveyors. There were no additional features to add to the map. I verified with them we'd meet out there again the following morning to map in the site with their equipment. Then they left. Mark and I were standing in the middle of a field beside a raging river. "Do you see yourself doing consulting for long? Do you enjoy it?" he asked.

Right then and there, I knew I'd been deluding myself. There was no way this was going to work. Who was I kidding? Other than attending SFU and being consulting archaeologists, Mark and I had nothing in common. In fact, Mark was still in love with field archaeology; he couldn't get out of the office enough. "I don't think I'm in a good position to answer that question. I like dead people."

He nodded, "And dead people don't pay. I get it."

We walked through the field and back to the road. I reiterated what Mark wanted to see in my report. "You want to see everything in and around the site, including garbage, features, depressions and any landforms."

Then he corrected me. "No, I need to see every bit of debris on the map."

I'd just said that. I stuffed down my pride. "I'm still going to recommend monitoring on the construction."

"I think you should recommend avoidance of the sites rather than monitoring. I want them as far away from these Fur Trade Period sites as possible."

I stood flabbergasted for a moment. "Mark, these are my recommendations. You can't tell me what to recommend; I'm the Consulting Archaeologist. If you wanted to recommend the work, you should have done the fieldwork."

Mark was suddenly very quiet. Then he said, "I look forward to reading your report," and left.

I was left wandering around the gravel road, bewildered and not slightly belittled. Opportunity, right! Another scenario that blew up in my face. I wondered why I bothered trying.

I drove back to Grande Prairie then sat in the parking lot of my hotel and called Sebastian. "How's things?"

"Theo's taking care of things." I could already hear that he hadn't been sleeping, probably hadn't slept since I last talked to him.

"I'm sorry, Sebbie."

"It's okay. Mom never liked her anyway." I rolled my eyes. Great. It's not that I liked Trisha, she wasn't a bad person. But Trisha didn't stand a chance against Theo. She'd be lucky if she got her own savings back after this and that wasn't fair.

I signed off then. I didn't want to get any more involved in my brother's life than I already was. I had enough shit to handle in my own life, even when I wasn't trying to grab opportunities.

Chapter Eleven

The Land of Acronyms

I spent a whopping four days in Calgary doing all the safety paperwork to go back up to Fort McMurray for a new project and to finish digging the sites I'd started back in June. This was the only reason I was home. For once, I wish I hadn't gone home.

Speaking of which, I had three messages on my home phone. I already knew who they were from. First was Ashely asking if Sebastian really showed up at my work. The next was Sebastian thanking me for telling him to talk to Trisha. The last, however, was mildly shocking. It was my mother. "I would like to have everyone over for dinner one night. I know you are busy, Elise, so please call me and we'll work around your schedule." I don't know which shocked me more, that she called or that she was acknowledging my schedule.

I called each in turn and told my mother that, when I returned in two weeks, dinner was feasible.

I was to finish my reporting and Mark's precious surveyed map for the Peace River valley during the winter. It was now September and everyone was in a rush to get clearance for their oil and gas development.

This happened every year – a mad rush in September and October for oil and gas companies to get historical clearance so they could do winter construction on their developments. You'd think winter came once every five years. July tended to be slow. In August, oil and gas companies talked a lot. Then, suddenly, it was "OH MY GOD, we need clearance now!" What did these people do all summer? It was a secret to me. All I know was that winter was predictable; it came the same time every year. Yet oil and gas companies always left historical clearance to the last minute. That's when we had to remind them that, "We can't dig in the winter."

Well, we could. It's just not pretty. Kinda like the units of the first site my crew excavated this summer; nothing like chipping away at frozen dirt and freezing your ass off. It's bad archaeology and it's unsafe. Besides the fact that it's really expensive for everyone involved.

Fort McMurray. Again.

Three times in one year. It was just too much. The flashbacks began assaulting me as soon as I stepped into the Calgary airport. Air Canada Jazz is the only one that frequented Fort Mac. I knew these airport gates well and there's only one good thing about them: Tim Horton's.

The next day I was back among my crew. Or, at least, they looked like my crew. They certainly didn't act like it.

Jacquie still had the crew split in two so that more digging could be done. Scott was back at home writing his interim permit report to come back up after me to finish up.

"Ellen," I bellowed, frustrated already, "where are the other clipboards? We had one in each bag."

Ellen ran over, and breathlessly sang, "I'm so glad to have you back, Elise. I missed you."

I was too perturbed at the disorganization and disintegration of the crew to appreciate Ellen's sentiments. Ellen plucked a box from the back of the truck and flipped it open to show me a stash of clipboards. "I had to hide the stock. Things started to go missing. Scott was dishing out supplies left and right. He was handing it out to everyone but everyone kept losing it."

What the fuck?

An hour quad ride later, I was still stewing. The newcomers, four in all, were still getting used to their quads and hadn't had the benefit of our initial day of quad training back in June. It didn't help that I'd noticed Chad standing on his quad pedals again.

I took stock of where we'd left the first part of the excavation. Leaves and caterpillar carcasses littered the floor of the square excavation block. I looked at the crew, "Okay, peeps, this is how were going to do things. You each get a bag, like before. It's yours. You lose anything in it, tough shit. You have to do your job without it. And you <u>will</u> be doing your job, properly, otherwise I send you home." I hadn't appreciated how much of a threat this was until I'd learned that most of these kids depended on their arky jobs to pay their tuition and live through the year.

"First, we're going to clean up this site, then we're going to set up the screens. Equipment goes there," I pointed to a tree. "Screens go there." I pointed again. "We have two days to dig. Let's move."

I got a few cheers. The others, newcomers since I was last up in July, were in shock. Yes, this is Elise Marquette, Nazi permit holder from hell. Get used to it. If I had to hold this godforsaken permit, it was going to be done right.

After the first day, my half of the crew trained the newcomers and then everything seemed to fall back into place. My crew and I got back to camp at four. I didn't realize how exhausted everyone was until my half of the crew showed up for supper with bedhead and sleepy eyes. The other half didn't even show up.

I leaned over to Ellen at the salad bar, "Where is everyone?"

"Jacquie won't get in until after six. Most go have a nap before coming to supper."

"What the hell is going on?"

Ellen shrugged as she dished up some grapes and mango. "Jacquie insisted on doing 12-hour field days. Scott agreed because he has no backbone. They said we had a schedule to keep."

I mumbled. This was insane. I hadn't been up here all summer, doing 12-hour days, and I was exhausted. I could only imagine what my crew had been feeling. Jacquie and I needed to have a talk.

By the time Jacquie walked into supper, it was past seven. There was practically no one in the dining room. The kitchen staff were cleaning up while TVs blared prime time shows.

Jacquie looked like shit. She was barely holding it together. Despite being out in the great outdoors and getting fresh air, Jacquie looked like she'd been through the wringer.

"Hey," I decided to try the direct approach when she sat down, "you're looking pretty tired. What kind of hours are you putting in?"

Jacquie answered me through mouthfuls of alfredo pasta. "Usually 14. Was up to 11 last night because we had a glitch in the numbering of the units."

Great. Everyone was so tired they were making mistakes. Blood and injury would be next.

"I'm going to pull rank here, Jacquie. I want you guys back in camp by four. The crew is exhausted, you're exhausted. I need you guys to function for at least another month and you're going downhill fast."

"We can't," Jacquie said. "Michelle made it quite clear that all excavation has to be done this summer. We can't slow down."

Shit. I was really beginning to hate Michelle.

"Well, I don't think Michelle would want you to burn out. Why don't you take it easy, at least while I'm here. I can go full bore while you lay low for a few days."

Jacquie nodded. The next day she didn't get her crew in until after six. Again.

I cornered Ellen at the screen the next day. "Why won't she do shorter days?"

"Jacquie wants to do a good job. She's afraid HSAC won't hire her again next summer unless she's finished her M.A."

"How many summers has she worked up here with HSAC?"

"Four."

I shook my head. Jacquie was so tired even her logic didn't make sense. "She's doing too much." Ellen nodded and picked up a flake of Beaver River Sandstone from the screen and slid it into a plastic bag. "Okay, here's the plan: I'm up here for two weeks. I can put you guys back into camp by four and, over the next week, get you rested. The next week, I start switching Jacquie's crew for mine. Got it?"

Ellen nodded, beaming. "We're also out of candy."

Now, that was just nasty. My crew should not be deprived of candy. No wonder they were tired and out of sorts. Measures had to be taken. Soon.

By the end of my two weeks, nearly all of my sites were finished and nearly all of the crew had been rotated. Most were again showing up for supper. I couldn't, however, get Jacquie to get into camp earlier. I also couldn't make her see that, for the longer day, her crew was getting less done than my crew. I trained Ellen in how to double-check the artifacts and records so, at least, she could help Jacquie get her after-supper-work hours down.

I left my crew at camp wishing them luck.

Ellen accompanied me on the drive to Fort Mac, reading her smutty romance novel all the way. It was glorious.

When Ellen dropped me at the airport to pick up the truck for my next project, she hugged me tightly. "I don't want you to leave. I like working with you."

This girl had a knack of bringing tears to my eyes. "I'll see you at the company Christmas party. We'll drink, okay?"

She nodded and drove away, but not before I'd given her strict orders to pick up more candy and chocolate for the crew.

When Morris dropped this new project on me I had one condition: I wanted Cam back.

The next day at 5am, my prized assistant was waiting for me in the hotel lobby. "Are you ready for this?" I asked.

Cam smiled, his freckles condensing as he raised his gallon-sized coffee cup. "Bring it on. After digging all summer in Oyen, this is a walk in the park."

Famous last words.

We were due on the lease at 645am to do an on-site safety orientation. This meant we had to leave Fort Mac at 5am.

Just when I thought that I'd tackled all the safety paperwork within the four days and the 11th hour before leaving Calgary two weeks earlier, I found out that, no, there was more. I didn't think it was possible. Two online courses and a drug and alcohol test weren't enough. The on-site orientation was required and had to be completed before the pre-impact assessment could start.

"Elise," Cam said, "I think he wants you to roll down the window."

Driving into the river valley in Fort Mac, I rolled down the window. It was the end of September and it was dark. It was also beyond foggy. It was the proverbial pea soup invasion from London. And I didn't like anything from London.

"You got no tail lights," yelled the guy in the passing van.

Oh shit.

I pulled over. Cam inspected. Yup. No tail lights. And fog thicker than paint in winter. At 5am. What can I say? I hadn't felt like doing a vehicle inspection in the dark.

"Okay, I gotta turn around or, at least, pull off somewhere safe," I said once Cam returned.

We pulled off and I phoned the rental company's road assistance. "Okay, let me get this straight," I barely managed to bury the growl that had been growing for the past 5 minutes, "You can tow us back to the airport where we got the truck, but I can't get another truck until 7am."

"Yes."

I snapped the cell phone shut. Fuck this.

So, at 7am, after a second breakfast, Cam and I headed to the airport, gathered another truck (with working taillights, as we discovered during the inspection) and high-tailed it to the lease for our orientation training that only took place on Monday and Wednesdays at 645am.

Thanks to our safe actions, my client bent the rules. Four hours later, we'd completed our safety orientation training. We were given temporary passes for the lease and were introduced to the bird crew, Jake and Alan. Jake was a small blond guy with black-rimmed glasses and a lisp that would make Sylvester the Cat jealous. Alan was a strapping young lad with dreadlocks. The two could not have been more different from each other and more out of place on a lease. They would be our drivers because we needed someone trained in how to drive on the lease and how to fill out the daily paperwork. Jake and Alan would save us time. Really.

After lunch, we had precisely three hours to perform as much fieldwork as possible in 90% humidity and 100% mosquitoes. I'd never encountered a September this muggy. On the bright side of things, Jake and Alan were awesome. I was beginning to create a proposal in my mind regarding the need for HSAC to give up archaeology students as assistants and, instead, hire unskilled labourers. Jake and Alan didn't complain. In fact, they loved working with us. It was something interesting to do. It also got them away from cleaning the air cannon used to scare away birds from the tailings pond. And, boy, could they dig. After the initial "here's how you dig a square hole," they were digging so fast, I could hardly keep up. They and Cam were digging the holes, while Cam and I looked for artifacts in their back dirt. The three of them would have put my Fort Mac crew to shame.

After that first day, I was hopeful that we would actually get done the assessment on time, despite all the time wasted on paperwork and training.

The client had a safework policy -- so did HSAC -- that stated we couldn't work more than 12 hours in any one day. That included drive time. As the return drive time from the lease was three hours, we had nine hours in which to dig. Theoretically.

The next day, Cam and I arrived back at the lease at 730am fully expecting to start fieldwork right away and, hopefully, get a good eight hours in.

No such luck. Although our IDs had been created and were ready to go, we could not receive them. We didn't have the all-important MSE General training; the training, for which the lease employees only know the acronym, was not in the library already lining our brains and wallets.

I was fully convinced that if I had to obtain one more safety or training certificate, I would need another wallet.

The next hour was blown -- we had to figure out where to take the online MSE General training, find someone to help us find where this place was, find someone to help someone else get the computer training started, find where the printer was to retrieve the certificate of completion, and finally, pick up the ID passes we had, at long last, earned.

I was beginning to wonder how many trees it took to drive a truck across a lease.

At 9am we started fieldwork. At 330pm, our babysitters, Jake and Alan, had to be back at the main building on the lease to take the bus back to Fort Mac. In total, we achieved a startling six hours of fieldwork that second day.

By the next day, I was fully prepared to push our pace. Morris had scheduled three days for me to do this survey. It was already Day Three and we were only half done. Cam and I arrived at the lease to meet Jake and Alan at 8am. I kept pushing back our start time because Jake said they had other standing paperwork duties to perform outside of babysitting us.

Cam and I sat in the coffee room and waited. An hour later, Jake and Alan walked in. They'd been on site since 5am. "We had an air cannon dithappear into the tailingth pond. We had to fith it out and clean it," Jake said pointing to the spattering of black along his overalls. I understood the black to be bitumen.

Alan said, "Now we have to fill out the paperwork. Sorry, guys. Hopefully this won't take long. Have a coffee."

In the meantime, I figured out how to download music on my cell phone, I played several trials tunes for Cam, and attempted several of the games. Outside of my Halo-time with Mikey, I don't do computer games. I got bored pretty quickly. I even dodged phone calls from both Theo and Sebastian. Sebastian had found out about Theo's words to me. I was caught in the middle again. Fantastic news, all in all.

At 11am, Jake and Alan were ready to dig some holes.

I laid out our map on the coffee room table. "We need to get in here," I pointed to the river that traveled through the far reaches of the lease. "Is there a road we can take to get close?"

Jake and Alan conferred and decided on the best route. We ate lunch in the truck as we made our way through the traffic and buildings of the very busy lease. We got to the intersection of the road we'd picked. "Oh, you've got to be kidding," Alan said.

The south road we needed was blocked. Some sort of construction. "What about going around the other way?"

"Yeah, yeah," and Alan turned the truck back to the east. That way was blocked too.

Alan pulled the truck around. "What do you think about the Strawberry Hill road?"

Jake gawked. "Are you th-eriousth?"

"It'll take us right there."

"You uthsed it before?"

"Yeah, I used last year when the vegetation guys were back in there doing their assessment."

Alan drove the truck back into the heart of the lease. Then we drove out of the lease and right into the open pit bitumen mine.

"Whoa!" Cam and I were both plastered against the back truck windows in awe. I'd never seen trucks so big. They were Tonka trucks on serious steroids. No wonder Cam and I needed escorts who knew how to drive on the lease; these trucks wouldn't even feel it if they drove over us.

The road was slick from the recent rain. Alan was an excellent driver, but I was beginning to understand why trucks get so beat up on leases. The truck slid sideways then bumped over ruts and holes. My head hit the ceiling. Cam's head hit the window.

I couldn't help it. I started to laugh. This whole thing was ridiculous. I think I may have actually lost my ability to reason at that point.

We broached the crest of a hill and I began to appreciate how big that Oilsands mine was. I'd been to football games. I know what 50 yards looks like. This mine was bigger than that. Much, much bigger. It was a crater.

Alan drove us down into another section of the mine, one not so busy. He pointed to the top of the mine in the east, "That's Strawberry Hill road." I could barely make out a scratch along the pit wall.

"Oh, that'th it?" Jake asked. "I know that road. Yeah, we can do that."

We continued down into the bottom of the mine, Alan continuing to swing the wheel and maneuver us through the oil-slickened mud and holes. "Is that a road?" He pointed to the right on the floor of the mine. "We need a road across the mine to our road."

Jake peered through the window. "Yeah, thure. Let'th try it."

Alan floored it and we flew across the floor of the mine to the road he and Jake identified as one perhaps meeting up with the elusive Strawberry Hill road. We crested another hill and were within about 50 metres of our new road when our current road suddenly disappeared. So did the hill.

It was a quick drop of about 20 metres to the mine floor. Alan did some quick driving and we slid to a halt. "Shit. That was close."

The road was discontinued. In the mine, there were no signs. That's what radios were for. "I heard they did thith to the thoil crew thith past thpring. They went in to a thection to get thamples and while were working, the road was discontinued. They couldn't get back out." Alan snickered at Jake's story. "They had to thleep in their truck until a crew came and made a new road."

I was laughing again. It was a whole other world in the mine. It was crazy. Forget the assessment, I just wanted to make it off the lease alive.

We paused and reassessed. It had been an hour driving around in the mine. "Okay, we still have a few hours," I said. "We can still go over to the other area on this side of the river and finish that up."

Everyone agreed and Alan turned the truck around. Twenty minutes later we were back at the lease. The Jake's phone rang, "Bird crew," he answered. After a brief conversation, he hung up and turned to us. "You guys wanna go thave a duck?"

I gave up. This day was utterly shot. "Sure," I said. "What the hell?" I was laughing at the ridiculousness of it all again.

Cam was beaming. This was definitely one for the books.

We turned around and drove back into the mine. "It'th at Nipple Lake."

"Nipple Lake?" Cam piped up. "You're kidding, right?"

Jake shrugged, "It'th a mine full of men."

This I had see. I suddenly had visions of a lake with a hill protruding from the middle.

We drove / slid passed the 'road' we'd tried before. Jake had to call a couple times for directions to Nipple Lake, but eventually Alan found it. Just in time to see the duck fly away.

We stopped and exited the truck. I'd never seen bitumen. It was everywhere. I bent down and picked up a hunk. It was dirt saturated with oil, the thickest oil I'd ever seen. Kind of like tar, but it definitely looked like oil. And, geez, it reeked of oil outside the truck.

Alan and Jake conversed with the guys that had called the duck in. We were in a different section of mine; it continued on for another few football fields. It was hard to imagine this was all forest before men dug this crater.

By the time we made it back to the lease, without having done any digging that day, it was three. Cam and I offered to drive Jake and Alan back home the next day if we could push and do a long day. They called into their supervisor. Jake grinned, "Overtime, here we come!"

I phoned Morris that night and gave him the 411, "We didn't finish today. Today was a complete write off. Lease duty over-rode our measly arky assessment. I'm going to need another couple of days."

But Morris was prepared. "I've already talked to the client. They know what's going on. However long it takes you to finish, that's fine by them."

Day Four. We abandoned any idea of driving to where we needed to go. We walked. Six kilometers in, three kilometres along the east side of the river to do the assessment, and six kilometres out. And Alan and Jake were still loving the arky work.

Maybe they were delusional. I had to wonder what their job was normally like. Again, I was wondering if my job was really that bad.

We found a couple sites and, in the process, Alan and Jake began to pick up the knack of identifying artifacts. I wanted to kidnap these guys and take them back to Calgary.

Jake hitched a ride back to Fort Mac with us that night. He and his girlfriend lived in a basement suite of a mansion with a three-car garage. All the houses in the hills of Fort Mac were like that. And, I learned a couple years back, that some of the people who owned these houses requested food baskets from the local Food Bank at Christmas. They had a ski-doo, a mansion, two vehicles and a boat, but they couldn't afford food. Fort Mac had priorities.

Day Five found the four of us on the west side of the river, finishing up what we'd started on Day One. Two sites and forty shovel tests later, we finally finished.

Cam and I dropped Jake and Alan at the lease office at the end of the day. I told them if they ever needed a job, look me up.

When I reported to Morris that we'd finally finished, he announced I had to do some helicopter recon, then had to head over to Cold Lake to do another assessment.

The weather forecast was calling for snow next weekend. The crunch before winter had arrived.

I called my mother and told her that I could do dinner in two days. It would have to be an early night because I had to leave the next day. I could hear her lips curl over the phone.

Dinner on Sunday it was.

Chapter Twelve

Sinking

I arrived with a bottle of wine. I wish I could have brought scotch. I know Ashley would have tried, if she hadn't already been into a bottle before arriving herself.

Sebastian opened the door. He was wearing an apron. I was surprised. I was expecting Ashley, as usual. "Hey!" he burst and hugged me.

Now I was stunned.

I entered my family home via the foyer where mother scolded me for getting my dress shoes dirty and where dad tugged my hand, saying we'd sneak out later and buy another pair. Besides my own differences with my family, I never understood its foundations: mom and dad. I hardly ever saw them kiss or hug. Dad was always making up to my mother, the disciplinarian. I must have noticed this disparity early in life because I remember asking Dad why he and mom were together. He merely said, "Because I love her."

There must have been something in her to love. I'd forgotten what, but my Dad never did. I wish he'd have let me in on the secret before he died.

Mother was pulling the lamb from the oven as I entered the kitchen. "Mom, let me do that." Sebastian plopped my bottle of wine on the counter and fled to help.

I turned around and left the kitchen immediately. Might as well get the firing squad over and done with, I thought as I entered the formal dining room. My mother fought tooth and nail to keep her home sparkling with three children racing around. It still sparkled. The dining room table could seat fourteen if the leaves were in. It was an heirloom from her side of the family. I pulled up a chair and sat across from Theo and Ashley. Theo nodded. Ashley smiled and grabbed my hand from across the table. "Theo wants to say he's sorry for yelling at you," Ashley began as Theo burst out then grumbled it back. "He didn't know Sebastian came to you."

And this is why Ashley and Theo will never divorce. They know they are good for each other.

I smiled, reveling in Theo's discomfort. "Thanks, Theo. That means a lot." I nodded to Ashley.

But Theo attempted to regain lost ground, "I still don't like that you told him to confront Trisha. He should have waited and talked to me first."

I nodded and bit back a fighting remark. Instead, I said, "Note taken. Next time an extra-marital affair is in the works, I'll remember that."

I got a menacing side-glare from Theo.

Sebastian came in with the lamb and Mother brought in the side courses, as Ashley bounced up to help. "So glad you could make it," Mother's eyes finally found me.

Theo carved, as the eldest son should do. Dinner was only half done when the shit hit the fan. "I have some news," Mother began. It could have been news from her Bridge club, or one of the local charities she helped. Maybe Josephine's by-pass surgery had been successful. "Theo's going to make partner at the end of the year."

I stopped eating; indigestion was only a matter of time now.

Sebastian grinned, "That's great, bro."

My stomach churned.

My mother wasn't finished. "And Theo tells me that Elise is going to be working for him starting in January."

At this Ashley's mouth dropped open. "That's....um, fabulous, Elise." Her head was swiveling between me, my mother and Theo, looking for the grain of deception.

It was Sebastian who was wholly unconvinced. "You're kidding, right?"

I nearly threw up. I could feel the blood draining from my face, from my head, from my body. I couldn't say anything, but my head was shaking.

"No," Mother continued in to revel in her glee. "Theo said Elise was in need of a change of career. Margaret is going to train her to be a Legal Assistant."

My head continued to shake. I had noted how Theo kept silent during Mother's story.

My mother helped herself to the sliced lamb as everyone remained riveted to her tale. "It's a wonderful opportunity and we all know how unhappy Elise has been. It's about time she started a proper career and earned some real money."

"No," it came out in a croak. Ashley glanced my way and blanched. "No." I repeated, louder, and rose from the table.

"You're not excused, Elise," my mother said.

"I'm leaving." I pointed at Theo. "Fuck you and your partnership. You're not getting one more cent from me than what we agreed on, and in the way we agreed."

My mother put down her knife and fork; the picture of decorum. "Now really, Elise. You don't have to be so dramatic. Why don't you just sell that scrubby old cabin in the middle of nowhere and pay your brother back?"

All the blood from my body hit my feet and bounced back. Boiling.

"Fuck you, Mother." It came out as a whisper. I know Sebastian didn't hear me, maybe not even Ashley, but I know Mother and Theo did. Mother sucked in her breath.

The room became very quiet and still. And then my life came out in a rush.

"I will never sell the cabin: it's Dad's cabin. It made him happy. And all he wanted was to be happy. Being in the bush, with me made him happy. And you hated it. You did everything you could to take it all away from him and, in the end, you killed him." I could see my words strike her; I didn't care. For the first time in my life I wanted to inflict pain, I wanted her to feel what I'd felt when she'd taken Dad's happiness away from him, my happiness away from me. I wanted my words to ring in her ears, knowing the destruction she'd caused. "You made Dad feel so guilty that, in the end, he gave it all up. He gave it up and it killed him. No. I will never sell the cabin. It's mine, it's Dad's.

I don't care about money. I don't care what you think about my job, my life. I'm living my life my way and you can just go fuck yourself."

I looked at Theo finally, willing him to stand against me. "I don't care what you do, or how you do it. You can take me to court, sue me, garnish my salary; I will not work for you. You either take the $400/month I'm giving you now or nothing."

At this Ashley shot to standing. "Theo, what's going on?"

Sebastian rushed around the table to me as I strode for the door. I'd reached the foyer before Sebastian caught up to me. I heard Ashley pry the story from Theo; Mother was uncharacteristically quiet. "Elise," Sebastian grabbed my arm, then seeing the venomous look in my eye, quickly removed his hand. "What the hell is going on?"

I glanced at him then threw the door open. Sebastian followed. By the time I'd reached my car, I was shaking. Then the tears started. God, I was lousy at confrontation. Sebastian held me as I cried. Finally, it subsided enough that I could talk. "Theo lent me money for school because I couldn't get a loan. He wants me to pay it all back so that he can make partner."

I could feel Sebastian's body freeze. "When did this happen?"

"May."

"Why didn't you say anything?"

I sniffled. "I didn't want Mother to know."

Sebastian pulled back and shook me. "For Christ's sake, Elise. I would have lent you the money, or given it to Theo. You could have asked."

"You would have told Mother."

Sebastian grew quiet again. "No." He straightened then. He pulled a tissue from his pocket and handed it to me. The crickets in the river valley sang and a cool wind blew the trees. "I was envious of you and Dad, you know?" I gaped at him, my nose running. Sebastian snickered as he indicated the dripping snot. I blew and he continued. "Yeah, I was. You two were always so happy. I remember when you came back on Sunday nights and, even though you were covered in mud and sweat, you were glowing. I envied that. You don't know what it was like living with Mom while you two were gone." I remembered his face in the window when Dad and I left, but I never saw him when we got back, late Sunday nights.

"I'm sorry, Sebbie."

He shrugged. "It's okay. Nothing I couldn't handle. I just wish I could have gone with you guys, at least once, just to know that kind of happiness." Sebastian smiled and ran hand around his neck. "You know, little sister, I kind of admire you."

"Bullshit."

He nodded. "You stood up to Mom. You always did."

"I never have."

Sebastian shook his head and wagged a finger at me. "No, you may not have actually said anything, but you did your own thing despite what she thought or said. I wish I could have done that."

"There's no time like the present," I nudged him.

He laughed and rounded my car. "Go home and get some sleep. I'll work things out here."

I got in and rolled the window down. "Thank, Sebbie."

"Promise me something." I nodded. "Take me to the cabin some-time."

"Absolutely." I said goodnight and drove home.

Yeah. That's right. This is Cold Lake, I thought as I drove to the hotel the next night. Seven hours of driving, thinking about my family and their crap, and all I could do to get my mind off my family was food. Stopping at every second gas station to pick up a coffee, another juice, more chips and chocolate bars went a long way to ease the mental torture I was going through on that lonely drive. That scenario could have also gone a long way to explaining why I'd gained so much weight.

When I arrived in Cold Lake, I was still hungry

I remembered this pizza and donair place I'd stopped at last year. I'd picked one up and eaten it down by the lake. Best damn donair I'd had in a long time. So it was settled. I was having a donair and getting an extra one for lunch in the field the next day.

But driving through Cold Lake just didn't make any sense. The road construction, of course didn't help. But nothing looked the same as it did a year ago. The maps I'd looked at, had printed off for the safety paperwork, flickered through my mind. Yup. The hospital was over there on the hill and the donair place was down here, on main street. I kept thinking how I'd just driven into town last time, then drove through town, and out of town. Just like that. It was one of those drive-thru small towns. Now it certainly wasn't. I drove around more, looking for the main street. Maybe it was down by the lake.... The lake had been easy to find last time. Eventually I got lost and had to backtrack. This should have been my first tip-off that the echoes of stress were taking their toll.

What the hell was going on? For not the first time, but the first time in a long time, I started to contemplate the idea that maybe the Twilight Zone wasn't just an idea.

I finally gave up. No donair tonight.

It wasn't until I looped back around to the intersection of Highway 55 and Highway 28 that it suddenly hit me: the donair place had been in Lac La Biche, not Cold Lake.

I had a flashback to laying in bed in a hostel in Barcelona. For a lengthy 30, maybe 40 seconds, I'd been a hair's breath away from a panic attack. It'd taken a vacation from the pub in Galway and done eight countries in two weeks. I'd done hostels the whole way and consequently wasn't getting much sleep. Whether it was just too much traveling, or too little sleep, I don't know. All I know was that for those 30 seconds, I was scared shitless. I couldn't remember where the hell I was. It was a terrifying moment, one that even ten years later still stuck in my mind. Barcelona was the first time it happened. It hadn't happened when I got back to Ireland. Or even in England this past February. It happened again after returning home.

Every now and again, it would hit, always upon waking; this sudden, horrible anxiety of not knowing where THE HELL I WAS!

You know you've traveled too much when...

Usually, now, it was just a matter of mixing up stores or restaurants with cities. It had been especially bad when I'd moved to Vancouver after growing up Calgary, then back to Calgary after living in Vancouver for 3 years. Trying to find Granville Island in Calgary just wasn't going to work, but still, on occasion, I would have a go of it.

After I'd inserted my brain and heart back into their rightful places, I decided on a safe bet for supper. Boston Pizza. They had predictable, decent food and they were in every small town. It was only a matter of time before those, too, started to run together.

It was October. Far too late in the year to be doing fieldwork, in my opinion.

It was hard to remember that a mere week ago I was paranoid about heat exhaustion for the umpteenth time this season.

"Fuck," I muttered as I pulled my muddied boot out of the snow-capped muskeg.

I took a step, shovel in hand, and sank my other foot into the frosty muskeg up to the knee.

I was now beyond expletives.

It all started by waking up a half an hour before my alarm, with a headache. Why my body was waking up a full half hour before the alarm instead of, say 5 or 2 minutes, I couldn't quite figure out.

Then I walked out of the hotel. An inch of fluffy white snow covered everything. "Oh, bugger."

When you think that things can only get better after having a crappy morning, don't delude yourself. Things can definitely get worse.

It was a good thing I'd left the hotel early. It took a full hour to drive from Cold Lake to the Range. I was 40 minutes late.

The roads shone. Brakes didn't work. And at 6am, it was rush hour in Cold Lake. I did a hesitant 80 kph all the way to the Cold Lake Air Weapons Range, pulling a trailer with an ATV. When I arrived, I had to peal my fingers from the steering wheel.

It was under these conditions of extreme distress that I managed to forget to check-in at the CLAWR Orientation Office. I forgot about the amazingly efficient Francine and the ever-moving bombing zones on the Range.

I had to use the special radio on the Range this time. There was no getting around it. We were back in the booniest of the boonies on the Range. And because we were using an ATV to get into the back-of-beyond, I couldn't use the little portable radio I'd rented last time. No. This time I had to use the 40-pound radio. It's a good thing Canada hasn't had to fight a war in a while; their technology hasn't improved since WWII. Plug in the antenna to the radio, plug the radio into the argo, call in when you are about to leave high-grade gravel road. Disassemble the radio. Drive the argo. Reassemble the radio. Call in when you've left high-grade gravel road (two feet later) and are going somewhere. Disassemble the radio. Drive the argo. Reassemble the radio. Call in when you get there (10 minutes later), etc., etc. The radio is too bulky to leave on while you drive the argo. You must disassemble and reassemble it each time. Fun!

The ATV we were using was an argo – an amphibious-type of all-terrain vehicle that had eight wheels and drove like a mini-tank. It could sit up to five people and haul their gear. Sounds good in theory but the thing was a bitch to drive. It really wasn't all that 'all-terrain' either.

We'd done the assessment areas with easiest access first. I didn't like saving the worst or harriest assessment areas for the last. I liked getting the hard stuff over first. But it was cold and wet so we chose to do the easy stuff first. I was expecting to have trouble getting into the last of the assessment areas. I was picturing big swamps, muskeg, cutlines that ended suddenly. However, we surprisingly found good access. We drove a cutline straight in and managed to avoid the big swamps. The second to last assessment area was located in muskeg - a write-off as far as historic resources are concerned (nobody wants to camp in wetness).

I wanted to cut across country to get to the last assessment area. The route on my map looked fairly straight-forward. It was only 500 metres west. It should have only taken us five minutes of straight cutline driving to get there. I radioed in then steered the argo away from our southern entry route and turned onto a west-bound cutline. The argo plunged seat-deep into the frosty muskeg. "Oh shit."

After several minutes of unwinding the winch, finding a suitable tree to hook up to the winch, hoping the cable wouldn't break, and finally hoping the winch wouldn't break, Christine and I finally gave up and walked away. Or tried, at least.

I stood upon some grasses, my feet slowly sinking through the snow and into the muskeg and counted to ten. I surveyed the scene and counted to ten again. "If we were driving quads, this wouldn't have happened." I muttered again and again. Finally, I called the guy I rented the argo from. "Hi Jim. I sunk your argo. Do you have a pair of quads you can bring me tomorrow?"

Unfortunately, Jim only had a pair of 500 quads. These were too big for Christine and myself to handle. I was stuck with a replacement argo. "Don't worry. I'll bring another tomorrow, we'll pull out the stuck one and you can have the new one to carry on with," Jim said. Apparently this happened all the time to Jim.

Meanwhile, I stared at my map. To walk cutlines through the bush for the remainder of the day or to retreat and start the hour long walk back to the truck? In the end, I decided that venturing further into the bush when already wet and straying far from our safety equipment wasn't a good idea, especially in the snow and cold. I radioed in our new situation then we donned our backpacks (mine being a good 30 pounds of safety equipment that no one would ever use), picked up our helmets and shovels, left the 40-pound radio, and began walking.

Two pairs of my wool socks were now soaked. Not good. I was beginning to wonder if I would finish this project by Christmas. Then I revised my thought processes: would I be out of the field by Christmas?

We walked out of the bush via the cutline we entered by and found the truck sitting happily on the gravel of the well site. I cranked the heat as soon as we slid in. I dropped Christine at her truck and headed home, heat and music cranked. And still I forgot to check-in with Francine at the Range Orientation Office.

The next day, Jim met us at the well site. We all rode in his brand new argo, down the cutline, the old argo sitting seat-deep in the frozen muskeg. It was with my relief that I watched Jim pull the old argo out. But things got bad again. "Jim," I pointed, "It's got a flat tire."

"No problem," he said, his smile breaking through his balaclava, "I can make it back to the truck. You take this one."

I had already planned on buying Jim a Tim Horton's gift certificate. The dollar amount on the card just went up.

Christine and I threw our gear into the new argo and took off. I was bound and determined to finish the project that day, come hell or high water.

Then hell came.

"Oh shit. I forgot to call in." I dug the radio out of the back of the argo and connected all the wires to the argo. Christine went into the bush. I assumed she was going for a pee.

"Security this is Heritage One. Over."

"Go ahead, Heritage One. Over."

"Heritage One requesting clearance to travel from high grade road to LSD 15 – 12 – 50 – 4 – West of the Fifth. Over."

"Heritage One, request denied."

I paused, mouth open with the word, "Roger," on my lips.

"What do you mean, 'request denied'?"

"Target Zone Red was altered last night. You are not allowed into that section until tomorrow."

Shit.

"Christine!" I bellowed then remembered to sign off. "Roger, Security. Heritage One out." No need to tell them I screwed up. No need to tell them that I kept forgetting to check the locations of the Red and Blue Zones on the map in the Range Orientation Office. No need to tell them that we were located in a zone designated for active bombing.

I threw the radio into argo and ran toward where I last saw Christine. "Christine! We need to leave NOW."

Christine was nowhere in sight. I listened for a rustle in the woods. Instead, I heard fighter jets.

Double shit.

"Christine!" I gave one last spin around before I took off for the argo myself. Then she stepped out of the woods up the cutline, looking at the ground.

"Christine," her head snapped up. "We need to leave now."

I ran back to the argo and started it. I looked up and saw Christine walking down the cutline, picking up stray twigs as she walked.

I shut off the argo. "We are in a Red Zone and will die if we don't leave now." Did I hear jets again?

Fuck.

Christine hesitated. Did she need a translation? I was getting one ready when reality finally set in and she quickened her pace.

I didn't even bother with my helmet. I started the argo and was already turning around when Christine finally managed to arrive. "Just get in and hang on."

I didn't know how fast an argo could go but I was going to find out. I cranked the handle and made like I had stolen my friend's dirt bike. Face into the wind, I jerked the handles back and forth, trying to make the awkward mini-tank stay within the cutline. Christine had one hand on the side bar and one gripped on the roof handle. We must have got up to about 40 kph. But it was not fast enough.

I saw two jets coming toward us, flying north. They were really low.

I cranked the throttle some more.

We flew over the crest of a hill and hit the ground hard. Christine flew up. I saw her go up, hit her head, then I saw her hand come off the roof handle.

I grabbed her limp body and pulled her toward me. Shit.

I worked the handle one-handed while I hung onto Christine and hoped those jets were going somewhere else.

Up ahead, I saw the patch of muskeg where we got stuck yesterday. I'd forgotten that was this cutline.

I pulled Christine closer to me and wrapped a leg awkwardly around her. I grasped the handlebar with both hands and prayed like

I was a Catholic in the Vatican on Easter as I picked an undisturbed part of the muskeg patch and cranked the throttle.

It worked. I made it through. I glanced back, saw my tracks darkening in the snow-covered muskeg, and laughed. I'd barely touched the muskeg I was going so fast. I'd have to remember that.

It was only another few hundred metres to the well site. I hadn't seen any more jets. That didn't mean they weren't out there.

I flew off the cutline and had to jerk on the handles hard to turn. The argo nearly flipped. I'd forgotten about the ditch around the well site. When I had all eight wheels back on the ground, I dipped the argo into the ditch and climbed out the other side.

I skidded to a halt beside the truck and jumped out before the engine stopped.

"Christine," I slapped her face. No response. I repeated. No response.

I scanned the skies again. I didn't see anything, but I definitely heard them.

Thankfully, Christine wasn't a big woman. And thankfully, it was winter and she was wearing plenty of clothing. I hauled her out of the argo by the collar of her coveralls and drug her around to the passenger side of the truck.

I've heard stories of people lifting vehicles to save their injured loved ones from the scene of an accident. It was all adrenaline. Frankly, if it hadn't been for the adrenaline, I probably wouldn't have been able to lift Christine into the truck.

I didn't even bother with the argo.

It seemed like it had taken me an hour to get out of the bush. By the time I hit high grade, it had probably only been five minutes. Time really does slow down when you're in a hurry.

I raced through every speed limit sign and gave no thought to the icy road. I didn't stop until I got to the hospital in Cold Lake, 60 miles away.

Once Christine was on a gurney and inside, I popped my phone from my jacket pocket. The screen read "One voicemail message." Great, I thought. Security is already panicking. I called Range Patrol without checking my voicemail.

"This is Heritage One. I am off-site and at the Cold Lake hospital. My assistant had a concussion. I had no time to call in. Sorry. Please tell Jim I'll get the argo back to him tomorrow."

They reamed me out a bit. I was ready for it. I had a good excuse. They still didn't know I had been in the Red Zone.

I called my voicemail. It was Gavin Cleary. Since last time, I'd looked up the country code for Ireland. I dialed his number.

"Hello?" His Irish accent resonated in my ear.

"Hi, Gavin. This is Elise. We've been playing phone tag all summer."

"Ah, Elise." I could hear his smile from across the Atlantic. "I was just composing an email to what I hope was your email address. I must admit I was getting desperate to contact you and did some internet searching yesterday. I came across your email at Human Strata Archaeological. Is that correct?"

I'd forgotten I'd given him my old card from Simon Fraser University and not my archaeology one. "Yes, that's fine. I'll get whatever you send me."

"Well, while I have you on the phone I might as well ask you."

"Okay." I was all a-fluster. I may have actually been blushing. Even a 40-kph argo ride through the bush with fighter jets on my tail couldn't do this.

"I have received funding for the Dahkleh Oasis Project...."

I couldn't help it. I burst in, "You got the funding? That's fantastic."

"Ah, you remember!"

"How could I forget," my mind flashed back to the café where we'd eaten lunch that afternoon. God, that'd been the best day of my life. "It sounds amazing. Congratulations."

"Thank you. Well, actually I am in dire need of a physical anthropologist with excavation experience." My heart skipped a beat. "Everyone I know is either lab-bound or doesn't know a bone from a Roman coin. My proposal's got approval and I can offer you a paid position. I know we've barely met, but when I read your biography on your company's website, I knew you were the one I was looking for."

It was a no-brainer.

I'd just died and gone to heaven – but that was okay because my family couldn't reach me in heaven.

"I hope you'll say yes, Elise. I'm...I'm hoping to see you again."

I'd definitely died and gone to heaven. My family was so wrong about my happiness.

I signed off with Gavin and stood with my cell phone in my hand for a moment, contemplating the wonders and turns of life. I debated calling Morris and giving him my two weeks notice right then and there. But, after all he'd done for me, I owed him an in-person resignation, at the very least.

I called Sebastian, "I'm going to Ireland."

"For how long?"

"I've been offered a three-year contract."

There was silence. "Will this make you happy?"

"Yes, it will."

"Mom knew about Theo putting you through school. Becoming partner was a rouse to get you to sell the cabin. Mom was behind the whole thing. Thought you should know."

I felt tears well in my eyes. "Thanks, Sebbie."

"Send me a postcard. I'll miss you."

Acknowledgments

Many big thanks go to my friends, family, and colleagues who have given much encouragement and support during both my time as an archaeologist and as a writer. I couldn't have survived either experience without you!

About Author

Yvonne lives in Alberta and was a Consulting Archaeologist for almost six years. She now has a desk job, is able to come home every night, and no longer feels as if she's on call. However, she still feels the need to dig dirt out from under her fingernails and excavate previous traumatic events in search of writing material.

If you enjoyed this novel, visit Yvonne's blog or her Facebook Page, *The Reluctant Archaeologist*.

Her website is yvonnekjorlien.com

Also By Yvonne Kjorlien

Elise Marquette adventures

Memoirs of a Reluctant Archaeologist

Ballast (a short story)

Fate series

Waiting for Fate

The Skirts of Fate (coming soon)

Non-Fiction

Why I Quit School and Got a Life and You Should Too: Finding True Identity Outside Academia (coming soon)

Don't miss out!

Visit the website below and you can sign up to receive emails whenever Yvonne Kjorlien publishes a new book. There's no charge and no obligation.

https://books2read.com/r/B-A-TTBU-XWRZB

Connecting independent readers to independent writers.

www.ingramcontent.com/pod-product-compliance
Lightning Source LLC
Chambersburg PA
CBHW071431200726

48294CB00002B/596